# SUNDAY *afternoon*

*David* ELIAS

# SUNDAY *afternoon*

COTEAU BOOKS
WWW.COTEAUBOOKS.COM

Edited by Edna Alford.
Cover and book design by Duncan Campbell.
Cover photo, "Sunlight on Messy Bed," by Neo Vision/Photonica.
Author photo by Wendy and William Elias.
Printed and bound in Canada by Gauvin Press.

**Library and Archives Canada Cataloguing in Publication**

Elias, David H., 1949-
Sunday afternoon / Dave Elias.

ISBN 1-55050-301-4

I. Title.

PS8559.L525S85 2004     C813'.54     C2004-904622-5


1  2  3  4  5  6  7  8  9  10

COTEAU BOOKS

401-2206 Dewdney Ave.
Regina, Saskatchewan
Canada   S4R 1H3

*Available in the us and Canada from:*
Fitzhenry & Whiteside
195 Allstate Parkway
Markham, Ontario
Canada   L3R 4T8


The publisher gratefully acknowledges the financial assistance of the Saskatchewan Arts Board, the Canada Council for the Arts, the Government of Canada through the Book Publishing Industry Development Program (BPIDP), the Government of Saskatchewan, through the Cultural Industries Development Fund, and the City of Regina Arts Commission, for its publishing program.

Canada Council   Conseil des Arts
for the Arts     du Canada

SASKATCHEWAN
ARTS BOARD

Canada

CITY OF REGINA
Regina Arts Commission

*For Brenda*

*(Africa!)*

# PART *one*

WHEN A BLONDE IN A YELLOW CONVERTIBLE pulled up to the barricade, the young private posted there could hardly believe his wild luck. He certainly hadn't expected anything so terrific looking to come driving down such a lousy little road. In fact, he hadn't counted on much in the way of traffic at all, since the road came to an abrupt end only a few hundred yards farther up. But already he'd turned back a half-dozen vehicles, all of them with the same yellow and black plates from someplace he'd never heard of called Manitoba. The drivers all spoke with an accent he didn't recognize, said "vee" instead of "we" and "rade" instead of "ride." Whoever they were, they seemed a compliant bunch, their manner more sheepish than annoyed, and he had turned them all away without incident. Here was something else, though. A honey in a convertible with California licence plates.

The private slung his M-14 up on his shoulder, the way he'd been trained to, and stepped up to the passenger side of the car. There, sitting behind the wheel, wearing a pink angora sweater and white pedal-pushers, was the most beautiful woman he'd ever seen. He stared down at her, unable to speak.

"Well?" said the woman behind the wheel.

"Ma'am?" he managed.

"What is it? What do you want?"

"Want?"

"Are you going to let me through?"

The young private tried to pull himself together. He'd never been this close to a woman so attractive.

"I'm sorry, ma'am," he said, "but you can't get through this way."

"No?"

"No, ma'am."

"Are you sure?"

There was a teasing bit of cleavage at the top of her sweater. She threw back a strand of silky blonde hair that had fallen across it.

The soldier swallowed. "I don't think so, ma'am."

"You're not sure?"

"Yes, ma'am. I mean no, ma'am. I mean, I can't let you through."

"And why not?"

"Roadblock, ma'am."

"I can see that. But what is it for?"

"It's to keep anyone from getting through."

"What's going on up there?" She was looking up at him with enormous apple green eyes.

"Up where, ma'am?"

"There," said the woman, and pointed past him. "All those men. All that equipment. What exactly are they up to?"

The young private didn't really have a story he was supposed to stick to when it came to the reason for the barricade. He hadn't needed one up to now. The others had turned back without any questions. But he was going to have to come up with something now. He tried to think back to the conversation he'd had with his commanding officer in the barracks earlier that morning.

"What do I tell them, Sir?" he'd asked.

"Tell them?" The sergeant was sitting behind his desk with his head down.

"Yes, Sir."

"Tell who?"

"The people, Sir."

The sergeant lifted his hands and placed one on each side of his helmet.

"What people?"

"The people who come down the road."

"There aren't going to be any people, you idiot. It's a dead end for chrissake." He took off his helmet and rubbed his forehead deeply. "Jesus," he said, "I got such a fuckin' headache." He was fighting another tremendous hangover. There was an element of surprise, of alarm, in his voice, as if such pain were unfamiliar to him, even though he used the same words to describe his suffering every morning. "If it was up to me we wouldn't have bothered with a roadblock in the first place." He took a bottle of pills out of the desk drawer and shook some into his hand. "But it isn't up to me, is it? Or to you, for that matter." He threw some pills into the back of his mouth, picked up a glass of water and drank quickly. "We just follow orders."

"Yes, Sir, but..."

"But what, soldier?"

"The missile, Sir."

"What about it?"

"It's right out in the open, Sir."

"Tell me something, private. What site number is this? Well?"

"One thirty-seven, Sir."

"That's right, one thirty-seven. And what does that number mean to you?"

"Mean? I'm not sure, Sir."

"I thought so. I'll tell you what it means, soldier. It means there's a hundred and thirty-six more of those goddamn things..." and he pointed out the window of the bivouac at the

3

massive Minuteman Missile lying on its truck bed, "... squirrelled away around here. You understand what I'm telling you, private? I'm saying that folks around here are probably used to it by now. I'm saying the goddamn place is goddamn crawling with fucking missiles."

"Yes, Sir, but what if someone should come, Sir? What reason do I give?"

"Reason? Goddammit, son, you don't need a reason. You've got an M-14 semi-automatic rifle strapped to your shoulder. That's all the reason you need."

The sergeant was being flippant with the private because the entire operation had been out in the open for some time now. When it came to the local inhabitants, there had been a casual atmosphere of dismissal from the beginning. It had started with the senior officers and filtered down through the men in the ranks. A lot of it had to do with the fact that the people installing the missiles, soldiers and officers alike, were all from someplace else. Places to the south and east and west that, by comparison, had a lot more going for them. As far as they were concerned, they'd been posted to the outermost reaches of their country, to a place none of them would ever want to live, a godforsaken place by any American standard. Only dreams constructed on the smallest of scales could be lived out in a place like this. Even if you were one of the lucky dirt farmers who'd been paid a small fortune to have a nuclear missile buried under one of your fields. Even then, you might just want to take the money and find some place else to spend it.

Besides, if the people who lived and worked there did so mostly because no other Americans cared to, they should welcome an opportunity to have the place transformed into a new frontier. And if they objected – on the grounds that a nuclear frontier was not really what they had in mind – who was going to pay the slightest bit of attention? As for the people on the other side of the border, clustered together in their villages across the green and fertile valley, they might as well not have existed at all. From the very beginning – from the highest rank to the lowest – they had not been given so much as a single moment's thought.

"But I have to tell them something, Sir," said the private.

"I don't give a rat's ass what you tell them." The sergeant's head was pounding. "Tell them anything you want. Tell them – tell 'em there's a goddamn bridge out."

The woman in the yellow convertible was waiting for an answer. The young private felt himself getting dizzy. He was trying very hard to come up with something, but all he could seem to think about was the curve of her pink angora sweater, the way her white pedal-pushers hugged her hips. He was desperate now for something to say, but all he could remember was the last bit of advice from the sergeant.

"Bridge out," he spluttered.

"Bridge?"

"Yes, ma'am. It's out. The bridge."

"There's no bridge on this road."

"Yes, ma'am, there is."

"No, there isn't."

"It's a new bridge, ma'am." The young private was pleased with his quick thinking. He had a momentary sensation of victory. He was getting the upper hand. "They're just putting it in," he added.

"Who is?"

"You know, them."

"Who's them?"

"Up there," and he nodded in the direction of the missile site.

Up ahead, men and equipment were moving around. There were trucks and earth-moving machines and cranes. But all of it was just far enough away to make the precise nature of their activities indecipherable. The focus of their attention, however – the object they were all milling around, like ants around a queen – was unmistakable.

"What about that thing?"

"Which thing would that be, ma'am?"

"That thing on the back of the truck." It was impossible to miss the Minuteman II Missile, big as a cottonwood tree, lying on the bed of an enormous olive green semi-trailer, its red tip gleaming in the sun. "That looks like a rocket to me."

"I can't say, ma'am."

"You can't say whether it's a rocket or not?"

"I mean I'm not allowed to say." It was all coming apart again. The young private had very little experience with women, and none at all with one this distracting.

"They're getting ready to bury it, is that it?"

"I'm just following orders ma'am," he said desperately. His breath came in short gulps and gasps.

"Isn't that right?"

"Please, ma'am," said the young private. He was pleading now. Pathetic. Beaten.

If the woman behind the wheel had been a Russian spy, sent to infiltrate the site and sabotage the missile installation, this would have been the moment she pulled out her shiny Luger and shot the young soldier point-blank between the eyes. He was certainly at his most vulnerable – mouth half-open, eyes glazed – mind empty but for one thought. The Cold War was at its height, after all. Throughout the US – the world – there was tremendous paranoia about spies. About infiltration.

But if the young private failed to make any connection between this woman's alluring appearance and the possibility of sabotage, he was going to get away with it this time. Lucky for him – for the free world – she was not a spy. She had never even played one in the movies.

"What do you expect me to do?" she asked, even though she knew perfectly well.

"You'll have to go back to the highway, ma'am."

"But I've just come from there."

"I know."

"You mean I have to turn around?"

"I'm afraid so, ma'am. Sorry for the inconvenience." He watched her put the car in reverse. "I can do that for you, ma'am," he said. "If it's a problem."

"Do what?"

"The car, ma'am. I can turn the car around for you."

"That won't be necessary. Thank you."

She manoeuvred the big convertible around expertly until it faced the opposite way on the narrow road, and drove off. When its yellow sheen disappeared behind a billow of dust, the young soldier wondered immediately if she had been real or not, if maybe he'd been out in the sun too long.

But the woman in the yellow convertible was real. Her name was Katie Klassen, and she was on her way up to Canada from California. She had come down the road only because she'd thought it might be the quietest way to make her entrance into the village. The one she was on her way to. The one that lay just across the border.

A closer inspection of the dead-end road would have revealed a set of worn tire tracks that veered down into a shallow gully, wound through a stand of long grass, and up over a ridge onto the other side. If a vehicle followed those tracks in good weather, it would emerge high and dry in an entirely different country, at the end of a single, tree-lined street running the length of a quaint, old-fashioned village.

The people who lived there sometimes used the shortcut to smuggle cheap tobacco or whisky or blue jeans, or even television sets, back into the village from the first American town across the line. The name of that town was Wallhalla, and it lay nestled against the last of the Pembina Hills that ran down out of Canada. They formed the western edge of a fertile valley there, but on the American side, they continued for only a few more miles before they melded into grassy knolls and bluffs and disappeared altogether.

But Katie Klassen wasn't trying to smuggle any contraband over the line. She had come down that particular road for an altogether different reason. She'd decided to try the shortcut only because it would allow her to come in from the south end of the village, which happened to be where her parents lived. That way, she wouldn't have to travel along the entire length of the street to get there. She wasn't interested in making an entrance. In drawing a crowd. She hadn't come back for that. But as it was, she'd have to go through customs, and come in from the north.

Katie would soon discover why so many people from the valley wanted to use the shortcut instead of going through customs; why even the ones without anything much to smuggle didn't want to cross there any more. The place had always had an atmosphere of low-level tension about it, of possible reprimand or mild punishment, but that had lately been replaced by something much more sinister. By the possibility of real violence. The first indication that things had changed were the two young soldiers, each armed with a machine gun, cordoned behind a wall of sandbags four feet high across from the depot. It wouldn't come as much of a surprise to Katie, though. More than once, coming up from California, she'd sensed that she was driving through a country preparing for war.

Driving through the desert with the top down – was it only yesterday afternoon? – radio playing, still trying to figure out what she was up to, she'd become aware of a slight, steady thumping in her ears, a sensation that became heavier, more insistent, as she drove on, until she spotted a squadron of helicopters flying low over the horizon. The thumping grew stronger, deeper, and the helicopters just kept coming, more and more of them, and then still more, filling up the sky, louder and louder, too many to count, coming straight for her. She hadn't thought there were that many helicopters in the world. They swarmed, low and menacing, over the top of the open convertible, green and ugly, a deafening plague of giant locusts, their concussions thundering down on her, shaking the car, the earth. Smothering her until she couldn't breathe. She screeched the car to a halt in the middle of the desert highway. Heard her own muffled cries only after she put her hands over her ears.

When the last of them finally chopped off into the distance, the silence that returned seemed altered. As if something had changed. Something inside her. Something in the world. So many things seemed to take on a menacing edge after that. Later the same night, driving through the darkness, refusing to stop, she thought she heard them again. A sense of dread overwhelmed her. They were coming back for her. But this time it was more of a pulsation, a series of low-level rumblings coming out of the black distance. Then she spotted a bank of lights, impossibly bright, across the miles and miles of open desert, the sky a brilliant, eerie green above them. Then flashes of red. Streaks of blue. A deep sense of apprehension. Difficulty breathing. She drove on.

By that time she knew she was going back. All the way back to the valley. Had admitted to herself that she was returning to the place of her birth without so much as a change of clothes. All the way up from California, through the desert, into the Dakotas, she'd told herself that it wasn't happening. Had clung stubbornly to the idea that she was just out for a ride. That had been the plan, after all. Just a drive up into the mountains to get some air. But she should have known something was going on when it was late afternoon, pulling into Las Vegas, and still there had been no signals, no urge to turn around and go back home. She'd stayed the night there, and next morning when she got into the car, instead of turning back – as she was sure she would – she kept going, heading north and east.

And now here she was, about to cross the border into Canada. She wondered if the customs agents would search her purse and find the roll of cash she had stuffed into it. If it would make them suspicious. It was a lot of money to be carrying around – far more than she usually had. For some reason she'd stopped at the bank on the way out of the city on the day she left and asked for a ridiculous amount. The teller had given her a peculiar look, as if she knew Katie was up to something. How could the teller have known that Katie was up to something, when she hadn't known herself?

E VEN IF KATIE KLASSEN had been allowed to use the short-cut, her entrance into the village would not have gone unnoticed. She would have encountered a group of young girls – banished from their homes, as all children were on Sunday afternoons – who'd come to play hide-and-seek among the tall grass and wild hollyhocks at the end of the village street. By now the girls had trampled down a network of paths for them to run along, and exposed a steel marker, half-hidden in the long grass, with the words "United States of America" on one side, and "Canada" on the other.

They ran, all but hidden from view, until one of them stopped abruptly at the edge of the ridge, next to the marker, and pointed at something across the line. The other girls gathered around. There was never anything much to see on the other side, but this was different. Something was going on. Something to do with the talk around the supper table, lately. With the animation in the voices of the men around the cooler at the village store. Something big. Something important.

They squinted under the bright sunshine, small white

hands cupped over their eyes, and wrinkled their noses. They could make out uniformed men moving around some kind of construction site, some of them barking orders, others carrying them out. There was a lot of arm waving and manoeuvring. A very tall crane, with ropes and chains and cables hanging from its boom, seemed to be lifting something off the bed of a truck. Something long and sleek and shiny. The idea seemed to be to hoist this enormous object into a vertical position from the bed of the impossibly huge truck, so that its red tip pointed at more and more of a steep angle into the bright blue sky.

"What is it?" said one of the girls.

"What does it look like?" said the oldest. "A rocket, silly." She wore a plain cotton sundress that fell to her ankles. The others had all gathered in a small cluster around her.

"It's so big."

"It's scary-looking."

"It's so close."

"It's got a bomb in it," said the oldest.

"What kind of bomb?"

"It can blow up the whole world."

"There's no such a thing."

"There is. They invented it."

"Who are they?"

"They're The States, silly. And they send it up in that rocket."

"It goes up into the sky?"

"It goes up to the top of the world."

"Like John Glenn?" The girl who said that stood out from the others because of her frilly pink dress, which barely came to her knees. Most of the other girls in the village weren't allowed to wear anything like that.

"Who's he?" the older girl wanted to know.

"Never mind," said the girl in the pink dress, and blushed a little. She'd just remembered she wasn't supposed to tell about that. She'd been roused from her sleep one night by a lot of banging around downstairs and her mother's voice, wanting to know what was so urgent that her father had to drag a thing like that into the house in the middle of the night. "Something very important," she'd heard her father answer. "Something that can't wait." By that time the girl in the pink dress had made her way down the stairs, and only a few minutes later, found herself nestled next to her mother on the big four-poster bed where she was never allowed. Her father moved two shiny rods around on top of the television set until the grainy black and white flecks on the screen became the unmistakable image of a man, strapped into a chair, with a funny-looking suit on, and a helmet over his head. His puffy arms darted across the screen in quick, jerky movements. Every few seconds he babbled something unintelligible in a thin, milky voice. The man's name was John Glenn, her father informed them. He was an astronaut, and he was talking to them from very far away, high above the earth, a place he would only explain as "space." The little girl in the pink dress remembered all of it, including the promise she'd made to keep the whole thing a secret.

"What happens after it gets to the top of the world?" she said quickly now, hoping the older girl wouldn't notice her discomfort.

"It falls back down, of course."

"That's all?"

"No. When it comes back down, the bomb goes off and blows up all the people in the world."

"There's no such bomb."

"There is. And that's where they're going to keep it. Right there under the ground."

"But why do they have to bury it?"

"So no one will see it, silly."

"But we can see it."

"They don't care if we see it."

"Pa says we're being punished," said a girl in a flowered kerchief. "He says it's all because of people like you." And she pointed at the little girl in the pink dress.

"What's that supposed to mean?"

"He says there's going to be a war. An atomic war."

"There's going to be a war..rr, there's going to be a war..rr," sang a girl with braided blonde hair, and disappeared along one of the trails.

"All they have to do is push a button," said the older girl, "and 'Boom!'"

"There's going to be a war..rr," sang the blonde-haired girl as she ran among the hollyhocks, and as she did, the pigtail at the back of her head swung from side to side between her delicate shoulder blades.

"I think you're lying," said the girl in the pink dress. "You're making it up. You're just trying to scare everybody."

"After the bomb goes off there's nothing left."

"Nothing? No people?"

"A few. But they get sick and turn into monsters."

Everyone gathered closer. Even the girl running through the hollyhocks came back to listen. She hadn't heard this part of the story.

"What do they look like?"

"Like the Martens brothers," said the older girl.

Everyone knew who they were.

"They're scary."

"I never look at them."

"I heard Ma say they'd be better off dead."

"I want to go home now," said the girl in the pink dress.

"Go ahead," said the older girl. "Scaredy cat."

The little girl in the pink dress began to cry. The girl with the flowered kerchief put a freckled arm around her. "You don't have to be scared," she said.

"I don't?"

"Not if you've taken Jesus into your heart. Because then, if you die, you just go straight to heaven. My Sunday School teacher said so this morning."

"But you said the bomb could kill everybody."

"Almost everybody."

Then the little girl in the pink dress said something that frightened everyone – even the older girl – into a long, deep, silence.

"But what if it kills Jesus?"

For a while they all stood silent, under the sunshine, until the older girl spoke up, but not so bravely as before, and without the same sense of authority she'd had only a moment ago.

"No bomb can kill Jesus," she said.

O N THIS SUNDAY AFTERNOON, Abe Wiebe was not in his bed-room the way so many of his fellow villagers were. He and the Martens brothers had made a trip over the line to take in the Sunday matinee at the new movie theatre. When it ended he wasn't ready to go back yet, and so they were having a quiet drink now, at Jack's Bar, just down the street. Abe was sipping Jack Daniels, while Jake and Cornie drank Schmidt Bigmouth beer as usual. Those two were arguing about the huge, three-dimensional letters that ran along either side of the marquee and spelled out the name of the theatre, but Abe hadn't been paying much attention.

"'Halla,'" said Jake. "'Walla' on one side, and 'Halla' on the other."

"No. It's the same on both sides," said Cornie.

"It isn't.

"I'm telling you, it is."

"That doesn't make any sense. If it's the same on both sides, that spells 'Walla Walla.' What kind of a name is that?"

"That's what the letters say."

"No, they don't. They say 'Walla' on one side, and 'Halla' on the other. Get it? The Wall – halla theatre. That's the name of the town."

"But that doesn't spell 'Wallhalla.' That spells 'Wallaaaah – halla.' It's not Wallaaaah – halla. It's Wall – halla."

"Exactly. That's what it says."

"No, it doesn't."

"Yes, it does."

Getting in the truck and heading over the line with the Martens brothers was something Abe did from time to time, especially on a Sunday afternoon, when being back in the valley got to be too much. There was something about maddoch schlope that depressed him, made him want to get out of the village. Out of the valley. Out of the country.

There were others who felt the same way. More and more of them lately, scattered through the crowd inside the movie theatre. You could pick them out, once your eyes got used to the dark. They were easy to spot. There was a look about them – unmistakable on their shiny faces – of hungry naïveté. Today he'd spotted a young mother, her husband probably asleep back in the village, with two children, one on either side of her. The children sat at the very edge of their seats, mouthing popcorn and candy bars, while she reclined well back in hers, luxuriating in the plush red velvet, as shadows from the big screen flickered across her face. She was pretty, Abe remembered thinking, except for a bruise on her cheek that even the semi-darkness couldn't hide.

Abe had been to church that morning for the first time since he'd come back. Instead of going out to the workshop, as he would have on any other Sunday, to put a final coat of wax on the new schlopebank he'd just finished, something had made him give in to the impulse to join the weekly pilgrimage of the other men and women of the village and follow them to the plain white church at the centre of town.

The bench would have to wait, even though there was a wealthy and very attractive young American woman coming to pick it up that afternoon. The benches Abe built were a traditional item of furniture found in the sparse sitting rooms of every household in the valley. Simple in design, they were used as much for storage as for sitting on. "Schlopebank," literally translated, meant "sleep bench," but they were as hard as church pews, and curling up on one to take a nap would have bordered on self-abuse. You could open the seat like the lid of a chest and fill the space underneath with blankets and linens. They were usually made out of spruce or pine, but Abe made his out of cherrywood. There happened to be a lot of it around – an entire orchard his grandfather had planted years ago.

"They all look at me," his grandfather had said one Sunday afternoon, "as if I'm crazy. Even your own father." Abe was still a boy then. "They don't understand why a man would want to take up so much land for something so frivolous. Land that could be used for wheat or corn or even rhubarb. Jacob, they say, what do you want with all those cherry trees." By that time the trees had grown tall enough for the two of them to walk side by side under a canopy of pink, sweet-smelling blossoms, Abe reaching up to hold his grandfather's great hand. "The fruit won't be any good, they say. Ornamental at best. A few measly jars of over-sweetened jelly is all you can hope for. Have you lost your judgement? Are you insane? This is how they talk to me, Abraham." His grandfather was the only one who ever called him Abraham. "How can I tell them I don't care about the fruit? How can I explain to them?"

They stopped. Bits of blue sky sparkled through the bower of blossoms above them. On a branch overhead an orange and black oriole sang brilliantly. A gust of wind shivered the trees and then it was snowing pink flakes over their upturned faces. "Here," said his grandfather, and gestured with both arms in a wide sweeping motion that was as poetic as anything Abe had ever seen a man do. "Here is my answer."

When his grandfather died years later the trees died soon after. They'd survived the harsh climate as long as they had only because of his loving care and attention. No one cut them down. Their dried skeletons remained as a testimonial to his grandfather's folly. When Abe returned from overseas, one of the first things he did was to walk among them, as he had all those years ago, and try to recapture something he was sure he'd lost along the way, and that was when the idea struck him. He would build benches with the wood. The kind you would sit on, under the grandfather clock, on a Sunday afternoon.

He went back to the yard for a bucksaw and cut one down, milled a few crude boards out of it, and built his first schlopebank. Slowly. Carefully. The old way. The way his grandfather had showed him all those years ago. Peg and dovetail. No nails. When it was done, the more he polished the warm grain of the wood, the more spectacular it became.

He had one sitting in the sun on the front porch one Sunday afternoon, newly waxed, when an American couple stopped in front of the house and asked if they could come over and take a closer look. They offered to buy it immediately. Mentioned a ridiculous sum of money. By that time Abe had built three of them. He accepted their offer, not so much for the money, which he needed, but for his grandfather. It would drive people crazy to think that something as plain as a schlopebank should be an object of desire, a symbol of wealth, all because it was made from the wood of those useless cherry trees. "Here," Abe could hear his grandfather saying. "Here is my answer."

But this morning Abe had decided not to go into his workshop. Instead, he'd made his way to the church, managed to get inside and into a pew without incident, even though he

17

was forbidden, technically, from entering the building at all. The village elders had decreed his excommunication because of his service in the army, but their rules and verdicts had never been enough to stop him, he thought, so why should it be any different now?

He'd needed to be there that morning. Not so much to hear what the preacher had to say about the missile silo going in over the line, in plain sight of anyone who cared to stand at the edge of town – or even at one of the unadorned windows on the south side of the church – and watch it being installed. That was bound to be a disappointment. No, it was more that he wanted to be there with the others. That, in spite of himself, he felt the need to congregate. He was surprised and relieved to see that others – people like Martha Wiebe and the Martens brothers and the young poet – had given in to the same impulse and were already sitting in a small cluster at the far end of the church. He went to sit with them, their collective presence providing some insulation from the frowns and scowls of people like the Zacharias sisters. He half-expected a gang of burly and bearded men, sent by the elders, to come and hustle him down the aisle out onto the steps, but they never did.

Halfway through the preacher's sermon he almost wished they had. Nothing had changed inside that building. The preacher spent his time browbeating the congregation into handling the presence of these terrifying weapons, and the possibility that the entire valley might become engulfed in a nuclear firestorm, with massive doses of prayer. It was through prayer and pacifism, he'd insisted, that such problems should best be addressed.

The preacher was an educated man. He had been to Bible College in Otterburn. But the fact that he had more formal education than the sum total of the entire congregation did him no good whatsoever. There was really no one to intimidate with such learning. Certainly not the church elders, who rarely, if ever, allowed themselves to be bullied by anything so fanciful as reason or intellect. Besides, it was difficult to sustain such abstract ideas – to give them the kind of weight and solemnity and prestige they deserved – in Plaut Dietsch, a language so devoid of any higher vocabulary.

Abe Wiebe could have told this preacher a thing or two about the effectiveness of prayer in a conflict situation. He had been in war. Had shot people. Had himself been shot. He was certainly no pacifist. Didn't think it was really possible to be one – in or out of the valley. And yet, he'd always had a strong sense – even more so since he had returned – that the best part of him – of any man – was a gentle thing.

He didn't think he really believed in prayer, except perhaps under the most desperate of situations. Had always thought of it as overused and abused by people like this pretentious preacher, to suit their own ends. Even in Korea, when he'd felt the bullet plunge into his torso, even then he hadn't prayed – convinced somehow that one bullet wasn't enough to kill him, so there wasn't really the need.

Abe didn't even think it was such a bad idea to have a weapon that could protect them from the Russians. But the idea of one so close to the children of the village bothered him. He couldn't seem to shake a scenario that haunted him, of his nephews and nieces lying under their down-filled comforters at night, their sleep invaded by a barely audible hum that never relented – the sound of the missile waiting to be released from its underground lair. That, nightly, its vibrations would penetrate the houses, the straw ticks people slept on, and agitate their dreams until the village, the entire valley, flamed up into one giant fireball, while they ran, feet in molasses, unable to put any distance between themselves and the death that was coming at them. It was this, more than anything else, that had made him want to go to church that morning, to sit there with the others and try to find a way to make sense of it all.

But, heavy as it weighed on his mind, even that had been eclipsed this afternoon by what he'd seen up on the screen inside the movie theatre. Something every bit as powerful as an atom bomb.

And now, as if that wasn't enough, here was this American standing next to him, trying to be friendly. Abe had seen him sitting up at the bar for some time, chewing on a cigar, staring over at them, and guessed that he'd finally worked up the courage to come over to the table.

"Say, can I buy you fellas a drink?" said the man, and held up a fresh glass. He was a big man, big-boned and carrying too much weight around on his chest and belly. The Martens brothers stopped arguing and looked over at Abe for a reaction. They knew he was in a mood. That something inside the movie theatre had caught him off guard. Something he'd seen up on the big screen. But they weren't going to try and talk to him about it just yet.

"Mind if I sit down?" said the man.

Abe gave a little nod.

Cornie and Jake bolted down their Jack Daniels, chased it back with loud gulps of Schmidt Bigmouth. They'd worked up a thirst arguing about the letters.

The man sat down noisily, his face red and puffy. He pulled a nasty-looking cigar out of his mouth and took down half of his drink in one gulp. The stub of the cigar, wet and mangled into shreds, poked out between two fat fingers. He leaned forward and put his elbows on the table. His suit jacket was too small, the shiny sleeves riding up his shoulders, his thick and hairy forearms exposed. The fedora hat he wore was equally disproportionate, and ridiculously small for his large head. He pushed it back over his greasy forehead and stared, closely and intently, first into Cornie's face, then into Jake's. Then he stuck the cigar back into his mouth and chomped down hard on the end of it.

"Jesus," he said. He took the cigar out of his mouth and finished the last of his drink, clanked the glass down on the wooden tabletop and stared at each of them again. "Jesus H. Christ," he said. His breathing was laboured. Hard.

"Is there something we can do for you?" said Abe. Said it in a way that let the man know he wasn't going to put up with much more.

"Arty's the name," said the man, and put out his hand. Nobody took it. "Arty Sigurdson. I sell real estate around here. I know everybody. I've seen you boys in here before."

Jake finished up the last of his Bigmouth. Held the empty bottle up for the real estate agent to see.

"Say, you boys can really put it away. I heard about that. Heard about the way you people can drink when you want to. Howie!" The real estate agent yelled up at the bartender. "Bring us another round here, would ya?" and held up his glass. "There was something I wanted to ask you fellas." And he looked again into each of the Martens brothers' faces.

"Wait," said Jake, and sat up rigidly. He leaned over to examine his brother, Cornie, whose head had tilted awkwardly to one side, square jaw set, mouth open wide.

"What is it?" said the real estate agent. "What's wrong?"

"I think he might be getting something."

"Nothing catching, I hope?"

"He's pulling something in."

"Hey," said one of the men at the bar. "That crazy bastard is at it again." He and some of the others left their bar stools to come and stand at the table. "Watch this," he said, and put one hand on the real estate agent's shoulder. "You're not gonna believe this."

Cornie opened his mouth wider, allowed Jake to pivot his head slowly, in tiny increments, from side to side, tilting it slightly one way, then another.

"It usually takes them awhile," said the man from the bar, "but it's worth the wait."

"Wider," said Jake.

Cornie opened his mouth even wider, as if he were executing an excruciating, silent, scream. His facial contortions made him look even more hideous than usual. The real estate agent lifted his drink off the table and sat far back in his chair. He'd come for a closer look, but now he was getting more than he bargained for.

It was true that the Martens brothers were two of the most gruesome-looking creatures the valley had ever produced. Their faces were too torturous for most people to stomach. They were recognizable as faces only in the weakest sense of the word, since the usual features, such as noses, lips, and eyelids, were no longer discernible. The incredibly hot fire had consumed those parts of their anatomy. The remaining skin had been pulled tightly over their bone structure, like the skin of a drum. They were disfigured to the point where ridicule or self-consciousness were completely out of the question. There was in the presence of their unassailable ugliness something so compelling that strangers – people like this real estate agent – caught themselves staring shamelessly, against their will, unable to break free of the disturbing mixture of attraction and repulsion. As for the Martens brothers, they carried the compelling horridness of their appearance around with them as easily as a wart. A hangnail. A blister.

"Christ," said the real estate agent, still catching his breath, "is he all right? Is he okay?"

"He's fine," said the American standing next to him. "Just fine."

"But what the hell is he doing?"

"He's trying to get himself lined up."

"Lined up? Lined up for what?"

Jake put a hand on Cornie's shoulder. "Maybe we should

try that other chair. You were in that chair last time, remember?" He looked over at the real estate agent. "Say, would you mind?"

"No. But what the...?"

"Wait."

The sound of hollow static, like glass shattering in a far-away room, crackled out of Cornie Marten's mouth. Then they could make out thin, wispy traces of music, snatches of voices singing in garbled, yodelling harmony.

"What the hell is that?" said the real estate agent.

"Goddamndest thing you ever saw, hey?" said the man from the bar. "He's picking up the signals."

"Signals?"

"From that goddamned TV tower. The one they just put up over there in Pembina."

"Fifteen hundred feet high," one of the other Americans bragged. "Taller than the ones the Russians built."

"Tallest in the world."

"He can pick up the signals with his mouth."

"Hang on," said Jake. He reached up and tilted Cornie's rigid head down slightly, and the signal came stronger. The skin stretched tightly across his face acted like a speaker and amplified the sound coming out of his gaping mouth. "That's better," said Jake. They could make out what it was now. The noise was really music. It was a jingle. A television commercial was playing out of Cornie Marten's mouth:

*Brylcreem,*
*A little dab'l do ya,*
*Brylcreem,*
*You'll look so debonair...*

"What do you think of that?" said the man from the bar. "Isn't that the goddamndest thing you ever heard?"

The real estate agent chomped down hard on his cigar. "How the hell does he do that?"

"Fillings," answered Jake matter-of-factly. "He's got a mouthful." He took down a large swallow of beer. "Too many sweets. After the fire, Mr. Klassen over at the store told us we could have all the candy we wanted, anytime we wanted. Felt sorry for us, I guess. We sure took him up on it, though. Teeth went bad. Cornie there, he went to the dentist. Drilled and filled about every tooth he had left. Said he'd never seen a mouth that bad. I wouldn't let him touch me, though." He grinned hideously to give the real estate agent an unobstructed view of his own teeth, some missing, others little more than rotting remnants.

"I bet those two could make some money," said one of the Americans farther back from the table. "You know those shows they have in the circus?"

Abe, who hadn't been paying much attention up to now, stiffened in his chair. "And what shows, exactly, would they be?" He was staring through the crowd, daring the man to answer. The Martens brothers knew that if he answered badly, there would be trouble. There was one word Abe would not allow anyone to use around them.

"I said, just what exactly what kind of a show would that be, mister?"

The American sensed that he was in a tight spot. Something about the way things got so quiet made him say, "I didn't mean anything. Really. Not a thing." He didn't want to say what it was any more. The thing that had gone through his mind – that went through a lot of people's minds when they got their first look at the Martens brothers. The thing that had brought the real estate over to the table in the first place.

"*We interrupt our regularly scheduled programming...*" A deep baritone voice sounded out of Cornie's gaping mouth.

"He's at it again," someone said, glad to break the tension.

*"President Kennedy has just announced...state of alert."*

"What'd he say?" Static was breaking up the message. *"...embargo on all ships heading..."*

"What was that last part?"

Jake adjusted the angle of Cornie's head, the aperture of his mouth *"...Cuban...missile bases."*

"It's that Castro bastard."

"Nah, he's just the front man. It's that baldheaded little cocksucker – what's his name – Kruschev. He's behind all of this."

"Goddamn Russian sons of bitches," said one of the Americans and slammed his fist on the table. The noise startled Cornie into closing his mouth.

"Geez, now look what you did," said Jake.

Cornie shook himself, as if he had just come out of a trance. "That was a good one, eh?" he said, then sat back and took a long swallow of Jack Daniels.

"They gotta send in the army," said another American. "Send in the troops and clean that mess up."

"Never mind that. I say send a few of those rockets over there. Wipe 'em out. The whole goddamn bunch of them."

"Show's over, boys," said Abe.

The Americans went back to their tables and bar stools. There was plenty for them to talk about now, one way or another, thanks to the Martens brothers.

"I'll let you boys in on a little secret," said the real estate agent. "This business with the Russians? Best damn thing that ever happened around here."

"Just how do you figure that?" said Cornie, who seemed completely normal now, as if nothing out of the ordinary had happened. The real estate agent found this a little unsettling, but kept right on talking just the same.

"Easy. All this Cold War stuff means more missiles. And

where are they putting them? Right here, boys. Right under our noses. You could throw a rock in any direction and hit one. It's a gold mine, I tell you. Say one of you has a little farm around here. You try to make a go of it from one year to the next but you don't know how long you can keep it up. And then, out of the blue, some guy in a uniform shows up at your door with a wad of cash. Offers to buy a few acres of your land for more than your whole place is worth. Wants to put one of those missiles in the ground. A gold mine, I tell you. Land prices are going through the roof. Good for the farmers. Good for me. Good for everybody. "

The real estate agent waited for a reaction and when he got only silence, kept on talking. "You boys are from over the line, that right?" he said. "That's Hutterite country up there, is it?" The Martens brothers looked over at Abe. Ordinarily, someone making a remark like that around Abe would have had to pay for it, but they could see that he was taking little, if any, interest in what the real estate agent might have to say. He wasn't himself this afternoon, they realized. Hadn't been since the movie. They knew he'd seen something up on that big screen that had disturbed him, but they weren't sure what it was and Abe wasn't talking. But he sure was in a mood. Everything about him seemed crooked – shifted. Even the way he'd walked out of the theatre – at an odd angle – the slant of his shoulders now, sitting at the table.

"Mennonites," said Cornie. "We're Mennonites."

"But you're clean-shaven. How's that? I thought you people all had beards."

"Beards," said Jake, and stroked a polished red chin. Cornie did the same and they both laughed. Ever since the gasoline fire, they'd lost the ability to grow facial hair.

"Hard workers, too" said the real estate agent. "I've heard that much."

"And pacifist," said Jake. "Don't forget pacifist."

"Must stick in your craw to see those things going into the ground right under your noses."

"We don't think about it too much," said Cornie.

"No. We're too busy working," said Jake.

"And praying," Cornie added.

"And trimming our beards." They both laughed.

"You wanna know how come they're putting them in so close to the border?" The real estate agent took a quick, sloppy gulp out of his glass. "Closer all the time? I'll tell you why. Logistics. That's what. Simple logistics." He was getting himself good and wound up, puffing up a grey plume of smoke from his rancid cigar, and for some reason, Abe Wiebe was letting him. The Martens brothers didn't mind all that much, since they were getting free drinks out of the deal. "Shortest way to Russia. Simple as that. Straight over the North Pole. Closer to the border, the better.

"The Russians. You know what the goddamn Russians are doing? They're installing their own goddamn missiles down there in Cuba – the sons-a-bitches. It's not like we really have a choice in this thing. We've got our interests to protect. You can understand that, can't you? Let me tell you something about the inhabitants of your little valley up there, boys. If it wasn't for us..." The Martens brothers were looking over at Abe again, waiting for him to say something.

But Abe wasn't really listening. Hadn't been from the start. He was thinking about the movie they'd just come from. About what he'd seen up on the big screen. It shouldn't have come as a surprise, he kept telling himself, to see her up there. He should have known it might happen. He knew as well as anyone she'd gone down there to be in the movies, but up to that moment he'd never really believed it. Never wanted to, somehow. Not that he didn't wish her well. Not that he didn't think she could hold her own with the most beautiful women in the world.

It was just that he hadn't expected it to be like this. One minute he was watching a harmless scene from another gangster movie, and the next, there she was, stepping out of a bedroom doorway in a rundown tenement, traffic noises coming in through grimy curtains of the open window. The man she was talking to pulled on a suit jacket, and slipped a snub-nose .38 revolver into his shoulder holster. Katie straightened down the front of her dress, smoothed back her long blonde hair, folded her arms. The man turned to her, put his hands up to her shoulders.

"I guess this is it, then," she said.

"I guess it is."

"But why does it have to be like this?"

"I don't know. I wish I had an answer for you."

"It doesn't make any sense. Not any of it."

"Maybe it isn't supposed to."

Sitting there, hands clutching the armrests of the plush velvet seats, eyes frozen to the big screen, Abe couldn't believe what he was hearing. It didn't seem possible. He knew every line of this dialogue.

"What exactly do you think you're going to prove?"

"I've asked myself that same question a hundred times. If I knew the answer I'd tell you. But I don't. I only know there's something I have to find out."

"And you can't tell me what it is."

"I'm telling you I don't know what it is. I only know I'll never find it here. And neither will you."

"So you keep telling me."

"You know it's true."

Hadn't he and Katie spoken these very words to each other the day he left? He knew exactly what she was going to say next – the line about him making a mistake.

"I think you're making a big mistake."

The man put his hands around her shoulders.

"I'll come back. I promise."

She tore herself free. Slapped him hard across the face. "How dare you?" She stared into his eyes. "How dare you promise me a thing like that."

He turned to go.

Abe was sure his imagination must be playing tricks on him. How could it be the same conversation – word for word – they'd had that last night they were together? Even the actions were the same. She was about to embrace the man one last time.

Katie threw her arms around his neck. "I won't let you. I won't let you go. Not like this. I'm sorry. It's just that... What if we both stayed? We could get married. What about that? Get married and have babies? Lots of babies. And then we wouldn't have to think about any of this again."

"It's never going to be that simple. Not for either of us. We both know that."

And this was where Abe had reached up and pulled her hands away. Hurried out through the door. He hadn't known about the part where Katie put her hands up to her face, sobbed into them.

If Katie had been there with him she could have explained all of these uncanny resemblances to Abe. Could have told him all about how the script came to sound the way it did. Look the way it did. Especially, she could have explained to him how easy the crying part was.

The rest of the movie was a blur for Abe. All he could do was sit – unable to breathe, unable to swallow – and wait for her to come back onto the screen, for the loveliness of her to crush him once more into the plush velvet of his seat. But she never did. And now he was wondering whether the whole thing had been his imagination – everything blown out of proportion by the lights and cameras and the big silver screen. That's what movies did, he told himself. That was their power.

But all of his second-guessing couldn't erase the fact that the sight of her had shaken him badly. Shocked him into this dark, brooding silence.

As for the bothersome man at the table with them, it was easy for Abe to ignore him. He understood what the real estate agent was trying to say. How important it was for him to believe, like so many Americans, that they really didn't mean any harm.

IN THE VILLAGE OF NEUSTADT – the one Abe Wiebe had escaped from and Katie Klassen was on her way back to – some of the men and women supposedly having maddoch schlope were, instead, secretly watching their newly acquired television sets. They had smuggled them over the border along the shortcut Katie had been turned away from, the one the young private was busy guarding.

These secret television watchers were allowed to engage in such sinful Sunday recreation without tipping off their neighbours thanks to a remarkable stroke of geographic luck. Ordinarily, to pull in a decent signal, they would have had to install a bulky antenna up on the roof of the house. But the inhabitants of the valley had no need of such cumbersome and revealing technology. Purely by chance (unless you believed the afternoon conversations of the men around the cooler at the village store), the tallest television transmission tower in the world had just been constructed only a few miles away, across the US border. Even the cheapest little set could pick up the signal. All you had to do was give the rabbit ears a twist or two, and, thanks to your close proximity to the tower, an amazingly clear, crisp, black and white picture of American network television beamed out at you from the screen. Then, like any other secret television watcher in the valley, you could simply sit back and let it do the rest – which it would, hour after hour, day after day, for as long as you let it.

These watchers had seen the special news bulletin, the one Cornie Martens had broadcast out of his mouth. It wasn't the first time that regular programming had been interrupted, and it wouldn't be the last. In fact, when it came to such unexpected intrusions, they were in for plenty more in the coming months. This bulletin had reported that the American president, John Fitzgerald Kennedy, would be making a special address to the nation later that day. The subject of his speech would be the embargo that had been placed on all ships sailing into Cuban waters. He would tell the American people – and anyone else watching – what was really going on down there. How Castro was allowing the Russians to secretly install their nuclear missiles on Cuban soil. How they were continuing to install them, against the express wishes of the United States of America. Most of all, he was going to tell everyone how he, JFK, leader of the armed forces of the United States of America, wasn't going to take it any more.

All the secret television watchers in the valley were tuned into the same American network television station, not because their tastes were so predictably homogeneous, but because it was really the only thing they could pick up. The signals from other stations – Canadian ones, for example – were broadcast out of more modest and distant transmission towers, and required an antenna up on the roof in order to pull them in. And because that would put an immediate end to any notion of secrecy, they were nowhere to be found in the valley.

The only house that had one belonged to Martha Wiebe. She'd installed one, not so much because of a preference for Canadian television programming, but more because she had no qualms about such a brazen display of worldliness. The antenna sat on the roof of her house as a testament to her defiance of the unwritten code of secrecy. It shimmered there, luminous in the afternoon sun, like some gigantic aluminium garden rake, so that all the valley might see the kind of illicit pleasure-taking going on in that particular household, the shameful depths of worldliness to which the occupant had allowed herself to sink, and know that she didn't give a damn.

She was about to watch television just now, along with her aging and captive father. She had never been able to convince him to stay in the same room with the television set on, but today was going to be different. Today he was going to stay. It was cruel, she thought, and a little humiliating, but she was going through with it because she was fed up. Tired of listening to him shout at her from the other room about what she was up to in there.

"That goes but all against," he would say in his most judgmental tone, "what you there do. To the devil goes that." As if she were engaged in some kind of satanic ritual. And always with such an annoying air of authority, when he didn't have the slightest idea what he was talking about. In this regard, she knew, he was just a typical Mennonite man, but even so, she had had enough.

It was just the two of them now. All her brothers gone. Her mother long before that. Martha remembered her as a fine-boned, soft-skinned creature, easily tired and not up to the demands of the life she had married herself into. She'd never been a strong woman physically and had died, not from hardening of the arteries, as the doctor had insisted, but from exhaustion. The boys, and Martha's father, had simply worn her out. As for Martha, who had a robust and athletic if not terribly feminine body, the job of looking after five grown men who conveniently refused to take care of themselves had not had the same effect on her. She had inherited none of her mother's delicate features. Any finesse had been smothered by the harsher aspects of her father's genetics.

When their mother died Martha had agreed to take over

the household chores temporarily. Promised herself that it would be something she would endure only until the boys married and left home, or her father managed to find a new wife. Certainly it was not unusual in the valley for a widower to remarry in as little as a month or two. There wasn't much to fear in the way of censure. Even people like the Zacharias sisters agreed that if a woman had the nerve to die on her family unexpectedly, she could expect to be replaced in short order. A man had to eat, after all. Had to have his kitchen looked after. His house kept in order.

But her father had been content to remain a widower. And the boys had refused to marry, until the daily ritual of domestic duties blended one day into another, one year into the next. Her father hadn't once, in all that time, talked to any of them about the decision they'd made. Had certainly never broached the subject of Martha's spinsterhood with her. Had never asked her why it was that she didn't seem interested in men, just as he had never asked his sons why they shunned women. It wasn't all that unusual for a village to have a household of brothers or sisters who never married. By staying together in one place, living in each other's company, their combined numbers formed a kind of insulation between themselves and the larger community – an alliance forged against the disapproval and second-guessing that came along with such a lifestyle – the closest thing the valley had to anything resembling a monastery or nunnery.

The boys had all taken their leave rather suddenly, one after another, within a few months of each other. People like the Zacharias sisters said it was out of loneliness, but the boys had never really suffered in that regard the way people thought. Martha knew it wasn't loneliness that had killed them, but drink. All their lives, they had insisted on ingesting the hard water that came out of the well in the yard – water saturated with enough minerals to fossilize every organ in their bodies. Even the most rudimentary forensics, she was certain, would have established the cause of death in each and every one of them as hardening of the arteries. After their mother's death it seemed to Martha the boys began to drink the water that was surely killing them with a kind of added zeal. They seemed to take extra pride in the way they dispatched glass after glass. There was an unexplainable and dogged willingness about it that infuriated her.

"What mean you," her father would scold, whenever Martha protested that they should drink the rainwater from the cistern, boiled, the way she did – the way any sensible inhabitant of the valley would. "Look once on my boys," he would offer in Plaut Dietsch. "Where has that them hurt done by. That water does those boys nothing harm. Or me." Her father drank the same acrid water, just as the boys did, and never hesitated to offer himself up as a testimonial to the frivolous nature of his daughter's concerns.

Martha had to admit that they certainly seemed the picture of health in their rolled-up shirt sleeves and tanned, muscular arms, their good teeth and square jaws. Occasionally, when she got on them about it, they became playful. Took turns flexing their muscles at her, stuck out their chests, pounded their hard stomachs, as if they were part of some backcountry, body-building pose-down.

"It's not where you can see it," Martha would persist. "It's on the inside."

"Oh," they would look at each other with raised eyebrows, wink. "The inside." They would open their mouths and look down each other's throats. Peer into each other's ears. Make her feel foolish in spite of herself. This was their power. The power of men. To make a woman feel foolish for showing concern. Compassion.

Her brothers' early demise was taken as proof by the local inhabitants that a life devoid of marriage and children was not suited to longevity, that the companionship of a good woman

was essential in helping a man reach old age. They had not
died from hardening of the arteries, the local wisdom insisted,
but from hardening of the heart.

So now it was just her father left, still stubbornly gulping
down glass after glass of the same water that had surely killed
his sons.

"Now must I look," said Isaac. He spoke in Plaut Dietsch,
the same crude dialect all of the people in the valley had been
born into, and addressed his only daughter with the same tone
so many of the men used. The one that transformed all of their
conversation, including questions, into declarations.

"Yes." This time she was not going to help him out of the
room. This time she was going to make him sit through it, no
matter what it did to his delicate psyche.

"Here."

"Yes."

"You are oh but very against, daughter."

"It's time you saw for yourself."

"Now must I."

"You must."

"That will I not."

"You will."

"Sitting will I. Oh, but looking will I not."

She got up and turned up the dial for the volume on the
front of the television set. The program she wanted to watch
would be coming on at any moment. She didn't want to miss
the beginning. It was a western called *Have Gun Will Travel*. It
wasn't so much the show she wanted to watch as its star –
Richard Boone. Martha liked him very much. Liked the look of
him all dressed in black. The way he wore his fancy black hat –
fancier than a Stetson – and smoked those little black cigars.
He was such a ruggedly handsome man, with such a good
chest and wide shoulders. Martha thought he could easily have
come from Mennonite stock.

"That will me nothing hurt do, you think."

"You won't feel a thing."

"It is all wickedness."

"Nonsense."

A handsome young man's face appeared on the screen, rubbing something into his shiny hair. From the speaker came the sound of singing:

*Brylcreem, a little dab'l do ya.*
*Brylcreem, you'll look so debonair.*

Martha looked over at her father to see how he was taking it. He stared at the television set – head cocked to one side, eyes wide – the way a dog might at something it is unable to decipher.

"Where." Jacob sat up. Then, "Who."

"Where what?"

"There." He pointed at the television screen. "That man. Where is he."

*Brylcreem, the gals'l all pursue yaaaaah...*
*They love to run their fingers through your hair.*

"What goes there on."

"It's like a movie," said Martha, but, of course, her father had never been to a movie – never would go. Martha understood that he had no concept of projection, of screens. That he was unable to make the leap to electronic imagery. He lived in a literal world. Concrete and fundamental. Abstract ideas did not present themselves to him readily. Nor were they part of the language he spoke.

"But where are they."

"Who?"

"That people there." A shapely young woman was running

her fingers through the sticky substance the young man had just rubbed into his hair. Even with her back turned to the camera, Martha thought she looked familiar.

"They what there speaking do," said her father. Isaac got up out of his chair and shuffled over to the television set. "How can that." He leaned forward and touched it gingerly, the way a cat might touch its paw to a pool of water. He inspected the surface of the screen closely, blocking it out so that Martha lost sight of the woman she was trying to identify. Then he went around to the back and peered into one of the many small round holes, trying to get a better look at the inner workings.

"That looks me as a radio there in." He leaned around to see what was happening on the screen. "How are they there in so small." There was a different commercial on now. A well-dressed man sat down next to a sophisticated-looking woman on a fancy sofa. She had a cigarette in her hand and he was lighting it for her.

"But where. How can that people give. And furniture," Isaac wanted to know. "They do there smoking," said Isaac, and leaned over to peer into the opening again. "Oh but this is all cracked." He sniffed loudly. "That smells me nothing. How can there smoking be and yet not to smell it."

"The people are on the screen, Papa. Like a picture," said Martha. But she knew it was no use. She understood that her father was no different than any other old man of the valley. He had an idea in his head now, and like any self-respecting Mennonite – right or wrong – he wasn't about to let go of it. This particular idea, she was beginning to realize, consisted of her father's stubborn conviction that the people and artifacts on the screen actually existed somewhere inside the television set.

She got up and crouched next to him, one hand on his shoulder, trying to coax him back to his chair.

"How can that there all packed in be. That goes not."

"They're not real, Papa, they're not really there."

"Midgets." And he made one last attempt to peer through the small opening before she pulled him away and took him back to his chair. Instead of *Have Gun Will Travel*, a reporter came on to tell everyone that regularly scheduled programming had been interrupted to make an announcement. Martha got up and turned off the television. She decided that she'd upset her father enough for one day, and if he figured out what they were talking about it would only make things worse. She had a pretty good idea what the bulletin was going to be anyway. She knew all about how President Kennedy and Nikita Kruschev were flexing their muscles for everyone to see.

"I'll go make us something to eat," she said, and went into the kitchen to fix them some fastba. When she checked on her father a few minutes later, he was still in his chair, still staring blankly at the now inanimate screen. He had fallen into a quiet agitation by that time, an unsettled reverie in which he was nothing more than an addled spectator, watching helplessly as several powerful ideas took turns butting up against each other in his mind.

Martha went back to slicing pickles at the kitchen counter, and thought about the woman she'd seen in the television commercial – the one with her back to the camera. There was something familiar about her. A bright flicker of light shimmered through the window. She looked up in time to glimpse the sunshine bouncing off something moving between the cottonwood trees along the street. Something shiny and yellow.

BECAUSE IT WAS JUST PAST ONE when the car with the California license plates came gliding into the village, many of the adult inhabitants weren't up to see it. After a

morning of sermon and song, followed by summer sausage
for lunch, all the respectable mothers and fathers of the valley had continued their celebration of the Sabbath by retiring
into their cool dark bedrooms for maddoch schlope – a
leisurely afternoon nap. And so it was mostly the young –
children playing hoops and hopscotch along the dirt-packed
street, adolescent lovers stretched out under the shade of the
giant cottonwood trees – that witnessed the unexpected
arrival. The woman behind the wheel took off her dark sunglasses, brushed back her shiny blonde hair, and smiled at
them with perfect white teeth. They marvelled at her apple
green eyes, her wine red lips. They stopped what they were
doing, even the adolescent lovers groping at each other's
newly-minted body parts, when they saw what appeared to
be a movie star in a shiny yellow convertible riding past
them.

It was purely an act of the imagination for them to identify
her as such, since none of them had ever seen a movie star in
the flesh. A small but increasing number had witnessed one
from the luscious velvet darkness of the Wallhalla theatre by
that time, since more and more of them were sneaking out of
the village on Sunday afternoons for just such a purpose. They
only had to make their way around the half-hidden marker at
the end of the street and down the road a few miles. The most
formidable deterrent to such an act of defiance had never been
geographic, but rested, rather, in the strict and rigorous hierarchy of the village elders. Once that was no longer enough to
stop them, the rest was easy.

It was obvious, even to these sheltered and unenlightened
youngsters, that this visitor had come from far away. The
license plate was a dead giveaway, even if they had only a
vague idea where California might be. As she floated by under
the cool canopy of the cottonwoods, all the brush-cut blond
boys in their itchy wool pants and long-sleeved shirts, all the

braided blue-eyed girls in their plain sundresses and bare feet, sensed that they were in the presence of someone truly special.

"Maybe she's come for a schlopebank," said the girl with the braided hair. She played with one of her pigtails between her fingers as she watched the convertible go by. They had finished their game of hide-and-seek among the wild hollyhocks at the edge of the village, and were making their way leisurely up the shady village street, inspecting the ground now and then for dirty things the boys might have scratched there. They were actually on their way to the schoolyard, where they intended to take turns pushing each other on the big swing.

"She's pretty," said the girl in the pink dress.

"Prettier than that other lady."

"Much prettier."

"Pretty in a different way," said the oldest, who could make final pronouncements on such matters.

The girls were comparing this visitor with another woman who had come into the village only last week. That one had stopped and asked them for directions to Abe Wiebe's place. They had watched her turn into his yard, seen him come out of the house to greet her, help her out of her car and into his workshop. Word around the valley was that Abe Wiebe's schlopebanks were becoming a bit of a collector's item with wealthy young women from across the line – farmers' wives some said, who had suddenly come into a lot of money.

The girls remembered that it had been a long time before Abe and the woman emerged. When they finally did, he was carrying a bench, which he loaded into the trunk of her car. They'd watched her drive away with a strong sense, childhood innocence notwithstanding, that something more than simple commerce had taken place inside the workshop. After that particular visit the talk around the village had shifted in a new direction. More than one of the girls had overheard the gossip that it was not the schlopebanks, but Abe Wiebe himself who was becoming something of a collector's item.

But this woman didn't stop to ask for directions, only smiled and waved as she drove by. The girls waved back and continued on their way to the school grounds. They had no way of knowing that it was this woman, above all others, that Abe Wiebe would have wished into his yard. But then, there was a great deal they could never have suspected about her. The fact, for instance, that unlike other visitors, the more unique aspects of the village held no special novelty for her. She took no particular notice, for example, that in every shady yard on either side of the street, the houses and barns butted up against each other, so you couldn't tell where one ended and the other began. Such peculiarities often baffled other visitors, especially Americans, who passed through on a Sunday afternoon to gawk at the strange folk living across the border from them.

Sometimes it was an older couple, rosy with wealth and grooming, coasting through the village in a big shiny car with the windows up and the airconditioning on. Other times, a station wagon full of noisy, overfed children who yelled and pointed shamelessly out of their rolled-down windows at such a quaint way of life. As for the plain-dressed, plain-fed children who stared back at them from the side of the road, they were only just beginning to think of themselves – of their valley – as quaint.

If the woman in the yellow convertible seemed to take no particular notice of the unusual features the village offered, she had good reason to be so unimpressed. She'd grown up much the same as the children staring at her – eaten the same oatmeal and summer sausage, lived the same sheltered existence, allowed to take in only the smallest doses of the outside world through the carefully-constructed filter of religious piety. She had grown up in a housebarn just like the ones they lived in.

The last one on the right at the end of the street, as a matter of fact. The one she was on her way to now.

Katie took a deep breath. Tried to relax her shoulders. None of it made any sense. It all seemed so unlikely. So implausible. The whole thing felt like something out of a movie. There was nothing unusual in that. Ever since she could remember – long before she knew what a movie was – Katie had often thought of her life that way. As a series of scenes to be played out. A script. Even before she knew what a script was.

And what if this really was a movie script? thought Katie. No producer in his right mind would buy it. Rising young starlet returns to the small Mennonite village (nestled in an obscure, but scenic valley on the southern edge of the Canadian border) where she was born. He'd laugh it out of his office as too unlikely, too wildly contrived.

But even if he didn't, what actress in her right mind would take the part? Katie imagined a shot along the length of the shady village street, the camera panning down between the black and green cottonwoods, zooming in on the back of her yellow convertible. She couldn't decide which was stranger: the fact that she'd gone to California in the first place, or that she had decided to come back. Or had she? It didn't feel like a decision she'd consciously made.

Partly, she reasoned, her unexpected return had something to do with the times. Every day, it seemed, the unlikely was becoming more commonplace. That had always been true for a place like Los Angeles, but now it was spreading out across the continent. The globe. There was something going on. Everyone seemed to be on the verge of something. The edge. People were in a heightened state of awareness. The way they talked. The way they acted. There seemed to be a rarefied air hovering over everyone.

Katie was no exception. If people sleeping in their bedrooms on either side of the street had difficulty with the idea that she had become an actress, what would they think if they discovered that she had recently taken up the study of philosophy? In a way, she had Peter to thank for that. She'd packed one of his books by mistake when she left, stumbled across it again only last month when she pulled a cardboard box out of the closet, and examined it: *An Enquiry Concerning Human Understanding.* Something about the title had made her open it, later, in bed, instead of the romance novel she'd been reading. She didn't think, at first, that she really understood what the author was trying to say. She wasn't sure he himself did. The writing was couched in stuffy academic language that got in the way, it seemed to her. And yet, it had a certain allure, inaccessible as it was. She thought it was a pretty compelling thing for someone to want to write about. There was certainly a great deal she didn't understand about what it meant to be human. The way people acted sometimes. The things they did. Things that gnawed at her insides. So much about what had happened back there in the village felt unresolved. Unfinished. Perhaps, she thought, there might be a way to make sense of it after all.

She read the entire book over the course of a week. Then read it again. Made some notes. Went, for the first time in her life, to the local library and found other books on the subject. After that it was no more romance novels for her. The discourse of metaphysics and epistemology had become a kind of refuge for her now. A sanctuary. She found herself fascinated with the idea of an approach to life where human foibles and frailty were not allowed to be part of the equation.

The more she read the more it confirmed what she'd suspected all along: that in many ways the constructs of her existence, of everyone's existence, were not all that solid. It might have been this that attracted her to the movie business in the first place. She'd always had the nagging sense, even early on, that the world was a place built on illusion. That it might all

come tumbling down at any moment. And now, with everything that was going on, that kind of thinking seemed to be
making its way into the big and little events of people's every-
day lives. Everybody was caught up in it. Things were in a state
of flux.

In a lot of people's minds, World War Three was only days,
perhaps hours, perhaps minutes, away. Armageddon. The end
of life as everyone had come to know it. Catastrophe of biblical proportions. Scripture come to fruition. Back in Hollywood, people were very busy just now building fallout shel-
ters. They were all pretty sure there was going to be a nuclear
war. Some of them were converting their swimming pools into
concrete bunkers, stocking them with enough supplies to keep
the inhabitants alive for six months or so – long enough for
the bomb to do its worst. Perhaps it was this feeling of
impending doom, this idea that the world really was about to
end, that had sent her back home. But there was something
else. Something Katie couldn't put her finger on.

It was apparent to Katie, from all the children playing in the
yards, on the street, that lots of babies had been conceived and
born in her absence. Procreation was well in hand. If things
were still the same, she thought, then even now a goodly number of the villagers supposedly having maddoch schlope were
doing more than that. In many of the bedrooms, she speculated,
couples were engaged in the act of copulation – the women
lying dutifully under their hard-working men, allowing themselves to be quickly and efficiently penetrated and inseminated.
A goodly number of these same women being penetrated were
probably already pregnant, their husbands mounting them as
best they could, used to working around a swollen belly and
curved spine. Was it possible, Katie wondered, that in one or
two of the bedrooms the woman could be enjoying herself as
much as the man? A woman, perhaps, who was lucky enough
to be physiologically and emotionally programmed for quick

and easy orgasm? A woman who discovered, in the purposeful and efficient thrusting of her husband's genital machinery, that there was enough time for her to squeeze out a quick climax of her own?

As Katie drove slowly down the tree-lined street, the great cottonwoods on either side forming a shady bower for her to travel under, she noticed that in a few of the village yards, the traditional housebarn dwelling had been transformed into a granary or perhaps a storage shed. The former inhabitants had moved into a California-style bungalow complete with a picture window in the living room, the kind of houses she had seen so many of, but never lived in, while she was away in Hollywood. Katie was in the early stages of discovering that Neustadt, like every other village in the valley, was caught up in the unrelenting process of losing its identity.

She would soon learn that in some of the houses, instead of procreating, or sleeping, the mother and father were secretly tuning in American network television on crude black and white television sets, massive concoctions of wood and glass and vacuum tubes they had secretly smuggled into their bedrooms under cover of darkness to keep nosy neighbours from discovering what manner of sinful disobedience they were about to practise.

Some of the children watching Katie drive by had been into those same bedrooms when the adults were out of the house to take a quick look for themselves. They might have stayed to watch for only a few minutes, or perhaps for the better part of an hour. Either way, it would have been long enough to discover that the world inside their village, their valley, was not the one being depicted on the television screen. Katie Klassen could have told them as much, could have told them all about that other world – the world of television and movies, of commercials and consumerism – because she was just back from there. She had learned all the finer points of acquisition and disposal in a place founded on those very principles.

By village standards, she had become about as worldly as it was possible to get. It was the possibility of her worldliness that had started all the trouble in the first place – had made life in the village so unbearable. The people who lived there believed in just the opposite. Simple Mennonite worship. Toil. Sacrifice. There was no room for a woman like Katie Klassen, for the glamorous possibilities of her stunning natural beauty. And now she had studied philosophy, of all things. What would they make of her now?

It was notable that in a few of the yards there appeared to be nothing stirring at all. These places seemed too quiet – even for a Sunday. If the houses and barns seemed empty and unoccupied, it was because they were just that – abandoned. She would find her own house clean, in good order, and completely deserted. There would not be so much as a note. No explanation, except for a Bible laid out on the kitchen table, opened to a passage underlined in red – a passage admonishing the reader against the sinfulness of leading a worldly existence.

The fact that her parents wouldn't be there when she arrived would make things a lot easier in so many ways. She would be spared the hostile coolness of her father. The troubling neutrality of her mother. This way, there was so much she wouldn't have to keep from telling them. So much she wouldn't have to lie about. She'd long ago made up her mind that if she ever came back it wouldn't be to talk about where she'd been and what she'd done. No one was going to get much out of her on that score. Most of it wouldn't make any sense to them. Most of it didn't make any sense to her now, and she'd only been back for a few minutes. But already it seemed impossible that it could really have happened. That she should have undertaken something so improbable and succeeded. Already that world seemed as unreal, as unimaginable, as this place would to the inhabitants of Hollywood.

She hadn't had any contact with her family, or anyone else for that matter, since she left. In the beginning, she'd sent the odd letter – addressed to General Delivery – but it always came back unopened after a few months. There was no point in trying to telephone because that kind of technology wasn't allowed in her father's household – never mind a television set. And so Katie lost touch with everyone – with the village – with the entire valley. It didn't bother her all that much because she didn't think she was ever coming back. And now here she was. She'd spent the entire trip up trying to explain this to herself, but had been unable to come up with anything satisfactory.

She found just now, driving through the village, that she had no desire to conquer this place, the way she might have wanted to once upon a time. She'd always told herself that one day this place would have to acknowledge her as an individual it had failed to accommodate. It would have to squirm a little under her considerable presence. But that didn't matter now. Maybe it never had. She was not on a mission to gain acceptance or revenge, not in the way she'd thought she needed to.

As she drove through town, she felt, strangely, that she had come into a place of safety. Security. She hadn't expected to feel so at ease. She was sure, though, that it wasn't this feeling she had come back for. Back to this restrictive and unforgiving place. It was a feeling, she told herself, that could not be trusted. It was only because of the children. When the adults came out of their bedrooms it would be different. Katie Klassen hadn't forgotten about maddoch schlope. She had deliberately timed her entry for it.

ON THIS SUNNY AFTERNOON, while the people in the village nearby were napping or procreating or even secretly watching their television sets, Dickie Derksen was standing out in the middle of a cow pasture, his thick, flat face turned up to the sky. Dickie was not transforming fluffy white clouds into giraffes and kangaroos and kittens, although there were plenty of billowing beauties to choose from for just that purpose. Nor was he merely basking in the warmth of the summer sun while looking skyward for birds on the wing, even though the pasture he was standing in was a favourite hunting ground for many hawks and falcons in the area. No, Dickie wasn't interested in the natural world this afternoon. He was inspecting the upper atmosphere for military aircraft.

There was plenty to watch for. New varieties of jets and bombers seemed to be entering the air space over the valley every day. Some of them were enormous, such as the B-52 flying fortresses, which Dickie would have identified as such if he'd been able, but his ability in the area of language and auditory memory would simply not permit it, and so each different species of aircraft was classified in much simpler, less technical ways. Some of the aircraft hung in the sky on low-level, low-velocity flights, frightening the birds of prey as they circled overhead, throwing enormous shadows across the meadows and fields. Others, such as the tankers, equally enormous, flew tandem with the B-52s, refuelling them.

But the fighter jets were Dickie's favourite. They were small and fast and they could make a louder noise than any of the bigger planes. He was much too simple-minded to grasp the concept of flying through the sound barrier, but that didn't stop him from marvelling at the rolling thunder they could produce. And although he was unfamiliar with the aerodynamics of speed and manoeuvrability, he never tired of watching them perform their amazing feats of aerial acrobatics.

It was of no concern to him that all of this practising was taking place over Canadian soil, in Canadian airspace. That what was going on above his head constituted a violation of international law. Dickie wasn't about to blow the whistle. The thought of bringing it to anyone's attention never crossed his mind. In this regard he was no different than any other inhabitant of the valley.

Dickie just wanted to watch. Imagine himself up there. He'd always had a special affection for being transported through the air. When he was allowed to go to school, his favourite thing was for young Steven Zacharias to push him as high as he could on the big swing. There was such a feeling of freedom in that. Such a feeling of lightness. And even with his limited imagination, he wondered what it would be like up there inside one of those planes, so high above the ground. How wonderfully giddy it would make him feel.

Dickie had a lot of time on his hands these days. For awhile he had been allowed to go to school, since his retardation was not extreme, and because he did have some limited capability in mathematical computation and reading comprehension. The problem was that he didn't speak, and so his teachers had a hard time deciding whether he was actually learning anything or not. They found his presence upsetting.

His tenure as a student ended abruptly one afternoon, when, according to the administrative documentation, he carried out an unprovoked attack on his teacher, a Miss Agnes Thiessen, late of Steinbach, Manitoba. If anyone had bothered to ask the children their side of the story, they would have discovered that Dickie had been acting in self-defence, since at the moment he lashed out at Miss Thiessen, she had been flogging him across his thick back and shoulders with a stiff leather strap as if he were a disobedient dog. The entire student body would have been more than happy to give testimony to that effect, but, as usual, they had not been consulted on the matter.

Dickie had been expelled from school for that incident, was never to be allowed back into a classroom, and had plenty of time now to stand out in the middle of a pasture and look up at the sky for as long as he wanted to. He was back to spending his days on the rundown farm where he lived with all his brothers and sisters and his alcoholic stepfather in such spectacular squalor. People driving by were always amazed at the outright destitution on display there. They were troubled, but only mildly, that it should be allowed to exist in the valley at all. Such abject poverty flew in the face of Christian charity.

But Christian charity was practised in the valley only insofar as those on the receiving end were seen to be industrious and hard-working. Dickie's stepfather was neither. He was a drunk. The fact that he beat Dickie on a regular basis added little to the equation. The elders of the village went right on doing what they always did about that sort of thing. They simply ignored it.

Luckily, Dickie's skin was, literally, quite thick, and his bone structure hardy and tough. He could take a punch as well as a seasoned prizefighter. His stepfather, a burly man with a powerful chest and muscular shoulders, rarely succeeded at knocking him out. The fact that Dickie could throw a pretty good punch himself was of no use to him. He would never have allowed himself such an indulgence. He hadn't intended to strike Miss Thiessen either, had merely lashed out a fist at the source of the pain, a fist that his stepfather would have absorbed easily enough, and which would have made him double his efforts to pummel Dickie into unconsciousness.

Because the sun had passed the zenith, and was already on its way toward the western horizon, Dickie faced east to avoid the glare. Behind him, the Pembina Hills curled in a hazy blue curve along the western rim of the valley. They were not grand enough to be imposing, but too prominent to go unnoticed. Truly scenic only in the light of sunrise, they seemed content to lie in relative obscurity the rest of the day. They offered a pleasing, if not spectacular, view of the valley. A traveller standing on their crest could look east and see the entire valley laid out before him. Still, the greatest effect they had on the valley below was not visual, but rather climatic. They formed a kind of blind to incoming weather, which came mostly from the west. A day might unfold clear and blue until, without warning, a thunderhead swooped down over the valley, black and ugly and full of malice. It had gathered itself up on the escarpment, crept to the edge, lurked there, behind the cover of the hills, before it pounced on the unassuming inhabitants of the valley below, and caught them by surprise.

A villager might be pulling his plough, heading east down the field, his back to the hills, looking up at a clear blue sky, and see a shadow, dark and ominous, sweep past him, speeding out ahead of him over the field, feel the sudden cold edge of a wind blow his hat off before he could reach up to grab it, his bare head pelted with stinging pellets of driven rain or hail, nasty lightning flashes, thunder rolling across the low sky, his only recourse to crouch under the hot belly of his steaming tractor, a little stunned by the speed and ferocity of it all.

It was just such a thunderhead that was gathering itself up on the escarpment while Dickie stood out in the pasture watching for fighter jets. This thunderhead was preparing to generate a wind that would shake and shiver the enormous cottonwoods, flutter and roll their autumn leaves into a thousand spinning dervishes, bend the ripened wheat and barley low in wave after wave of wind and driving rain. And because it was an unseasonably hot and humid afternoon, this one had formed quickly and efficiently up on the escarpment, created its own charged world – one that would produce violent bolts of angry lightning, lightning that needed a place to go to ground. There wouldn't be much to choose from in the open prairie, except, of course, for the mighty cottonwoods. And Dickie Derksen.

Dickie, standing out in the pasture looking for jets, was not really thinking about any of this. He had no formal training in meteorology. He certainly knew enough to get in out of the rain, but didn't always feel like it. Especially if it meant making himself available for another beating. And so when the thunderhead snuck up on the little valley and swept over the edge of the escarpment with such stealth and silent speed, Dickie was too busy to notice. He was looking straight up. Listening.

He wanted to shout with anticipation, but there wasn't much chance of that. All his life Dickie had been trying without success to make some kind of sound come out of his mouth. He should have been able to bellow as loud as a bull. After all, he had the lung capacity of a barrel-chested opera singer. But not so much as a small squeal had ever passed between his thick lips. It was this unique feature which allowed his stepfather to beat him so severely without arousing suspicion from the neighbours. Not that the neighbours would have done much about it.

While the blows rained down on him, Dickie would often open his mouth in a desperate attempt to scream out the pain, but nothing ever came out. His stepfather would sometimes shout at his mentally disabled son, even as his fist crunched the bones of Dickie's face. "Come on you retarded son-of-a-bitch. Yell. Go on. Yell loud enough for the neighbours to hear." Dickie had long ago figured out what his father wanted from him. He understood that it was necessary for him to try and scream or yell or cry out in some manner. And he desperately wanted to. Tried with every lash. But the harder he tried and failed, the harder his stepfather beat him.

"Go on, yell, you idiot. Scream like a wild animal, you little cocksucker." A lot of the time Dickie's stepfather was very drunk and the beating less severe, simply because he could hardly stand, but other times it was just the right mixture of alcohol and anger, and then Dickie tried with all his might to scream. If only he could scream, he thought in his mind, if only he could do what his stepfather kept asking him to do, then he could make it stop.

It was Dickie's silence while he was being beaten that enraged his stepfather more than anything. It was the silence he couldn't stand. This afternoon he had found a new way of trying to make Dickie utter a cry. Today he had tried punching him in his little testicles, which should have dropped by now, but the blow only caused Dickie to exhale a muffled puff of air from his ample lungs and double over in pain. His stepfather took out his frustration at this failure by working his way around behind Dickie and kicking him very hard in the back, so that his head rammed into the side of the root cellar. This knocked Dickie out. After that his stepfather closed the door and left him there.

Dickie had regained consciousness, and stumbled out into the pasture to look for vapour trails, high in the sky, just the way the the young poet had taught him to. It was Steven who had first explained to him about sonic booms and sound barriers. Dickie understood little of it, but admired him very much for taking the time to explain it, nodded his head as if he understood everything.

The young poet had taken it upon himself to do so because he had decided some time ago that it mattered. Mattered more than most people ever thought it could. Mattered in a way that was just beyond his own comprehension – a way that was only hinted at in small, bright moments of insight, when he caught a brief and misty glimpse of what it meant for someone like Dickie to be alive in the world. It was through him that the poet had first seen a window into another kind of existence. Another way to be. Dickie, surrounded almost entirely by harshness, by cruelty, by ignorance, somehow carried it all on his broad, thick back in a way Steven could only marvel at.

He found in Dickie a humanity not easily accessible in others. In spite of his handicap – or perhaps because of it – he seemed more human than so many others around him. To Steven, he was not dull. He was not eerie, or strange to be near. It was Dickie's ability to make himself small that Steven wanted to learn. It was important to be able to do that, he understood, if he was ever going to be any good as a poet, if his poetry was going to be any good at all.

As for Dickie, he was smart enough to know that other children thought him stupid. And he liked it that the young poet treated him as if this were not true. He appreciated it very much. It made him feel better, just to have someone do that for him. It was a silent pact the two of them had made that first afternoon – the same afternoon Dickie had been sent home from school for trying to kill the teacher, Miss Thiessen. In fact, Dickie had only succeeded in knocking her into unconsciousness, after she lashed him several times across his thick broad back with the leather strap. In the aftermath, Dickie was expelled, and Steven had looked after him. In the process they had become friends, if such a thing was possible between two people so different – alike only in a few unexplainable ways.

The pact consisted of a tacit understanding that the young poet should explain things to Dickie, and that Dickie should pretend he understood them, and furthermore, that it was not a waste of time. The satisfaction, the pact insisted, would not rest in any measurement of how much was actually getting through, but in the act itself.

Dickie was still looking up into a clear blue sky when the first clap of thunder sounded behind him. He was convinced it must be a jet breaking the sound barrier, and intensified his inspection of the sky. He was excited, and took in an enormous gulp of air.

THE YOUNG POET was not there to see Katie Klassen come riding into the village. He was, at the moment, under the shade of a lone cottonwood tree in the no man's land that marked the area between the Canadian and American border. This strip of land consisted of a ridge, four or five feet high, and perhaps ten feet wide. Set squarely at the centre of the ridge, every now and then, was a steel marker with the words "Canada" written along one side, and "United States of America" on the other.

But these markers were not the true sentinels of the line. That distinction belonged to the stately cottonwoods that stood, mighty and rogue, at uneven intervals along the ridge. They had sprung up there, spontaneously, a long time ago, and been allowed to grow to maturity along the border stretching from the Red River to the Pembina Hills. It was only because of their location that they had been allowed to survive in the first place. It was all right to have trees in the village, around the yard, along the creek, in the ditch next to the road, and so on, but if they took up even the smallest plot of arable farmland they were quickly eliminated – cut down as saplings or, if they were smaller still, simply ploughed over. After all, what good were they?

But it was a different story along the border. Things were not so straightforward there. A sapling might have sprung up there that wasn't, technically, on anybody's land. On either side of the line, successive generations of farmers would have monitored the progress of such a tree along the edge of the field, as it got bigger and bigger each year. They would have taken off their mangled straw hats and scratched their heads, uncertain as to whether they had any jurisdiction over it. Was it an American cottonwood? Or a Canadian one? Unable to come up with an answer, they would have opted not to plough it under. In this way it had been allowed to grow there, perhaps for the better part of a century, until it towered, bold and solitary, over the fields on either side.

It was under the shade of just such a tree that Steven was sitting now. It seemed lately that he wandered more and more to this place. He was hardly seen any more in the village. It seemed some of the local inhabitants were having a bit of trouble with the idea of him sitting out in the open, perhaps on a crate next to the village store, or on the side of the bridge at the end of the street, or even on the steps of the church, God forbid, lost in reading – not the Bible – or writing profusely – not scripture – on some scrap of paper. Steven, a sensitive young man, was not unaware of this difficulty, and so had lately taken it upon himself to perform these unseemly rituals elsewhere. He could be seen at almost any time of the day or evening, walking out of the village and into the countryside with a book in his hand. He was just beginning to come to grips with the idea of being a poet in a place where there was really no room for one.

He was reading some poetry now, to the young woman next to him. She had agreed to accompany him to this relatively secluded spot, on the grounds that he would do so. He had discovered only recently that a surprising number of young women liked having poetry read to them.

Beth Unger didn't understand a lot of it. Didn't care to. But just now, she'd picked up a line – something about birds sighing.

"I wonder what that would sound like," she said.

"What's that?"

"A bird sighing," said Betty. "I wonder if there's really such a thing."

"I don't think it's something you hear with your ears. Not the way you hear a bell or a song."

"But then what does it mean?"

The conversation might have gone on longer except for the fact that Steven kissed her just then on the lips. It was a convenient time to do so. She was sitting on the blanket with her legs folded under her skirt, and he was lying on his side next to her, his head just below hers. When he looked up from the page, it was right into her eyes, her mouth only inches from his, and so he simply raised himself up on one elbow, and she bent down a little, and the kiss materialized.

About time, thought Betty Unger, who was eager to give herself over to the forces raging inside her, the ones her mother had repeatedly warned would get her into trouble. She didn't need any more poetry. A line earlier had put her over the top. It had the word dark in it, and also the word desire, and the way these two sounded next to each other had pretty much done it for her. Embodied within it was all the trouble she wanted to get into. Wonderful trouble. Dark and dangerous passion. She wanted to be overcome by her desire, in all its glorious darkness, to be swept up by it.

Unlike Betty, the young poet considered himself to be on a more noble quest. He was doing more than just trying to get something out of his system. His was nothing less than a search for truth. It just so happened that, at the moment, he was looking for it in the arena of carnal lust. All his life he had been taught that the pursuit of earthly pleasure was an obfuscation of the truth. That it could only be found in self-denial and sacrifice. That the only hope of finding it lay in the world to come.

But Steven couldn't afford to wait. Not when he could hear the sound of men and equipment working nearby. Could stand up and get an unobstructed view of them getting ready to insert a nuclear missile into the ground. Even now, as he read to Betty Unger, it was this business with the missiles that fuelled his imagery, channelled his energy, as much as any desire to explore the ways of the flesh. It had lately occurred to him that there might be as much poetry in one as in the other.

It had started when, along with the books of poetry his aunt Martha was always bringing him from the library in Winnipeg, she'd included something else. He'd gone to pick them up at her house and as always, she'd made him stay a while, long enough for him to tell her a little bit about the books he was returning, and for her to say something about the ones she was presenting him with this time. She handed over each one as if it were a gift. Which it was.

For this exchange they would sit on the schlopebank in her sitting room, with the books between them. Aunt Martha's sitting room was different than any other in the valley, in that it was not nearly so austere. Perhaps it was the oil painting on the far wall, a pastoral scene in the style of Gainsborough. Or the area rug, woven out of such colourful material, and spread so invitingly across the floor. It might have been the large and leafy dieffenbachia that grew almost to the ceiling in the far corner. Even one such item was a rarity in any other sitting room.

Or perhaps it had more to with the absence of things. There was, for example, a complete lack of white lace doilies on tablestops and armchairs. But more important was the noticeable absence of a grandfather clock on the wall. Every other sitting room in the valley, including his own home, had one. Great wood and brass chronometers, disproportionately ornate and elaborate for such austere surroundings. Children were often forced to sit on hard and unforgiving schlopebanks underneath them, the clock ticking above their bowed heads, while the father of the house read scripture in silence. Their relentless ticking, their intermittent chimes did not so much measure increments of time, it seemed to him, as dole out greater and lesser portions of weekly oppression, of another Sunday's tyranny over the valley.

But it was different at his Aunt Martha's. Steven found himself not only able to breathe there, but actually to relax. The last time he'd gone to see her she'd handed him a book titled, *Nuclear Warfare: A Formative Study.*

"Here," she said. "You should read poetry, but you should read this, too."

"Why?"

"Because this is what's really going on. Because it's important."

He'd taken the book only because he didn't want to upset her, read the first few pages with begrudging curiosity, then found himself completely absorbed by it – fascinated, not so much by the content, which was straightforward enough, but by the language it was written in. He might as well have been reading a book on the process of evaporation. The academic authors spoke of the end of the world – the nuts and bolts of it – with such an astonishing lack of sensitivity. Of humanity. They wrote of human casualty with such cold calculation, of unspeakable suffering with such abject dismissal, of devastating destruction with such stuffy scholarship. It seemed like nothing less than an amazing feat to the young poet, that the human mind could remove itself so entirely from the contemplation of pain and sorrow.

In spite of its frightening clinical prose, the contents of the book told him more than he wanted to know about what was going on only a few hundred yards away. The fact, for example, that in the event of all-out nuclear war, the missile installation area would be a major military target for the Russians. He found himself asking for more books on the subject, until lately it was becoming difficult for him to decide whether girls like Betty Unger were an obsession and the missiles a distraction; or vice versa.

To add to the feeling of impending doom were all the military aircraft flying constantly overhead. Lately, for instance, they had been practising refuelling manoeuvres. He and Dickie had watched them earlier that week, the two of them side by side on their backs, as a huge KC-135, carrying aviation fuel instead of bombs, pulled up just ahead of, and above, a B-52 bomber, and let out a long semi-flexible hose. At the end of the hose was a special flange, Steven explained to Dickie, which could be inserted into a nozzle above the cockpit of the bomber. When the coupling was complete, aviation fuel would be pumped out of the KC-135 and into the fuselage of the B-52 flying fortress. These manoeuvres were necessary, the young poet informed him, to make possible the long-range flights that would allow those same bombers to fly all the way over to Russia, where, on a command from the American President, they would deliver their payload of atomic weapons to specified targets inside Russian territory. If the president had been on hand he might have let it slip that they were stepping up such training exercises lately for another, more sinister, reason. True, there had been an escalation in the Cold War, but soon such aircraft would be needed to fly mission after mission, not over Russian territory, but over the blue and emerald glitter of the South China Sea.

On this particular afternoon, flying high over the heads of the sleeping Mennonite men and women of the valley, the pilot-in-training in the cockpit of the B-52 had committed an error. He had disengaged his aircraft from the floating nozzle prematurely, so that a tremendous amount of aviation fuel had continued to pump itself – instead of into the plane's fuselage – out into the rarefied air above the floor of the sleepy valley. Most of it vapourized, of course, on its way down through the atmosphere to the ground below, so that it did not actually rain fuel on the valley's inhabitants. However, the air was heavy with fumes, and as they slept in their beds, or copulated, or played tag outside, they were also inadvertently engaged in the equivalent of gas sniffing.

Steven thought he could smell it now, as he sat under the canopy of the lone cottonwood tree, watching the Minuteman Missile being readied for insertion into the underground silo a few hundred yards to the south. It had a distinctive bouquet, richer than car gasoline, almost like gunpowder, and he found it quite elevating to sniff. Liked, in spite of himself, the way it smelled, just as he liked the smell of explosives and explosions.

He wondered what a nuclear explosion would smell like. Of course he had ideas about what it would look like, had seen pictures in the books and on television at his Aunt Martha's house, but there was never anything about the smell of it, and for him, at least from a poetic point of view, that might turn out to be one of the most important things. The thing that would make it real. Until he could smell nuclear fission, he didn't think he could write about it. And he wanted to write about it.

It seemed to him that poetry about nuclear war, about the end of the world, was at least as important as that of love. True, he wanted to become a romantic poet, to focus on the properties of love, not war, but he was young, and only later would he come to understand that there wasn't really such a big difference between what was going on in the skies above and down here under the shade of the lone cottonwood. Already he suspected that it might be necessary to fall in love quickly and often, in order to refuel the engine of his poetry. Betty Unger would be the first to help him in this cause, but certainly not the last. He was just beginning to sense that in order for him to become the poet he longed to be, he would first have to devour the valley, not only poem by poem, solitary tree by solitary tree, but also young woman by young woman.

ONE OF THE PEOPLE who was not sleeping while maddoch schlope was supposed to be going on was the village preacher. He was lying in bed next to his naked wife, both of them breathing heavily. The two of them had just engaged in the most vigorous and intense bout of lovemaking in the history of their marriage.

"What was that?" the preacher's wife wanted to know.

"What do you mean?" The preacher knew perfectly well what she meant, but he didn't want to discuss it. He had already made up his mind that he was never going to do anything like that again. Never going to allow himself to lose that much control.

"You were...different," she said.

"Nonsense."

"Oh, but you were."

"Was I?"

"Yes."

"I don't know what you mean." The preacher was up at the side of the bed, pulling on his pants.

"You've never done it like that before."

"Like what?"

"You know. I think you gave me a couple of bruises." She gave him a playful shove. He pulled away and picked up his shirt. The preacher's wife wanted to talk about what had just happened because, up until a few minutes ago, the truth was that she had lost all interest in sex. Had relegated the act to a stifling performance of duty. From the very beginning her husband, a gaunt and rigid man with bad teeth and foul breath, had failed to arouse her. His lovemaking was a mixture of apathy and restraint. The two of them carried out their carnal duties as if it were more of a chore than a pleasure. Neither took much joy in it.

It had always seemed an irony to her, that in a culture where any kind of waste was frowned upon, her body should never have been put to its best and fullest use. She'd always had an instinct that, given half a chance, she would have been very good in bed. It was something she'd always felt in the deepest parts of her body. That she had a good body for sex. A good disposition for it. That given someone who knew what he was doing, someone who truly excited her, her sexuality would have been allowed to reach its full potential. She was sure of it. Her body was sure of it. But any traces of sensuality had long been paved over by the self-effacement and piety insisted upon by the role of a preacher's wife.

Until this afternoon, that is. Something had changed. Her husband had made love to her with such vigour. Such intensity. It was completely out of character, but it couldn't have come at a better time. It seemed an amazing coincidence to her that he should have chosen this afternoon to ravage her – when it was precisely the thing she wished for – even if it had been a little too rough. Raw. Angry. Instead of pumping himself into her with the usual lack of imagination or interest, he had mounted her with such urgency. Thrust himself into her with such force. Such animal brutality. And inadvertently, he had pleasured her. She had found it profoundly arousing to be handled so roughly. It was certainly better than boredom.

Maybe it was only because of what had happened this morning. The preacher's wife had never been in the least promiscuous, or even flirtatious. She knew her duty and had resigned herself to it long ago. And yet, just now, in spite of herself, she had done the unthinkable. Had imagined herself being made love to by a man other than her husband. Had found herself grinding her hips up into her husband's pelvis, all the while imagining that it was someone else above her.

"I didn't know you could be such a rugged lover," she said to her husband. She wanted to let him know that he had pleased her, even if someone else had been the catalyst of her desire. The preacher took one hand off the top button of his shirt, poised it menacingly above his wife's head. Lover. Just the word made him want to lash her across the face with the back of his hand. But he had never done that. Promised himself he never would. But lover. That was a vile word. A troublesome word.

"Don't ever use that word with me again."

"But why? I don't understand."

"I don't want to discuss it."

"I'm sorry. I only meant..."

"I don't want to hear what you meant."

"But why not? Why can't we talk about it?"

"Because there's nothing to talk about."

"But there is. It was good, wasn't it? Good for you?"

"That's enough."

The preacher was trying to come to terms with the fact that the best sex they'd ever experienced had happened for all the wrong reasons. And they had Abe Wiebe to thank for it. It was all his fault. His presence in church that morning was the reason everything had changed. As far as the preacher was concerned, Abe Wiebe had been a cancer on the community ever since he came back from the war. A boil that needed lancing. Clearly the man had no business there. He had been officially excommunicated several years before. The preacher himself, along with the elders, had seen to that. The ban had not been lifted. And yet, this morning, there he was, sitting in one of the pews, legs crossed in casual attention, as if nothing had happened. No one had gotten up to protest. The elders had not sent anyone over to confront him, force him to leave, as would have been the case with any other banished parishioner. The preacher himself did not want to overstep his bounds. He had no interest in making waves. It was his ambition to become an elder himself, as soon as he could manage it. That was where the power was.

The sermon had gone badly, even though the preacher had spent the entire week preparing it. The subject was, of course, the evil that was being allowed to take place just across the border, and the very real possibility that the entire valley might be bombed out of existence. He had often spoken about that very thing in his sermons. The end of the world. Judgement day. And now it was real. The world really was coming to an end. It might have been the most important sermon of his career. And Abe Wiebe had spoiled it.

His banishment should have been total. Unequivocal. Instead, he'd been allowed to sit there with complete impunity and corrupt the very air with his malignant presence. In spite of the fact that the church had excommunicated him soon after he came back from overseas, where he had gone – in direct violation of church teachings – to fight in the Korean War. And why did the congregation allow this? Because – the preacher hated to admit it – he was one of the best-liked men in the valley. Men, women, children; old, young. It didn't seem to matter.

Since his unexpected return he had made a mockery of everything the preacher stood for – he lived a life of sin and debauchery, and yet, in spite of all his insolence and stubbornness, he remained such a popular figure in the valley. It seemed he had a power over people. Power to make them see only what he wanted them to see. There was a kind of evil in that.

And now this morning the preacher's own wife had fallen victim. He should have seen it coming. Had been troubled on more than one occasion by the way she sometimes spoke about him. Defended him to the preacher's face. Said that even if Abe Wiebe had committed a few sinful acts, that wasn't reason enough to condemn the man. Worse, she had insisted on pointing out that he had also committed as many, or more, acts of kindness, and generosity, and outright Christian charity. Wasn't it he, she insisted, who had been a good and faithful companion to Cornie and Jake Martens, when no one else would go near them? And hadn't he taken the young poet under his wing, when he might have drifted away to the city and become a juvenile delinquent?

His own wife, of all people, wanted to ignore the fact that he had gone off to war, expressly against the tenets of their faith. That he had almost certainly topped Katie Klassen before they were married. That he had lately taken to fornicating with young American women who paraded their sluttish ways by driving right up to his place in their short skirts and tight blouses. The pretence that they came up to buy one of his schlopebanks was a shameless mockery. Abe Wiebe was going to the devil, pure and simple. Allowing himself to be enticed – time and time again – by liquor, by women, by violence.

The man was pulling the wool over people's eyes, the preacher's very own wife among them, throwing them off guard by diverting their attention from the truth with bold displays of uncalled-for familiarity. He could be seen at any time of the day, for example, hugging women, old and young, for no reason at all. Men, too. He thought nothing of taking a baby up right out of its mother's arms and kissing it sweetly on the cheek. As if he really thought he was fooling anybody. Or on the street, playing hoops and sticks with the village boys, laughing harder than any of them when he toppled into a ditch after stepping into a gopher hole.

"You do me a great offence when you defend him like that," he'd said to her only that morning. They were finishing up breakfast, getting ready to go to church. "After some of the things he's done."

"And you do me a great offence to condemn him so easily. To ignore all the good that he's done. No man is all good. Or all bad. Surely a man can be both, can't he?"

"A man cannot serve God and do the things he does."

"Wasn't it Abe Wiebe," she'd said, "who sat by Clarence Zacharias's bed for seven days while he lay dying. Doesn't that count for anything? Who else would have done a thing like that?" It was common knowledge that if Abe Wiebe was one of the most liked men in the valley, Clarence Zacharias had been one of the most hated. A cold and calculating man who used his position as a village elder to carry out ruthless acts of discipline. He was one of those vindictive people only the valley could have produced – allowed to exercise his petty authority, not only over his three spinster daughters, but over anyone else if he could get away with it. It was he who had initiated the excommunication of Abe Wiebe after his return from the war. By the time he lay dying he'd alienated so many people that no one – not even his own daughters – would stay with him. The preacher had made a cursory visit, but other than that Clarence was left in the darkened bedroom by himself. He had lived a life of bitterness and recrimination, the village wisdom decreed, and now he was reaping what he'd sowed.

But when Abe found out what was going on he couldn't stand the thought of it. It had nothing to do with who Clarence Zacharias was. Abe had seen a man die alone once before – in Korea. The memory of it had never left him. Lying not far off with a bullet in his own chest, unable to move, he'd been forced to listen to the dying soldier call, first for his mother, then for someone – anyone – to come and offer some comfort. Abe, his lungs and throat full of blood, had been unable to answer. Lay there listening to no other sound on Earth but that one man's quiet, pleading voice. And long after he'd healed and come back home, the loneliness of that moment haunted him. Left an ache there, deep in his scarred chest. It was the saddest moment he had ever been inside of.

When he heard what was happening to Clarence he couldn't let it go. Nobody deserved that. Nobody. It didn't matter who it was. It was about being human. About dignity. Decency. When he walked into the house the sisters never said a word. Never tried to stop him. They seemed be in a kind of collective denial about what they were doing. In the room, Abe merely stood over the bed until he was sure Clarence knew he was there, then sat in the chair next to the bed in silence. In all the time it took Clarence to die not one word was spoken between them. It wasn't about words. For Abe – perhaps for both of them – it became a kind of quiet meditation. A silent reckoning with the past. With the future that was to come.

"How many times did you go and visit him?" asked the preacher's wife.

The preacher blanched. Then reddened. "How dare you speak to me in this way. He's bewitched you. The same as everyone else."

"Nonsense. What has he done? Tell me."

"He's making a mockery of everything we cherish. It's him that drove people like the Klassens out of town. Him and those friends of his, and their drunken cavorting. That's why people have left. It reflects badly on me I can tell you." The preacher was talking about the families that had packed up and left for Paraguay only a few days before. "There won't be anyone left if we continue to let this go on."

"Hypocrisy. That's what I call it," said his wife. She was being very brave. Surprised at her own boldness. "You want to find fault with everything. Everyone. Even me. I'm always doing something wrong. Is that what it means to be a preacher?"

"Nonsense."

"You know it's true."

"Think what you like."

They'd left for church after that. But it wasn't that morning's conversation, or anything Abe Wiebe had done in church that had made the preacher want to hate him so much. It was what he had seen his wife do after the service had ended – out on the steps of the church – that troubled him so deeply. That was the thing that had made him lose control just now. He looked at his wife for a moment, lying on the bed – naked, content – and understood that it wasn't her fault. That she had been bewitched. He knew what he had to do. To make things right again. To bring his good wife to her senses.

KATIE SAT ON THE SCHLOPEBANK in the spare, cavernous sitting room and listened to the tick tick tick of the big clock on the wall. The wooden bench – part of the furnishings in every village household – looked and felt much the same as it had when she'd sat on it as a little girl. It was well-built, sturdy, and still as hard and unyielding as she remembered it. The house was silent. She had just discovered that the home of her childhood was empty of its occupants. At first, she'd felt a little like Goldilocks. A kind of dread that they would be back at any moment, and that she would be better not to be there when they returned.

But then she'd taken a quick look through the house, and discovered all the suitcases were gone. All the clothes. What few pictures she remembered. They had left in a hurry. She sensed, already, that they had left for good, that they were never coming back. That she might never see them again. But how could they have left these things behind, she wondered – the clock, the schlopebank? These were items, after all, that her grandparents had taken a lot of trouble to transport all the way from Russia to the new land they were travelling to. And why had they not bothered to take such family heirlooms this time? They wouldn't have taken up much space, would have given her mother comfort in her new and strange surroundings, wherever they were. And so she sat now, trying to make sense out of it all.

Perhaps they intended to send for them later. They certainly had not left them for her, since they had no idea she was coming. Then a nagging thought occurred to her. Could it have been because of her? Had they found out, somehow, that she was on her way back and left before she could get there? Impossible. She hadn't told anyone. Hadn't known herself that she was coming back. Perhaps someone had seen her on the television, in one of those silly commercials she'd made and the news had reached the village. She'd seen an antenna up on

Aunt Martha's house – remembered the broadcasting tower piercing high into the sky as she approached the border. Maybe other people were watching, too. Or maybe someone had seen her on the movie screen and news had spread all over the valley that for the price of admission Katie Klassen could be seen – half-clothed and caked with makeup – strutting herself in front of the whole world. There was that western where she'd had to wear the low-cut petticoat. Had her father been confronted with that, perhaps by one of the Zacharias sisters, and packed up the family and fled in shame from the ridicule of it all?

The clock above Katie's head chimed loudly – and then it was a Sunday afternoon and the house was full of people. The kitchen hot, noisy, crowded with women. Children playing in various locations, some inside, others out of the house – anywhere but the sitting room, where the men were seated with their dark beards and thoughts. The gathering had something to do with a wedding. Or was it a funeral? It didn't really matter much. The atmosphere in the sitting room, whether one of celebration or mourning, would have been essentially the same.

Katie was a little girl, and she had worked up the courage to enter there and seat herself quietly on the schlopebank under the ticking clock. She was wearing a new dress – just a frock, really, but there were flowers in the pattern and the sleeves were puffed out a little. She dangled her feet – complete with shiny black shoes – and looked up at the men in their itchy wool pants and jackets, talking severely over nothing she cared about.

She had decided to come in and sit down in their intimidating presence only because an idea had begun to form itself in her young mind. It was crudely formulated, to be sure, based as it was on the simplest notions of aesthetics, but nevertheless, Katie Klassen was beginning to suspect that she might be pretty.

She wanted the men to notice her. She wanted them to stop long enough to turn and look at her and maybe even say something. But she had been sitting for fifteen minutes now, and still not one of them had given her so much as a glance. She knew they must be aware of her presence – she was not invisible, they were not blind – but something in their manner made clear that they were very proud of their utter disregard for her charming and irresistible presence.

Katie had only wanted to be noticed, maybe even fussed over a bit. She had wanted to conquer these big scary men with their scratchy beards and enormous hands. Smile up at them coyly when they remarked what a pretty little girl was gracing them with her presence. Blush when one of them tickled her under the chin. Shake her shiny golden locks at them when they asked her if she had a boyfriend. She'd only wanted to get some sense of herself as worthy of their attention, as charming and feminine and far from plain. But she didn't seem to be having any effect on them.

The worst thing of all was that her own father was one of these men. He, too, failed to acknowledge her, as if she were something that did not belong to him, with whom he had no connection, so that at precisely the time when she most needed to feel precious to him, exactly the opposite was what she sensed. Dismissal. The longer she sat the more she felt herself becoming invisible. When she finally got up and left the room, she thought it might at least have been a secret reproach, but she glanced over her shoulder just before stepping out of sight, and saw the unmistakable look of victory on his face.

The feeling was with her now, in this flat stillness – the suffocating humiliation of it – as she sat on the same bench, the same clock ticking on the unadorned wall above her. Katie gave her head a shake and got up from the bench. Why was she allowing herself to think this way? It was happening already. Already the valley was getting a hold of her again.

She'd noticed that all the windows facing south had the curtains drawn and blankets hung in front of them. She looked out now, to see what they were meant to shut out and there, shimmering in the afternoon sun, close enough to reach out and touch, was the massive rocket – the same one she had seen on her way to the border – lying semi-erect on the bed of an enormous truck, waiting to be lowered into the ground. Katie couldn't keep back a smile. Then a grin. Then she thought she might laugh out loud. It was a terrible irony. That people like her father had first come to settle in the valley – built their homes there – expressly because they had been promised peace. Freedom from war. And now the most fearsome and destructive weapon of war the world had ever known was lurking little more than a stone's throw from those very homes.

And there was more. That the weapons were aimed at, of all countries, Russia. The very place they had fled to come here. And more still. Over in that country were weapons just like this one, equally destructive, aimed here. Perhaps it had been too much for her father to bear. He had refused to stay another minute. Gone. As far as their money would take them. Left in such a hurry they hadn't even bothered to sell their worldly goods or the house they lived in.

Katie correctly guessed that this was the reason for her deserted home, and those of the others she'd driven by. She would learn that the elders had promised to sell the house and property for her parents and send the money along later. It had never been all that unusual for a group of disgruntled villagers to suddenly pull up stakes and move – not just to another village or region, or even another province, but to another country entirely. Such drastic measures were usually occasioned by a conviction that things had become too worldly where they were now. It was the kind of thing that had been going on in the valley for years. And it had been a part of the culture for centuries.

She would learn soon enough that the group her parents had trundled off with had chosen as their new home, not only another country, but another continent altogether – a most inhospitable region of Paraguay, a place so desolate that not even the locals thought it worth inhabiting. But then that wasn't anything new either. The same had been true of every other place the Mennonites had ever settled. It had always been land that nobody else wanted.

This same valley had been rejected, first by the French and then the English, as uninhabitable – a place that simply wasn't good for anything. There was no water that was any good, they said. The soil was hard and brackish. But that hadn't been enough to stop her forefathers and mothers from putting down roots here anyway. And just as in every other place, they were soon not only surviving, but prospering – thriving – beyond all reasonable expectation. In the case of the valley it turned out that there was plenty of good water up in the Pembina Hills. All they had to do was find a way to pipe it down into the valley, which they promptly did. It turned the hardened sod, already loosened by ploughs and cultivators and harrows, into the richest farmland in the entire country. To hold the moisture and provide much-needed shade, they planted thousands and thousands of trees – cottonwoods and willows and maples – which grew to staggering height and girth in the rich, moist environment. No one could believe it. Least of all the English up on the escarpment, who looked down over the green valley, as did the French from across the Red River, and ground their teeth to think they had passed up such an Eden. They resented the inhabitants of the valley ever after for it, as they had been resented before, in every other time and place, for being so successful. The same thing was bound to happen in Paraguay.

Katie was suddenly very tired. She went into one of the bedrooms and lay down on the soft mattress. The cool sheets were still clean and fresh-smelling. She fell asleep thinking about her mother and father, her brothers and sisters, and how busy they must be right now – were they working on a Sunday? – far away in some distant country, trying desperately to scratch out a living. She hadn't really ever missed them that much. Why would she start now? She was alone in the house. She did what she had always done. She let a quiet loneliness settle over her like a blanket – the same blanket that had covered her so many nights in California, the one she curled up under – and stayed very still. The one that never quite kept her warm.

# PART
*two*

MADDOCH SHLOPE WAS OVER, AND ALL UP and down the valley, people were getting up from napping or having sex or watching television, and sitting down at the kitchen table to have their fastba. Martha Wiebe and her father were sitting down to dine as well, but they were out behind the house, where she had fashioned a patio of sorts. The two of them were seated at a small round table, on wrought iron chairs, under the shade of a cool maple tree. This afternoon, she had brought her father outside – very much against his will – because it suddenly made no sense to her that a man who had spent all his life out of doors, out in the sun and the rain and the wind, should now want nothing more than to sit alone in a dimly lit and poorly ventilated room.

The tradition of a modest afternoon meal, especially on Sunday, was something Martha rarely practised anymore, but she had decided that today would be different. And so she had brought out a tray of food for them. There was coffee to wash down the brick cheese, sliced bologna, homemade plum jam, and most unlikely of all, fresh-baked bread.

She had taken her father completely out of his element. The idea of the patio, of an area devoted exclusively to leisure, was foreign to a man like him, as it was to the valley in general. And when it came to eating, the landscape for him had rarely been anything other than a kitchen or a church base-ment. But she also knew how much he loved fresh-baked bread, and this afternoon he was going to have to sit out here on the patio – force himself to watch the hummingbirds drink weightlessly out of the lightly swaying hollyhocks and smell the grass – if he wanted to eat any of it.

Why was she deliberately making the day so difficult for him? What was it she wanted to prove? That she could win? That he was too old to keep up his end in a fight with his head-strong daughter, even if the topic was something as trivial as where they should eat? She felt a twinge of guilt, considering that she had already tortured him with the television earlier, and now this. But it wasn't enough to stop her. She was going to go ahead and do it anyway.

For the first time in more than a year, she had carried flax straw out of the barn this morning, over to the brick and clay oven that still sat in the middle of the yard – the last one the boys had built for her – fed the firebox, and left it to heat while she went back into the house to mix the batter. She'd kneaded the dough twice, left it to rise, then pieced it off into pans to take out to the oven. She'd slipped them in over the hot bricks and left them to bake, knowing the oven would cool on its own, but not before a magnificent golden crust had formed over each loaf by the time she came to take them out.

It was a year to the day since they had buried the last of her brothers, since she'd made a silent promise to herself, never to bake another loaf of bread. She never wanted to knead another pan of dough as long as she lived. The job of baking enough bread every day to feed five grown men – just one of the many chores that had fallen on her shoulders after the death of her mother – had gone on long enough.

But today something had made her want to go through the ritual again. She was surprised to discover that those same familiar textures and odours and sounds had taken on a whole new perspective. That there was a certain sensuality to working the dough – kneading it, rolling, pinching, stretching. Something suggestive in the playful sound of her bare hand slapping the shiny rounded surface of the dough. Something feral in the musty aroma of the rising yeast, the pungent odour of salt. She had found herself handling the dough as if it were human flesh. Responsive to her touch. Alive. Found that it aroused her. Most surprising of all, she found that she was not disturbed by this. She liked the idea that she could take pleasure in something that had once repulsed her.

Her father was wearing his Sunday best just at that moment, sitting obediently on a chair across from Martha. She'd made him comfortable at the table, in spite of his protests, and now she watched him pour coffee out of a cup and into a saucer, pick it up with both hands to bring it slowly up to his mouth, then sip, long and noisy, from the lip of the saucer.

She was barefoot, the warm black dirt curling up between her toes. Martha seemed to be spending all of her time in bare feet these days. She wanted to be in touch with the earth, to feel that she was grounded. She had always thought of herself as not so different from the hollyhocks that grew in behind the house or the cottonwood trees that towered above it. She felt that she had, quite literally, grown out of the landscape, as they had. That just as they had sprung up out of its soil, so had she. That her essential nature would always and forever be informed by the valley, regardless of where she went and what she did.

The place was an integral part of her – in a way she could never let go of. Never escape. And this had become her freedom. She'd accepted the truth of it a long time ago. Had managed to find her own liberty within the confines of the valley, not out of necessity, but out of choice.

"Thunder," Isaac said to his daughter. A percussion had just rumbled out of the sky, rattled his cup against the saucer just as he was about to pour out more coffee. He looked up, unable to understand how the sound of thunder could be coming out of a clear blue sky. "Oh but that is everything blue there up. How can that," he wanted to know.

"It's the planes, Papa. I told you before. Remember? The jets. They make that noise when they fly too fast."

"What mean you. Jets. Show me." Her father could speak English well enough, as could most of the inhabitants, but chose to speak Plaut Dietsch because he found English to be an anemic language when the finer points of declarative expression were called for, as they so often were.

By now most of the inhabitants were used to all the hissings and rumblings from aircraft flying overhead. It could occur at any time of the day, any day of the week. The B-52 bombers, massive enough to block out the sun when they came over low, did so on a schedule completely of their own choosing. Sunday was no exception. The fighter jets broke the sound barrier on a daily basis. The Sabbath meant nothing to them. Most people had stopped paying any more than passing attention to the sonic booms, but they continued to confuse farmyard animals, who insisted on running for shelter time after time under the mistaken assumption that a thunderstorm was approaching. Occasionally a storm really was on the way, and then it was inattentive villagers that failed to take cover who suffered the consequences.

"You can't see them," said Martha. "They're too high up." Her father's vision was not good. He would be unable to make out the fighter jets high in the sky, even if she tried to point one out to him.

"Oh but that hears me terrible loud." Another one had just flown through Mach 1. "How can that."

"I told you. It happens when they fly too fast."

"Then is it all exploded."

"No, no. They don't blow up. They fly through the sound barrier."

"What say you. That hears me stupid."

"Like flying through a wall of air. Compressed air."

Martha spoke English, not because she didn't really know the dialect any more – she could speak it as well as anyone – but it seemed to her that technical terminology was better in English. There weren't many words for that kind of thing in Plaut Dietsch. It was not a sophisticated language in that respect. Its richness lay in other, more earthy areas, where English could not keep up. But it was not a language of progress, of technology.

"Air compressors. Now talks she from air compressors. First it's that television, you call it. And now this. You want to make a person crazy, yes."

A lot of younger people in the valley were speaking English now. They did so, Martha understood, not out of any real need, but because so many of them wanted to distance themselves from the language of their fathers and mothers. They wanted to move into the new world – the one the tower was beaming at them, the one coming down off the big screen at the new movie theatre in Walhalla. They wanted to leave a language like Plaut Dietsch to the old and infirm, like her father, to places like the quaint valley they would soon be leaving behind.

"That hears me as a shot gun. Jake Wiens has there a ten gauge. Two barrels. He does there always by his culvert stink cats shoot."

"Nobody is shooting skunks."

"So hears me that. That the man there stink cats shooting does."

"It's nothing like that."

"Maybe yet Henry Reimer. He does there always stumps dynamiting in the slough."

"Not on a Sunday."

"That know you not," said Isaac. "That man is a dumb-head."

There was the smell of something in the air, but it wasn't gunpowder or dynamite, and certainly not spray from a skunk.

"It's the jets, Papa. It's how fast they go."

"All of them."

"Who?"

"All crazy."

It didn't matter. In a way she was relieved. No matter the explanations she offered, he would stubbornly cling to the notion that such noises were not really coming from the sky at all. That people like his daughter were mistaken. That something so loud could not be the result of a plane merely flying through the air.

But Martha wanted to get this thing through to him. She didn't really know why. He was not having a good day. If the television hadn't confused him enough, now there was this. He had never explained anything to her, really, as a child, or even as a teenager. It was amazing to her, when she thought of it now, how little she had seen of her own father while she was growing up. He had been disappointed in her, she knew, from the start. Had kept away from her as much as possible. He had wanted her to be delicate, feminine, passive. Like her mother. But Martha had never been any of those things. She had always been plain. And smart. And tough. Not the qualities he'd hoped for in a girl.

And now here they were, the two of them, not really knowing anything about each other, trying to talk across a solitude that could never be bridged. He really had no idea who she was, or what she was about. Her inner workings were an unknown quantity, not only to him, but to everyone else in the valley.

Until recently, Martha hadn't paid much heed to her own needs and desires, but lately had felt a troubling restlessness about her own capacity for sexual fulfillment. It seemed ironic to her that, at such a relatively advanced age, she should want something like that for herself. Something she hadn't wanted – or hadn't admitted she wanted – in her reproductive years. Not that she hadn't had the urge to bear children. But in a way she'd raised four big children on her own. Her brothers had never really matured into men in some ways – had lived much of their lives as children do, thanks in part to her.

But it was all different now. Everything was different. The way she felt about her father. The way she felt about herself. About the valley. And now this urgent need to satisfy herself. In a way she never had. This need to bring about a climax of her own. It always seemed to be strongest when she was standing at the window of her bedroom, late at night, looking out over the deserted street of the village. Sometimes she cried silently while she went about it. She seemed to be crying all the time lately. When she was alone. With herself. It wasn't loneliness. She had learned to deal with that long ago. It was something else. Something she hadn't been able to put her finger on yet.

There were times, after what seemed like hours, when she knew she must be close. When her knees weakened and her toes curled up under her feet so that she had to sit down on the bed, thighs shuddering, breasts shivering. But always, when she was so close, when the muffled cries and sobs of pleasure she allowed herself threatened to explode into shouts and screams, always she stopped just short. In spite of the fact that she had every right to it. This thing that she wanted for herself. Was entitled to. Stopped just short of the moment she longed for. Had worked so hard for. Could not seem to give herself permission to accept. This gift she wanted to give herself.

Always, she came face to face with the same peculiar paradox. It had required almost superhuman control for her to come this far, and now she was supposed to allow herself to lose complete control? To let her body go to a place, a moment, where it became its own means, its own end. Reach a point where it continued on without her. It was this very idea, after all, which had kept her out of intimate relationships with men. Kept her alone. She had made up her mind back then never to give up that much control to a man. Had decided that sexual gratification would always and forever be a solitary act for her. That if it was an exercise in expectation and fulfillment, then she would be the author of both. And yet, she had not allowed herself the ultimate achievement. Had not really tried for it. Had been content with less, until now.

THE MARTENS BROTHERS were finishing up the last of their drinks and getting ready to head out the door with Abe. The real estate agent had bought a lot of drinks for them. Far too many for a Sunday afternoon. In exchange they had told him the story he wanted to hear, of how they had come to be so gruesome looking. Now he was back up at the bar, talking to the man next to him. Buying him drinks. The real estate agent needed someone to listen. He wanted to tell the story he'd just heard.

"Harry, did you say?"

"That's right."

"Well, Harry, it was gasoline that did that," said the real estate agent. He pointed a stubby finger at the Martens brothers. "Take a good look at them. Look at their faces," he said. He wanted to get his timing down, his rhythm. Tell the story as if he'd told it a hundred times. No matter how many drinks it cost him. "Isn't that the goddamndest thing you ever saw?"

"Ugly sons-a-bitches," said Harry. He was trying to sound interested. He knew it was important to do that if there were going to be more free drinks. All he really wanted to do was get drunk. Harry had seen the Martens brothers before, plenty of times. Had been living in the valley long enough to know perfectly well who they were. He'd even heard the story of how they got that way, but he didn't care about that. It wasn't as if he'd had a hand in it.

"The two of them were cleaning engine parts in the shop, leaning over the vat of gasoline, washing out these car parts and one of them – that one there with his mouth open – you know what he was doing?"

"No idea."

"Smoking. That's what."

"Crazy bastard," said Harry.

"Says they never worried about a fire. And look at them now."

"Serves 'em right. Serves 'em both right. "

"Says they dropped a cigarette into that vat lots of times and nothing ever happened. Thing would just fizzle out."

"But not this time." Harry was working hard now to maintain a certain pretence of interest. He knew he needed to come up with some better responses for the real estate agent if he wanted another drink.

"Says he must have rolled a bad one. They always roll their own, those people."

"Which people?"

"Mennonites."

"Oh," said Harry.

"From across the line. Never seen one yet with a cut pack."

"I never roll myself," said Harry, who had acquired a taste for American cigarettes. He thought of Du Maurier and Rothmans and Players as sissy cigarettes next to Camel or Lucky Strike. He was sucking on a navy cut Lucky Strike just now. "Haven't got the patience."

The real estate agent had no idea what kind of man he was talking to. That Harry was a Mennonite himself, but was pretending not to be. That he could pass himself off as just a regular American anytime he felt like it. He had no idea that

Harry was in such a celebratory mood because he'd just come from beating his retarded stepson unconscious, a feat he rarely managed, and wanted to reward himself for the accomplishment. The real estate agent didn't understand that Harry liked nothing better than to inflict pain on someone, and to know he was the author of that pain. That it gave him tremendous satisfaction. He was a monster, really, and, as with all such creatures, had allowed himself to become one. Not because someone had failed him, a long time ago – which also happened to be true – but because he had given himself permission. He was really a failure as a human being. The real estate agent had no idea he was talking to a man like that.

Harry was always thinking up new ways to humiliate and torture people. He was very enterprising in that regard. His latest creation involved fingers. Breaking them. Snapping the bone inside one like a twig. Then waiting patiently for it to heal before he moved on to the next one. Already he had broken three of his stepson's fingers – both little ones, and one ring finger.

"Any second now," he would say. Speak softly, tenderly to his stepson, like a loving parent, all the while applying a steadily increasing pressure. Harry loved the anticipation. Bent the finger more and more, while his stepson lay on his back, arm outstretched, rolling from side to side on the dirt floor of the root cellar. Kept it up until the bone inside the little finger could bend no further. "Just a little more," he'd say soothingly, "a little more." Until it finally came. The snap. The crackle and pop of knuckle and bone. Such a satisfying sound. He loved the look on his stepson's face as he tried to deal with the pain. Tried, mouth open, to come up with some kind of cry. That was Dickie's job. To try as hard as he could to scream throughout the entire procedure. Nothing came out, of course. It never did. Only grimaces and facial contortions.

Afterward, his stepson would cry silently, his hand folded into the crotch of his lap, rocking slowly back and forth on the floor of the cellar, playing the finger gingerly one way and another as the pain began to take a serious hold on him.

It was going to be another week before he could start on a new finger, and so today Harry had settled for something more basic. For the simple sensation of his boot sinking into puffy flesh. The crunch of his fist on his stepson's flat face. Today he'd simply beat the living shit out of Dickie.

He'd married Dickie's mother after her husband was killed in a farming accident, the way men and boys often were in the valley. In this particular case, Dickie's father had got himself caught in the hammermill. He was feeding hay into it at the time, from the back of a wagon, squatting down and peeling square sections off the end of an alfalfa bale, sliding them down the shoot toward the opening, when he lost his balance and slid, feet first, along with a section of alfalfa bale, into the open maw of the hammermill. There were hundreds of heavy steel blades there, spinning very fast and with tremendous torque. They were designed to pulverize things like alfalfa and wheat and other edible substances into more gastronomically manageable fodder for livestock. In the case of Dickie's father, they proceeded to shred the muscle and bone and tissue that comprised his body with equal efficiency.

Dickie was standing next to the hammermill at the time, waiting to throw another bale up onto the wagon. He was very strong for a ten-year-old boy, and could throw a bale up there with no problem at all. One variation on the story, first proffered by the Zacharias sisters, was that Dickie had thrown a bale too hard and knocked his father off balance and into the machine.

An innocent bystander would have informed anyone who cared to listen that this was not true. That Dickie's father had simply lost his footing for no good reason. Slipped. Simple carelessness. Lack of concentration. Just like any other farm accident. As for the rest of the story, the bystander would have confirmed that Dickie had, indeed, watched his father being fed into the machine. That he had appeared to call out – even though no sound came out – above the din of the hammermill and the tractor turning it. That Dickie's father had enough time to look down at his legs being shredded, then over at Dickie, before the rest of him disappeared into the hammermill. The innocent bystander would have described the expression on his face as one of resignation.

In fact, Dickie's father was just trying to be philosophical at the time, the same as he'd always tried to be about his son's condition. About everything. He was thinking, even as his legs disappeared into the chaos of the machine's interior, that the hammermill was just doing its job – precisely what it was designed to do – grinding material introduced to it into small pieces and sending them, by centrifugal force, up the curved shoot and then down into the grain bin at the far end of the barn, which, judging from the red spray clearly visible at that location, was precisely where portions of his legs already were, and where the rest of him would end up in another second or so. Dickie's father didn't think anything else after that. His time for philosophizing was up.

The funeral was one of the few closed-casket ceremonies in the history of the valley. There wasn't really very much to bury. Not even the most diehard conservatives – not even the Zacharias sisters – were interested in paying their respects to what was left of Dickie's father.

Not long after that Harry left British Columbia to get away from some trouble and arrived in Neustadt. He married Dickie's mother when no one else would. She was desperate at the time. Ready to sacrifice everything – even her retarded son's safety – for the sake of her younger children – to keep a roof over their heads and food on the table. That was nothing new in the valley.

And just now, contrary to his nature, Harry was trying hard to be nice. He wanted to get drunker and knew he didn't have enough money to pull it off on his own. He would humour the real estate agent long enough to get three or four more stiff doubles out of him.

"Says he must have left a gap with no tobacco when he rolled it," said the real estate agent. "Just paper, you understand. So when he gets to that paper, it lights up. Puffs up into a little flame. And him with both hands in that vat. So what does he do? Spits it out. Right into that vat of gasoline. With the tip on fire and all."

"Crazy Mennonite bastard," said Harry. He was getting into it now. Going along for the ride, pretending he didn't know who the Martens brothers were. They were hideous, after all, and it was really no effort to hate them.

"So now the whole vat goes up in a ball of flame. Right up into their faces."

Harry held up his glass to inspect the contents. He was thinking that the bourbon in his glass kind of looked like gasoline. He thought he smelled gasoline now, for some crazy reason.

"They're still leaning over, you see. Washing car parts. When the vat goes up they raise their hands to their faces. Like this. Both of them." The real estate agent demonstrated how someone would put his hands up to his face, as if he were about to cry into them. "Instinct. They're just trying to protect themselves from the flames. But their hands are soaked in gasoline, you see. So now their faces catch on fire, too."

"Serves 'em right," said Harry. "Stupid fuckin' bastards."

"They get up and stagger around and one of them knocks over that vat of burning gasoline. So now the whole goddamn place goes up." The real estate agent took a big swallow of his drink. Harry held up his glass to let the real estate agent see that it was empty. "Somehow they manage to stagger out of there with their faces and hands on fire like that. Blazing like a couple of human torches. Meanwhile the skin is melting right off 'em."

"Dumb fuckers," said Harry.

"They were burnt so badly no one gave them a chance. Thought for sure they were goners. But they survived it. There's the proof."

"Shoulda' let 'em die. I woulda' killed 'em myself. Shot 'em right then and there. Beat 'em to death with my bare hands if I had to. Better that way. Better than looking like that the rest of your life." Harry found himself enjoying the idea of beating each of the Martens brothers, in turn, to death with his bare hands. He wondered how long it would take to kill someone that way. With just your fists. He thought he might like to try it out on Dickie when he got home.

STEVEN ZACHARIAS had been kissing Betty Unger's lips for some time now, sitting next to her under the shade of the rogue cottonwood tree, leaning into her. These long deep kisses were the premise upon which he proposed to build the framework of his passion, which would, in turn, allow him to fall in love. He needed to fall in love as soon as possible – if for no other reason than poetry. Time was a factor. There might not be another chance. He had to hurry and write as much of it as possible. That was the most important thing now.

Betty Unger was just an average-looking young woman of the village, but because the young poet was not interested in average, in ordinary, he'd been working hard to discover in her physical features something extraordinary. Something worthy of poetic praise and inspiration. Right now he was concentrating on her lips, had been declaring them to be the most exquisitely sensual and luscious he had ever kissed.

He marvelled at the miracle of his romantic capability. Forgave himself the fact that it was largely a contrived situation. That the entire exercise had about it an air of calculation.

He did so on the grounds that it was not really a plan at seduction, as such. That the ends were more noble than that. He wanted to hear the word "yes," that much was true. But he wanted it for reasons more romantic than carnal. After all, the word yes, in almost any sense, was not an easy thing to pull off in a place like the valley. A word that rarely fell from the lips of its fathers and mothers, and even less often from its elders and teachers. It was most often smothered in the subtle folds and layers of authority and religion, of custom and tradition. Its scarcity was not so much a reflection of an individual as an idea. A mannerism. A silence. A refusal.

Betty Unger was blissfully ignorant of all this. She had no idea that she'd become a construct in a manufactured reality. When it came to such notions she was in way over her head. But she wouldn't have cared one way or the other even if she had known. She had ideas of her own. She was thinking – even as she allowed her lips to be met and tenderly chafed again and again by those of the young poet – that all this innocent, purely devotional bussing had become boring. Granted, it seemed genuine, honest and deep, and made her feel special. She couldn't recall being kissed in such a fashion, had never really thought of her kisses as sacred, which they were according to the young poet. Holy. He'd used that word, too. A gift from God to be cherished. But it was time to move on.

Betty had an agenda of her own, based, not on a deep sense of creative urgency, but on sexual curiosity. She, too, felt a sense of impending doom, as everybody did, and she did not want to die a virgin. She wanted to be made love to. So while the young poet was busy kissing her – lightly, sensitively – she was thinking of a way to get on with it. She'd already decided that he would be allowed the privilege of moving on to other things. A lot of other things. He just wasn't doing them.

They were still sitting in the same position, leaning into

each other, side by side, like two cartoon lovers on a valentine card, when she unbuttoned the top of her cotton dress, pulled down the sleeves, loosened the straps of her slip, and let the young poet watch as the rest of the shiny white fabric fell away from her shoulders.

Steven had imagined Betty's breasts as two creamy orbs of soft white, in the centre of each the perfect bud of a rose-coloured nipple. What he saw instead were two unremarkable mammaries, brown aureoles disproportionately large and mottled, nipples the colour of mud. Already in the first stages of becoming pendulous, they hung unevenly across the front of her chest, not particularly firm for someone her age, and far from spectacular. But because he needed them to be the most noble, beautiful creations he'd ever had the privilege of gazing upon, he did just that – stared and stared, desperate to reconcile this latest reality into his scheme of things – while Betty waited, the leaves of the cottonwood tree shimmering flecks of sunshine and shadow across her naked torso.

The breeze caused her nipples to swell and harden, made her breasts a little firmer. She thought of them as highly desirable, since they were ample, and she had been misled into believing – like so many other girls – that bigger was better. And now she expected the poet to touch them. Fondle them. Play with them in some manner or other, as a number of boys had already done on previous occasions. But he was just sitting there, staring at them as if they were made of marble.

"Well?" said Betty. She was beginning to feel a little uncomfortable.

"They're beautiful," he said.

"But you haven't touched them."

"No."

"Don't you want to touch them?"

"Of course."

"Well?"

The young poet continued to stare down at them intently.

"You could at least say something. Poetic, I mean. I never had anybody say anything poetic about my tits."

Steven winced a little. "I wish you wouldn't call them that."

"What?"

"Tits."

"Why not?"

"Well, it's not a very lyrical word, is it?"

"But that's what they are." She put a hand under each one and held them up like fruit. "They're tits." She spat out the word. "Tits." Then louder. "Tits tits tits."

"Stop it."

She shot out a hand, grabbed his wrist, and pressed his hand against her breast. "There," she said. "How does that feel?" She felt something on the back of his hand and pulled it away to inspect it.

"What are those?" she said. There were angry red scratches across the back of his hand. She followed the fresh line of one gently with the tip of her finger. "How did you get these?"

"They're nothing."

"Does it hurt?"

"It's fine."

He didn't want to tell her about what had happened earlier in church. About the dream he'd had. He didn't want to even think about it. He had decided to attend that morning, as so many others had, not out of any sense of duty, but because like them, he thought perhaps this one time, the preacher might have words of wisdom for them. Perhaps, against all odds, he might say something to put things into perspective.

Of course the sermon was a terrible disappointment. Nothing but the usual assault of platitudes and Bible passages. Massive doses of drivel that bludgeoned him into a troubled sleep, a dream, in which he found himself sitting alone under the rogue cottonwood tree, his back to the missile silo, when a white flash blinded him. He knew instantly what it was. Waited for his sight to return while the shock wave passed on either side him – wondering whether the trunk of the cotton-wood tree was strong enough to withstand the power of a nuclear explosion.

Then he could see again, and watched as lesser trees – willows and maples along the creek bed – leaned away from the bright blast until they were completely horizontal, until their roots tore away and they slid along the ground, leaves and branches ablaze. Then he saw houses and barns along the village street burst into flame and fold like cardboard boxes. A mushroom cloud billowed high into the blue sky above him, blacker and uglier than any thunderhead he'd ever seen. Mutant bolts of bizarre lightning shot from its thick convolutions and undulating folds. They cascaded out in all directions, high over his head, like the electrified skeleton of some enormous umbrella. Concussions of atomic thunder punctuated the deep and terrible rumbling of the earth and sky.

And then, quite suddenly, it was quiet again. The ferocious, hot wind stopped. A slip of blue sky reappeared over the hills to the west as the enormous mushroom cloud moved east, carried away from the valley by the prevailing westerly wind. He got up and walked around to the far side of the tree. The trunk there had been stripped of its bark. The wood scorched, still smouldering, as if a gigantic blowtorch had been held there. He followed the trunk up into the branches and saw that all the leaves were gone. At the tip of each bare and blackened twig a small flame still burned, as if the tree had been transformed into an enormous charred candelabra, alight with a thousand tiny fires.

He wandered toward the creek, stripped of its trees now, and down into the dried bed, let it take him back toward the village. When he came around a bend the smell of singed fur and seared meat invaded his nostrils and there, naked and steaming, lay the skinned and cooked carcasses of an entire herd of cows, piled against the far bank – as if someone had stacked them there. The overpowering smell nauseated him, until he was throwing up, over and over. Until there was nothing coming out up of his stomach but bile.

Then he was walking along the smoky village street, past collapsed housebarns and granaries, some still on fire, some no more than blackened ruins. On either side, the branches of the tall cottonwoods, stripped of their leaves, smouldered. The air crackled with the sound of dying fires. Everything smelled of char and cinder, of ash and soot, and mixed in with all of it was the odour of something else – something that needed a metaphor to describe it – a metaphor he searched for and failed to find. The odour became more and more acrid, until it was stinging his nostrils, the sour vapours choking him, burning into the back of his throat.

He opened his silver cigarette case. The one he'd been saving for just this occasion. Took out the tiny pencil and one of the small blank pages. But he couldn't think of anything to write. Nothing came to mind. He found himself completely at a loss for words. Would it be this way with all the new aspects of a nuclear explosion, he wondered? Would they fail to allow themselves description? Would metaphors fail at this level? Would language? Would reason? Could these things, along with the houses and trees and hollyhocks, have been blown into extinction? Disintegrated by the force of the blast?

Perhaps in an explosion of such magnitude, changes took place that were undetectable by scientific equipment. Who could say what might have been altered? If the structure of molecules and atoms – the essence of physical existence – had been transformed, then perhaps other, less corporeal phenomena had also been changed. The structure of language, for example. Of thought.

Perhaps in a post-nuclear environment these things, too, had been warped, disfigured into something else. Perhaps language had been bludgeoned back into the grunts and groans of cavemen and cavewomen – the very people so vehemently denied by his Sunday School teachers. Who could say what had remained intact and what had been forever reconfigured? What guarantee was there for any human convention?

Two young men walked casually up the village street toward him. The Martens brothers, laughing and horsing around, stopped in front of him.

"Everybody looks like us now," said Cornie. The two brothers looked at each other and grinned widely.

"Look," said Jake. Suddenly the street was full of people, staggering and moaning, hands out in front of them like zombies, all of them burned beyond recognition, skin hanging in shreds and patches from their hands and faces. The Martens brothers mimicked their suffering with heartless cruelty.

"Ooooh, help me, help me," moaned Cornie. He held out his hands in front of him and hobbled around in a small circle.

"I'm burned sooo badly," mocked Jake. "Ooohh my, what will become of me? Oh, boo hooo." They bumped shoulders and laughed uproariously.

A girl in a pink dress came walking up the street. She was carrying a little doll in her hands and playing with it, talking to it as she walked along. She stopped in front of Steven and looked up. It was Betty Unger, except that she was a little girl in a pink dress. She and her dress had been perfectly preserved. When she lifted her face to look up at him she screamed silently, noiselessly, and ran away down the street.

"Wait," he called after her. She ran on.

"Why isn't she burnt like all the others?"

"Because she took Jesus into her heart, dummy." It was another girl talking now, a little older, and plainly dressed. "Don't you know anything?"

"What about them?" He pointed at the Martens brothers. "They're the same as before."

"That's because they're immune," she said.

"We've always been immune," said Cornie. They laughed again and jostled him back and forth between them, shoved and taunted him.

"What do you think about that?" said Cornie. "Now we're the good-looking ones."

"Good-looking compared to you anyway," said Jake. They both laughed and elbowed each other.

"What do you mean?"

"He wants to know what you mean," said the older girl.

"We mean, stupid, that you're even uglier than us now."

"What are you talking about?"

"Your hands." They pointed and laughed. "Look at them."

The young poet held his hands out in front of him and saw that the skin was falling off in ragged red shreds, leaving patches of exposed flesh.

"Your face." Cornie put one of his own shiny hands up to his mouth to stifle a laugh. He looked over at Jake.

"Your face isn't any better," Jake shook his head.

The young poet put his fingers up to his own face, pulled away patches of scorched flesh that came off in his hands.

He woke with a start. Someone was nudging him. He looked around wildly and there was Cornie Martens on one side of him and Jake on the other, both of them grinning over at him. When he tried to scream all that came out was a barely audible gasp, but it was enough to disrupt the preacher, who looked over at him, hesitated a moment, then went back to his sermon. Steven realized that he must have been having a nightmare, right there in the church, while the preacher droned on and on. That Cornie and Jake had been trying to wake him up.

"What the hell's the matter with you?" Cornie whispered.

"Sorry. I must have been dreaming."

"Well," said Jake, "that must have been some dream."

"Why?"

"All that squirming around."

"Making faces."

"And look what you did to your hand." The young poet looked down and saw that he had scratched away at the back of his hand with his fingernails until it bled.

"Fireweed," he said to Betty now, and pulled his hand away. "I accidentally touched some this morning. You know how it burns." He didn't want to tell her the truth. It was easier to just to make something up.

He looked out across the open fields, at what was happening only a few hundred yards away. They were clearly getting ready to lower the Minuteman Missile into the ground. It was suspended now, from a series of straps hanging from an enormous crane, and slowly, slowly, they were moving it into position over the silo.

JACK KENNEDY, president of the United States of America, was getting ready to make an important announcement on television. Regularly scheduled programming was about to be interrupted. The circuitry had been wired for a massive nationwide override. Stations had been posting bulletins to keep people up to date with the latest developments in the crisis, but now the time for bulletins was over. It was time for him to tell the American people that there was only one way to stop the Russians. At the advice of his closest and most trusted advisors, he was going to get them ready for all-out nuclear war.

The president was flipping the channel dial on the television, curious to see what shows he was about to pre-empt. He liked the idea of being able to bring people's lives to a standstill like that. He knew he was really the first president with that kind of power, and he intended to use it. He would turn it into the most powerful tool of his presidency. Of any presidency. Television was going to give him what no other president had ever had before. An entire country that felt a personal connection to their leader. A sense of ownership. Of worship. And there was nothing Americans liked better. Of course, in the bargain they were going to give him more power than anyone had ever dreamed possible, but that was a fair trade.

Two attractive young women walked into the room. Each of them carried a small hardshell case. They wore white blouses and tight black skirts over their slender hips. They stood in the doorway long enough to allow the men to undress them with their eyes. The men were mostly Secret Service, young and virile and dressed in their own black and white outfits – white shirts and black ties, dark suit jackets slung over their shoulders. Lyndon Johnson, the vice-president of the United States, was also in the room, leaning back in a chair against the far wall, a drink in his hand. His shirt sleeves were rolled up, his white Stetson pushed back from his prominent forehead. He ogled the two women shamelessly, but they were used to it. It was just part of the routine for them. One was a wardrobe assistant and the other a makeup artist. They walked over to the president, sat him back in his chair, and began to fuss over him.

"From now on," said the president, "it's going to be all about television, hey Elby?" He was calling the vice-president by his nickname, something he didn't usually like to do, but today he felt like being one of the boys.

"And you're just the man for it," said Elby. But there wasn't much enthusiasm in his voice. He was bored as usual. He didn't much like being vice-president. He preferred being in charge.

"It's like anything else," said President Kennedy, and this time he looked into the eyes of the makeup woman. "You have to know how to use it." She smiled coyly and kept on applying makeup while her companion worked on the president's suit jacket and tie. They were just getting used to working in the Oval Office. The whole thing still didn't seem real. Only a short time ago they'd been back in Hollywood working on a movie set when two men in suits came into Marilyn's trailer as if they owned it and asked if the two of them would please wait outside. The way they said it made it clear they weren't really asking. The next thing they knew the President of the United States himself walked right past them into the trailer and closed the door. It was a good twenty minutes before he came out again. When they were allowed back in it was clear they'd have to start all over on Marilyn's makeup and wardrobe. It wasn't long after that she disappeared and soon after two more men in suits showed up with a cheque for each of them and two tickets to Washington, DC. And now here they were, getting President Kennedy ready for the camera.

"You take that Ike Eisenhower," he said now to the men listening.

"Ike who?" said Elby. The men chuckled. ·

"Now there was a president people forgot about in a hurry."

"You sure left him in the crapper all right," said Elby. He had to admit that it seemed like ages since Eisenhower had been in the White House. That even the idea of him being president seemed foreign now. Alien. As if he had been leader of a different country altogether. On a different planet.

"He looked like a fish out of water on that thing," said the president.

"A pike," said Elby. He threw back the rest of his drink. "A goddamn northern pike." The men laughed again.

"Ike the pike," said the president, but nobody thought that was funny.

"But not you, Jack," said Elby. "Hell. You're a regular matinee idol on that goddamn thing." He grinned up at the others, and in behind that grin was something Jack Kennedy didn't like. He couldn't quite put his finger on it but it made him feel like an outsider. From the very beginning Elby had had a knack with the men that he'd never been able to match.

Elby was thinking how it was true that television really was made to order for a guy like Jack Kennedy. It was slick, accessible, and painless. Just like the man himself. And Elby was thinking how he himself was a lot more like Ike Eisenhower. That he could never match the charisma of a guy like JFK. Not on television anyway. He was really just along for the ride. Still, when these two were through, he was going to see about upping his average with one or both of them. It was always the president they wanted, of course, but Elby had discovered that there was no harm in letting them know second prize was up for grabs, too.

He got up to mix himself another drink, took off his hat, waved it in the air, and put it back on. The others winked and nudged each other. They knew the president didn't like Elby wearing his hat in the Oval Office, were all waiting for the day when he would try to make him take it off. They were bored, and craved any kind of excitement. Elby made a vulgar gyration in the direction of the women. "Hold onto your hats, boys" he said loudly, "We might end up miles from here."

The men laughed lustily. It was an inside joke. He'd used that same line after the president's announcement about putting a man on the moon before the end of the decade and returning him safely. Jack Kennedy was supposed to have said before the end of the century – not the decade – but it hadn't come out that way. So now there was no turning back. Things were moving pretty fast. They were all swept up in it. Everyone was along for the ride. The country had never set this kind of pace for itself.

"Kinda like we're speedin' along in a big ol' convertible," Elby said. "Jack there in the front seat, me in the back. You boys in a good ole pickup truck behind us. Out on a clear stretcha Texas highway. Both of us with one arm out the winda and the other on a big ol' pair of tits. Oh, pardon me ladies. Not that you don't qualify." The makeup woman blushed and kept on applying makeup. "And there's poor Ike coughing up dust in the rear-view mirror." He slapped the hat against his knee and laughed.

Sometimes it seemed to Elby that the whole world was speeding toward something, except he could never put his finger on it. That things had gotten out of hand and they might never regain control unless somebody did something. And this business with the Russians, with Castro, was the perfect opportunity. Elby felt sure this was it. This was going to be how they regained control. They'd finally managed to convince the president that he would have to take a stand. That there was really only one way to deal with the Russians. "Take the bull by the horns," as Elby had put it. And Jack had finally agreed, but insisted on going on national television first, to tell everyone what he was about to do.

"Do it first," Elby had told him. "Why give them advance warning? They'll never know what hit them."

"I can't do that."

"But what is there to tell them?"

"They have a right to know."

"It'll just give the Russians more time. I say do it first and worry about the fallout later. Goddamit Jack, we can't let those commies push us around like this. It makes us look like pansies. You don't want people to think you're a pansy, do you, Jack?" The truth was that Elby thought of the president as precisely that. For one thing, there were all those pills and injections. The country had no idea that without them Jack Kennedy would be a bedridden invalid. For another, he was always letting the people around him tell him what to do. As far as Elby was concerned it was no way to run a country.

Just then the door opened and a young intern stepped briskly into the room. Elby couldn't stand her. She was always interrupting. She was the only person who could walk into the president's office without knocking. Even he, Elby, couldn't do that. They were probably all going to have to clear out now for a bit. The whole thing never usually took more than twenty minutes, but still, he'd had the president on the ropes and now the moment had been lost.

"IT'S HER." The Zacharias sisters, teacups in their hands, were staring out the window at Katie as she walked by.

"Who?"

"Katie. Katie Klassen."

"First he has the gall to come back. Now her."

"Walking around here like she owned the place."

"Thinks she can just come back and take up where she left off. Well, we'll see about that."

"As if she had any right in this place."

They were spinsters, all three of them. This was not unusual in the valley. Just as there might be a group of men, like Martha's brothers, there might be a group of women, like these, living under the same roof, in a kind of small cloister, a nunnery of sorts, acting out the daily rituals of faith and self-denial and their own brand of spiritual depravity.

"On her way to strumpet herself for him, you think?"

"On a Sunday, yet."

"But she won't find him home. I saw him driving out of town early this afternoon."

"Gone to visit one of his whores in the States."

They were a bitter and bileful trio who stirred the village

into gossip at the slightest provocation. Over the years people like Abe Wiebe and Aunt Martha and Katie Klassen had supplied them with endless fodder for the mill of their disapproval, the fruits of their vilification. Second-guessing, censure, recrimination, all seemed to materialize effortlessly out of their collective reproach.

They were old order. Black skirts and black kerchiefs. All their lives they practised the custom of shunning religiously, so that in their old age – they were all in their seventies now – they spoke to hardly anyone in the village, since they had excommunicated themselves from almost everyone for one reason or another. They spent their waking hours discussing the affairs of the valley's inhabitants amongst themselves – talking about people, not to them. They did not even really speak to each other, as such. Their pronouncements on the weaknesses, the evils, the submission to temptation of those around them were not really spoken in a way that was meant to communicate anything to the other two. Each spoke to the others as if they were interchangeable. As if they were not really separate entities. They had no real identity, none of them, beyond their membership in the triad. But in that form, they had concocted a persona that was formidable when it came to village hearsay and slander.

After first Abe, and then Katie, left the village, there had been a troublesome void in the galaxy of their daily conversations, until they realized that they still had Martha Wiebe to depend on, and so doubled their efforts to find in her absence from Sunday church, her refusal to wear a kerchief on her head, her open defiance in displaying a television antenna on the roof of her house, all manner of wanton sinfulness, shameful in the eyes of God.

The god of the Zacharias sisters was as harsh as any furrow-browed Mennonite elder. They considered him to be as unrelenting and vengeful as their own father had been. They thought of him as an entity that would jump – as they loved to – on any opportunity to accuse, to cast aspersion, to doubt. Theirs was a god of steel-toed vindictiveness. As humourless and spiteful and petty as they were. More so, if that was possible. They revelled in a kind of insulated self-righteousness that no act of compassion – the kind Abe Wiebe insisted on performing from time to time – could penetrate. Their willingness to be inflexible was as ironclad as any suit of armour.

Lately, Abe Wiebe had been the main subject of their daily gossip. It was enough that he'd come back in the first place – something nobody in the valley would ever have suspected – and gone back to hanging around with the Martens brothers and causing all kinds of trouble, but recently there'd been that business with the woman from across the line. The one who'd had the nerve, the gall, to drive her American Cadillac right up to his place and step out in broad daylight wearing a tight sweater and a skirt cut right up to her thighs and pretend she was there to buy one of his benches.

And what had Abe Wiebe done? Taken her into his shop, where they stayed for the better part of an hour. What happened within the confines of that shop could only be guessed at, but whatever it was, the two of them would certainly burn in Hell for it. The Zacharias sisters had a firm belief in Hell. In a place where naked human bodies burned eternally. A place, in their collective imagination, where they conjured up deliciously disturbing images of people like Abe Wiebe (naked, and sporting an enormous flaming erection) fornicating savagely, endlessly, with people like Katie Klassen (also nude, and with such fine hips) even as their bodies burned – but were never consumed – by eternal fire.

Their zealousness in upholding the integrity of Holy Scripture knew no bounds. They revelled in their endless contempt for all those engaged in acts of filth and immorality, considered the thoughtless destruction of other people's lives by their gossip as nothing less than a celebration of their own piety.

Before Katie's car ever reached the driveway of her parents' abandoned home, the Zacharias sisters had already apprised themselves of the fact she had returned after all this time, looking more sinful and wayward and godless than ever. And now she was out walking the street, right in front of them, in a dress that revealed her curvaceous nakedness underneath, not to mention her calves and ankles, neck and shoulders, to anyone who cared to have a look.

"Where did you say she'd gone off to?"

"Hollywood."

"What did you say it was called?"

"Holy Wood?"

"No. Hollywood. You know. Holly. Like Christmas."

"Oh. I thought it was Holy."

"There's nothing holy about that place, I can tell you."

"Sodom and Gomorrah, that's what."

"She was down there, prostituting herself. Letting the men have their way with her. A different one every night. That's what I heard." Between the three of them they had concocted a scenario of Katie's activities based almost entirely on their own warped fantasies and musings.

"I heard two. One in the morning and a different one again at night."

"I heard two at the same time, sometimes three."

"Imagine."

"Humping her like dogs."

"Like cats."

"There's no place for a whore like her in this village."

"He's one, too, if you ask me. The way he lets those women come up here and...and..."

"She'll sing a different tune when she finds out what he's been up to."

"I'm not so sure."

"They deserve each other. The two of them."

"They can both burn in hell together."

"They don't care about that."

"About what?"

"About burning in hell."

"Their kind never do."

The three Zacharias sisters gawked out at Katie without the slightest reservation, the way they would have at anyone else walking by who was of interest to them. It was as if she'd never left. They took up right where they'd left off, without missing a beat. Katie might have been gone an hour or a day or a year. It was all the same to them. They were timeless in that regard.

"They'll come for her now."

"Who?"

"Men."

"First him. Women coming to sniff him out like bitches in heat. Now it'll be the other way around."

"I wonder how Abe will like that?"

"I say they get right back at it again, the two of them."

"They never could keep their hands off each other."

Katie could see the three Zacharias sisters, teacups in hand, staring at her from the window of their kitchen. They looked exactly the same as they had when she left. They did not appear to have aged, and their habits had not changed, since they used to stand in that very spot and look out at her when she was still living in the village. She told herself they could never get under her skin the way they once had. And yet, she found herself feeling not quite free of their eyes. Not quite immune to their unheard whispers. How did they do that? Those women in their black outfits with their tiresome righteousness, their gaunt self-importance. How could they still have even the tiniest part of her in their bony grip? What was the source of their power? Certainly not her shame. She felt none.

The irony was that Katie had kept herself whole in Hollywood. Refused to indulge herself in the very things they were so sure had ruined her. Not out of some sense of righteousness, but self-preservation. Her body would remain her own, she had decided. Not because she was saving it for anyone else. She would not sell it or compromise it or trade it, she decided, because she didn't need to.

Besides, she was different now, Katie told herself. She was not as vulnerable. She had learned that much. Katie turned and saw them staring out of the window. Looked back at them. Smiled and waved. They blanched a little and kept staring, as if such gestures, whether genuine or defiant, were a quaint and mildly troublesome novelty to them.

She'd changed into a summer dress she'd found in the house, along with some other clothes left behind. The dress was a soft, cotton material, patterned with flowers of yellow and orange. It was not an immodest article of clothing. Not revealing or improper in any way. Any woman of the valley could have worn it. She'd told herself none of that mattered when she put it on, and yet, walking down the village street in it now, she felt as though she might be on fire. This afternoon Katie burned.

She was walking by the teacherage now, the memories flooding through her. She felt a mixture of wonder and woe, a little numbed by it all. She knew she could never separate everything out, that it would always be a mix of the real and the imagined, just like the movies. There was really nothing to be done. Nothing to be undone.

She could remember back to the morning she'd packed her suitcases into the trunk of Peter Giesbrecht's car, parked in front of that same desolate house, right there, and let him drive her quietly out of the village. Riding past Aunt Martha's place, she'd seen her wave from the upstairs window, quite sure that it would be the last time she ever saw the place. And now here she was. Why?

Katie had been over at Aunt Martha's that last morning, as much for refuge and comfort as to say goodbye. She was leaving, but first she wanted to cry a little into Martha's ample bosom. Lay her head for a few minutes on one of her big shoulders. They were sitting in behind the house, on the wrought iron chairs, while the hummingbirds fed from the hollyhocks in the still of sunrise.

Word had come back to the village that Abe Wiebe had enlisted in the Canadian army and gone to fight in the Korean War. People like the Zacharias sisters wasted no time in explaining this development as a direct result, according to them, of having fallen in love with Katie Klassen. She had caused him to lose his senses, his better judgement, as any man would who fell under the spell of her unbridled enchantment, her worldly beauty.

"He wasn't ready," said Martha. "And neither were you. Now you'll have to wait – both of you – until you know yourselves a little better, that's all. He has to do it his way, and you yours." Katie hadn't told her yet that she was leaving, too. Martha wanted to explain to Katie why everything had fallen apart. Wanted to tell her how neither of them was to blame. How it was only because there wasn't enough room in the world – at least the stifling world of the valley – for both of them the way things were right now. How what had happened was unavoidable, even necessary. She wanted to try and capture in words the forces that had been at work. Something about two powerful energies – set one against the other. About being swallowed up, one by the other.

Certainly, she'd known for some time now that the valley would never be able to hold either of them for long, the way it held so many of its other inhabitants. When Abe Wiebe walked into a room, something happened to all the women. It went through the air, from one to the other. Suddenly – here was a man for whom everything might be up for grabs. Exactly the same thing happened to the men when Katie Klassen was in their presence. And when the two of them shared the same space there simply wasn't room for anyone else. Between the two of them they swallowed up all the energy in the room.

And somewhere in there, Martha was certain, the two of them had become afraid – perhaps not consciously – that they would lose themselves in such a process. Be swallowed up by it. By each other. That they would be consumed one by the other. By the very thing they each had so much of.

All of this was what Martha wanted to get through to Katie. Thought she needed to know. But none of it was working. Each time she started on a new angle of attack, it sounded shallower and more contrived. Martha didn't want to talk about love, an idea that had always been troublesome to her. Romantic love, she was convinced, was too close to lust to be trusted. Falling in love, she had decided a long time ago, was nothing less than debilitating. Got in the way of things that needed doing. Took up too much energy. But now, in spite of herself, she just wanted to say the thing she thought Katie needed to hear.

"He'll come back."

Katie lifted her head from Martha's shoulder and straightened herself up. "I won't be here."

"What do you mean?"

"I'm leaving." Katie, hands in her lap, looked straight ahead into the hollyhocks.

"What are you saying. When?"

"Now."

"But where? How?"

"It's what everybody wants, isn't it?" said Katie. "For me to get out? To leave? They'll be well rid of both of us."

"It doesn't matter what they want. It never has. It's what you want that matters."

"What I want." Katie looked down into the crumpled

handkerchief in her hands. "I've lost that. That's gone. Over. All I want now is to be away from here."

"You can't let them chase you off like that. It means they've won. Don't you see?"

"It's too late."

"You can come and stay with me if you like."

"No. I'm going. I have to do it now. If I stay another minute, I'll never go. I'll end up like..." Katie stopped herself, looked away.

"Like me. Is that what you were going to say?"

Katie turned back to look up at Martha. "I'm sorry. I know that you chose to stay. But it's different for me."

It was precisely times like this that had made Martha decide to stay. Times when she thought she might be of some service. To people like Katie. When they needed her most. The kind of people who were not completely at home here, and never would be, but who weren't ready for the world just yet. And here was Katie, in all her despair, her confusion, her heart quite broken by a man Martha respected and loved in her own right. She wanted to counsel her now. Tell her the right thing to do.

"But where will you go? You can't just walk out of here."

"Peter Giesbrecht is taking me to Winnipeg. He's waiting for me now. Over at the teacherage."

"Don't be ridiculous. I won't let you do it."

"I just came to say goodbye."

Martha looked hard at Katie. Leaned forward in her chair. "You're serious. My heavens, girl, you can't be." But when she looked again into Katie's eyes she saw that it was so.

"But why?"

"I told you. I have to get out."

"Yes, but not like this."

"It's all settled."

"But child, you can't possibly go through with this. Do you realize what a big mistake you're making?"

"I can't stay. And this is a way for me to go."

"But why him?"

"Who else is there?"

"Does he know?"

"Know what? About me and Abe? Of course."

"No, I don't mean that. Does he know what you're doing?"

"What does that mean?"

"You know exactly what it means."

"Yes. I think so. But he doesn't care."

"Think, Katie. Think what you're doing. You don't need to do it this way. You're strong. You're brave."

"Not that strong. Not that brave."

The two of them sat in silence for another moment. There didn't seem to be anything more to say. The hummingbirds buzzed among the flowers and the morning grew brighter. Much was understood then, that could never be spoken, as with all great moments between two people.

It was true that Katie had given Peter Giesbrecht little, if any, reason to entertain romantic notions about her. But now that his tenure in the village had ended (like so many others before him), taking Katie Klassen with him when he left was beyond anything he would ever have thought possible. It had all happened so quickly. First, without warning, Abe Wiebe, the man Katie was supposed to marry, had suddenly gone off to get himself killed in the war, and then Katie had quite unexpectedly allowed him to make overtures to her – not in a romantic sense, as such, but overtures nevertheless. If Peter Giesbrecht thought there was some calculation in it, if he suspected that Katie Klassen was up to something, it wasn't enough to stop him. He was going to do it for the same reason any man in the valley would – because she let him.

They would travel together to Winnipeg. Peter had purchased a house there, a bungalow almost as modest as the one he was leaving. There was a room for her. His parents, who lived nearby, would disapprove. He didn't care. He thought maybe he was in love with her.

That morning, riding in the car, Katie waved to Martha's camera with one hand and held a white envelope in the other. Martha had run upstairs and returned with it – told Katie not to open it until later – until she was out of the valley altogether. That first night in her new home, Katie had opened the envelope in the privacy of her small, sparse room. There had been three one-hundred-dollar bills inside, and a small note, which read:

Katie,

> In the village, your beauty was too much. Now, it will not be enough. The world is big. It runs on money. Here's a little to get you started.
> Go where you need to go.
> Do what you need to do.

Martha

Katie hid the money under her pillow when Peter knocked gently on the door. She'd heard him, in the bathroom, working very hard at grooming himself. She thought he must be a very exacting man in that regard.

Peter Giesbrecht had been getting himself ready for Katie. He was under the mistaken assumption that she would allow him some modest advances at intimacy. A kiss or two, perhaps, to begin with, nothing more. Katie had already told him there would be no such allowances forthcoming. Had made it clear from the beginning that there was really nothing in it for him in that arena.

But the evening preparations would become a ritual. Every night, with great care, and great anticipation, Peter would prepare himself. Each time he performed the same routine of tooth brushing and underarm cleansing, of hair combing and toenail clipping as if he were preparing for the most important event of his life. The moment when she would finally invite him in – the moment that would never come. Always, he would come by her door to say good night, stand for a moment on the far side of the door, wait for her to ask him in, and every night she would not.

He insisted on maintaining the scenario in his mind that one day she would let him in. He wanted Katie, not so much for earthly pleasures, as for stock. His motivation was not so much lust as a sense of history. The beginnings of an urban class of Mennonites was taking root in Winnipeg, and Peter Giesbrecht wanted to be among them. He had landed a job in the English Department at the high school nearby, and he wanted his children to grow up in a suburban bungalow – much better appointed than the one they were starting out in – and become doctors and lawyers and teachers like him. He was going to educate the children that Katie bore him in a way that would allow them to become the equal or better of any urban English children. They would be trained in the arts. They would play musical instruments. They would excel at sports. They would achieve in school. They would be living, breathing proof that Mennonite stock was as good as or better than any in the country. One or two might even feel a calling, as he had, to come back to the village of their forefathers and mothers and work there for a year or two. It would be a little bit like doing missionary work, but without the necessity and inconvenience of bustling off to Africa or some other backward place.

If he was patient and kind, he thought, eventually she would relent. Agree not only to let him in, but to marry him. Bear him robust, good-looking, and intelligent offspring. They were going to make beautiful Mennonite children together. He would get her pregnant early and often. From baby to baby, he thought, she would more and more come to be the wife and mother he desired her to be. If she lost some of her looks in the process, she could easily afford to.

As he mounted her on that wedding night, it would please him very much – the idea that he was inseminating someone so beautiful – that her unbelievably curvaceous and fertile body should house the product of his loins. They would raise urban Mennonite children together.

Katie, on the other hand – even as Peter dreamed, alone in his room at the far end of the hall, of pumping his progeny into her – already knew she wouldn't be staying long enough for children, for babies or families or domestic entrenchment. She understood, just as she'd known back in the village, that she was leaving. Not right away, but soon, and for the rest of her life. She acknowledged to herself that what she was up to wasn't very noble, but absolutely necessary. Peter would be disappointed, when the time came, but mostly for tactical reasons. Granted, he had taken her out of the village and given her a place to stay, but failed to take into account the fact that there was really nothing to keep her there.

She got up on that first morning well before Peter awoke, dressed in silence, and took a bus downtown. By the time she returned in the early evening she'd landed a job in the cosmetics department of the T. Eaton & Company department store. Had done so in spite of the fact she knew nothing of cosmetics – had never used any. It was only the first of many acts that would baffle Peter, catch him completely unawares. Aunt Martha would turn out to be right. Katie would prove early and often that she was capable of much more than she'd given herself credit for.

She had spent the morning learning how to dress – observed closely the fashionable women plying through the racks in the ladies' department to see what they were wearing. After that she went up to the cafeteria for something to eat, then returned promptly to the ladies' wear department and bought herself a new wardrobe of suitable clothes with the money Martha had given her, changed into them right there in one of the fitting rooms, and took the escalator down to the first floor. She walked up to the cosmetics counter in her new outfit, and, thanks to the presence of the sales manager, a Mr. Arthur Winkworth, was hired on the spot. Mr. Winkworth took one look at her, performed several acts of wishful thinking while he asked a few perfunctory questions, smiled ingratiatingly into her green eyes, and informed the gaunt and badly made-up woman next to him that Katie would be starting immediately.

Katie had no first-hand experience with cosmetic products. She'd never had the need to use any, not that she would have been allowed. Her beauty had come to her naturally. But she soon learned that she didn't need to know anything about the tube or bottle or jar she had in her hands in order to sell it. She only needed to get the woman on the other side of the counter to believe in it. She found she could accomplish this with surprising ease, simply by appealing to the unlikely combination of vanity and insecurity that so many women brought to the counter with them.

Katie soon discovered that the conversations which took place across the cosmetics counter were not real conversations at all, but rather intricate and extravagant rituals, in which the sales clerk pretended to give information, and the woman on the other side pretended to take it. Katie found that she could tell her customers almost anything about a product they were interested in and it wouldn't make any difference so long as they believed that it would make them more beautiful, more desirable. So many of these women, it seemed to Katie, just wanted to make themselves feel a little better.

Later, in Hollywood, she would be astonished at how many women there clearly did not feel good about themselves either. Even though they were movie stars. Even though they could count themselves among the most beautiful women in the world. In spite of this, a surprising number of them didn't seem to like themselves very much. The same would turn out to be true for the men.

Katie soon came to realize she had been working under a mistaken assumption. She had always thought that, out in the world, people would have a better sense of themselves. But it soon became clear to her that they were no further ahead in this regard than the men and women of the valley. Self-deception and wilful ignorance, to Katie's surprise, were as common out in the world as in the valley, except that the people out here were caught up in different kind of machinery – not of self-denial and sacrifice, but of consumerism.

Some of the women who came to the counter took the ritual of buying cosmetics to an even higher level of dishonesty. They worked under the tacit assumption that the woman behind the counter could not be trusted. That she would secretly withhold products that might end up making her customer more beautiful than she herself. If the customer already considered herself to be just that, extra precautions had to be taken. In that case, she might be shown something secretly designed to make her look, instead of more beautiful, less so. The women behind the counter would do so, these women believed, out of jealousy or spite or just plain cold, calculated bloody-mindedness.

Katie, however, worked under none of these handicaps. Her customers took one look at her and saw that they had no chance. That she was on another level. They saw immediately that they were not a danger to her, and so they trusted her, understood that whatever the product, it could never make them look as good as she did, and so they bought almost anything she cared to show them. Whenever one of them asked her if she used the product she was holding in her magnificent hands, the one they wanted to buy – would buy, no matter what she said about it – Katie always smiled, and managed somehow not to answer the question. This always satisfied them. Katie's sales were soon the highest in the department.

Men sometimes stopped by the counter, pretending to be interested in something or other. A lot of them were shy and ineffectual. A few were downright awkward and silly. But once in a while there was a man with real confidence who knew how to shower her with the kind of compliments and vaguely suggestive conversation that was designed to weaken her. They were intelligent, witty, sophisticated men who knew what they were capable of, who had seen their power succeed time and again. They were not afraid of a beautiful woman like Katie. Knew how to make her want to say yes.

And yet they always failed, not because she wasn't attracted to them, not because some of them weren't devastatingly handsome and charming. And certainly not because the whole idea of sleeping with one of them might feel like she was cheating on Abe Wiebe – never mind Peter Giesbrecht. No, Katie turned them down because as far as she was concerned it was just good practice. A way of cutting her teeth, of preparing herself for the men she would meet in Hollywood. She wanted to be ready, by the time she got to California. Ready for the time when she could sleep with some of the most desirable men alive, and would choose not to.

She soon learned to handle them easily enough. Made it clear she would reject them in a way that left their dignity intact, if they would just leave her alone. When they saw that she could not be manipulated by their charm, that she could not be penetrated by their flattery, they soon gave up. They were men who had only so much energy to invest, who had gotten where they were by paying strict attention to the finer points of acquisition and disposal, to the calculation of cost versus benefit.

It was also there behind the cosmetics counter that Katie Klassen first came to realize what she would later discover in Hollywood: that there were very few men in the world who could truly capture her imagination, and with it, her desire. Men who could make her laugh in a way that was more than mere politeness. Who could look into her eyes with the kind of honesty and intelligence and depth that it would take to reach her. Men who did not have a hidden agenda, or a false sense of their own importance. Who knew how to listen to a woman's breathing, in between the words she spoke. Whose eyes were open for inspection. Men who understood the importance of cultivating tenderness into strength. More and more it astonished her to think that the valley, of all places, had produced a man who possessed all of these qualities.

It was only a little more than three months, thanks to the generous commissions she earned at the T. Eaton Company department store, before she'd saved enough money to get her where she wanted to go. She had no qualms about leaving.

"I'm sorry," she said to Peter when it was time to leave. They were standing in the narrow hallway of the modest suburban bungalow that could never be her home. Katie had her hand on the knob of the front door.

"I guess I always knew this day would come," said Peter.

"Well, it has."

"I know why you're leaving," he said.

"You do?"

"Yes."

"Does it really matter?"

"It has nothing to do with me. Isn't that right? Isn't that what you were going to say?"

Katie hadn't expected to hear him talk this way. Had thought there would be pleading. Bitterness. She wanted to tell him that none of it had ever had anything to do with him, but now she didn't want to be cruel.

"You didn't really think there was any chance, did you?" she said evenly.

"Yes."

"But why? What cause did I ever give you?"

"None, I suppose." It was true. She had given him nothing. But Katie was failing to take into account the power of Peter's fantasy. The one he had been working so hard on all this time. The one where she was going to marry him. Have his children.

"You used me," he said. That was better. Katie wanted anger. Recrimination. She wanted to be thrown out. Felt she had it coming.

"Yes."

"You could have let me kiss you – just one time." He looked at her, eyes a little shiny. "But you didn't. Not even once."

"No."

"And you never would have."

"No."

"I enjoyed our time together." The truth was that they had spent almost no time together. A few quick meals, passing each other in and out of the bathroom now and then. A breakfast or two. "I wish you wouldn't," he said.

"I'm only taking what I've packed into my suitcases."

"Where will you go?" He folded his arms.

"You can have everything else. Or throw it out. Or whatever you want to do with it."

"Do you think you'll be happy?"

"I have to go now. The taxi's here." She pulled the door wide and picked up her bags.

"When I'm an old man, I'll look back and remember that once, a long time ago, when I was still a young man, I spent some time in the company of a beautiful woman."

Katie didn't want this. Wanted more anger. Scolding. Wanted to be screamed at. "Goodbye," she said, just before she stepped onto the concrete landing. She went down a couple of steps and turned slightly. "Thank you," she said.

And that was the last time she saw Peter Giesbrecht. Or spoke to him. Or even really thought about him. It seemed cruel-hearted to her now – the fact that she had been able to forget him so quickly, so easily. But there was a stark reality to it. What, really, was there to think about him?

DICKIE DERKSEN was out in the field looking up into the clear blue sky at the countless vapour trails criss-crossing each other. From where he stood, he could also see the Minuteman II Missile waiting to be tucked into its underground silo. He was in the middle of a pasture, not far from the southern edge of the village, where the little girls had been having their game of tag among the tall grasses and wild hollyhocks.

The pasture Dickie was standing in displayed the same features as so many others in the valley, with its small dugout for the cattle to drink from, and a stand of willow trees for shelter from the rain. The cattle in the valley could be seen standing under them more often than not these days – even when it wasn't raining. Even when a warm sun shone out of a blue sky. Intermittent thunder coming out of the skies, clear or cloudy, drove them there. The cows, not unlike some of the human inhabitants of the valley, were constantly under the mistaken impression that a storm was on its way.

In fact, they were spending so much of their time under the branches of those trees that they had taken to eating what foliage they could find hanging above them, and all through the valley stands of trees were perfectly manicured, as if by an expert gardener, to precisely the height that a cow's tongue could reach.

A few trails criss-crossed the pasture Dickie was standing in, running in various directions, along which the cows made their way morning and night, and along which most of their dung lay. Dickie was an expert on cow-pies, and had long ago classified them into various categories, by stages of decomposition. The system lacked a proper nomenclature, since Dickie lacked the linguistic skills to develop one, but the essential structure was there. One variety, for example, was still warm and fresh, with a slight tint of shiny green on it. When sniffed, it smelled more of mulched grass than manure. Another, at a later stage, had developed a brownish crust but was still soft inside, so that if stepped upon or kicked it would reveal a soft, faintly green interior. Still another variety was dried right through and surprisingly light. It was highly portable, and could be hurled through the air like a discus. Even a cow-pie that had disappeared altogether left its mark – a disk of brilliant green grass, where the manure had been turned back into pasture.

Lately, however, none of this was of any interest to Dickie Derksen. Nothing on the ground, including various species of cow-pie, could compare to what was happening up in the sky. He would stand for hours, the afternoon breeze sweeping across his flat, simple face, eyes turned skyward, looking up into the heavens. His large head tilted comfortably on a thick neck and heavy shoulders. His weight balanced evenly on the sturdy construction of his short, stocky legs. In all that time he would hardly move, except to shift his weight now and then from one foot to the other, swaying from side to side with a slow and steady rhythm.

Dickie was watching. Listening. Waiting for a boom of thunder to come out of the clear blue sky. Unlike the cattle around him, he knew what it was. Where it was coming from. Not that he understood the first thing about military aircraft, or Mach I, or the physics of breaking the sound barrier. He only knew that the great thundering booms that came rumbling down out of the sky shook the pit of his stomach in a pleasing way.

He had no appreciation for the fact that the men up there – flying F101-B Voodoos out of Grand Forks Air Force Base – were just doing their job, practising very hard for the possibility of World War Three, and that flying through Mach 1 was just a natural component in the course of their manoeuvres. Training had been intensified, stepped up, because they might have to try and shoot planes or rockets or who-knows-what – enemy aircraft travelling very fast, heading for ground zero only a stone's throw from where Dickie was standing – out of the sky at a moment's notice.

Dickie's imagination, along with his intellect, was limited. It failed to grasp the idea of aerial combat. Of strategic warfare. He knew even less about military installations. About the crisis that was facing the American Armed Forces. But he could grasp the notion of something flying very fast through the air, making a great and beautiful noise that shook the earth with its power. If nuclear war had broken out, and an atomic explosion detonated nearby, Dickie would have watched in fascination as the orange and black mushroom cloud billowed into the sky, towering over his little spot on the floor of the valley, shooting lightning bolts into the clear blue air around. He would gleefully have followed the progress of the shock wave as it swept toward him at twice the speed of sound. And even as the wall of heat smashed into him and burned, first his skin, and then his flesh, and then the bones of his stubby body into ashes, even then he would have marvelled at the intensity of it all.

In a matter of seconds the sky, which a moment ago had been blue from horizon to horizon, darkened ominously. The thunderhead that had been lurking on the edge of the escarpment swooped down over the valley. It had already taken the first step to sending a nasty shaft of crooked lightning down on Dickie. He heard it only as a little tick – felt the hair on the back of his neck stand up on end. But the lightning bolt had given itself away. Had done what any other lightning bolt would do before it struck, which was to set up a path for the energy to flow along. In this particular case, that path would lead directly through Dickie Derksen's thick, stumpy body.

Dickie didn't know anything about the nature of lightning bolts, and even if he had, it wouldn't have made any difference. There wouldn't have been time to do anything about it. The little tick he heard was a relatively small electrical charge – an exchange of information between the thunderhead and the ground – an agreement that before the actual bolt of lightning should come crashing down, a path needed to be laid out for it to follow. The small charge was a kind of preliminary strike, something the cloud and the ground set up between each other just to test the circuitry.

Dickie had no idea why his hair was standing on end. He was unaware that the little tick he'd just heard had originated from the top of his electrically charged skull. That a tiny rope had just been stretched down to the earth, along which the concussion of lightning would shudder and shock.

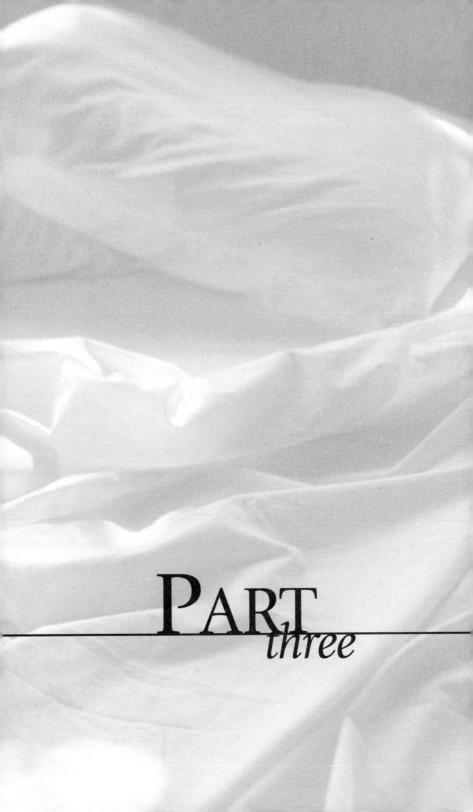

PART
*three*

WHILE THE INHABITANTS OF NEUSTADT were finishing up the last of their fastba, the young soldiers just across the line were in the last stages of readying the rocket for its insertion into the silo. They were busy operating pneumatic drills and rivet guns, tightening down explosive bolts, polishing the shiny tip of the nuclear warhead, all of them working with a mixture of eagerness and ineptitude. They were being heavily supervised, to minimize the chance for error. For every job, there were three soldiers to execute it. Everything had to be checked and rechecked. It was the same strategy the military was using in the space program, and the success of that operation would soon speak for itself. They were proving, once and for all, that redundancy was a concept to be valued, and that given half a chance, it could pay big dividends.

These young men gave not a thought to the possible moral implications of what they were up to, not a thought to the Mennonite villages, for example, that lay just over the border. Most of them didn't know there were any villages there to ignore. A lot of them didn't even know they were at the border. Some didn't even know they were installing an underground nuclear missile. None of that was important to them. None of that mattered. It was not their job to think anything at all while they worked. Most of them found this arrangement to their liking. What these soldiers enjoyed doing more than anything else was obeying orders. They had, in fact, been handpicked for this assignment because their psychological profiles showed a strong need to do just that. To follow directions blindly. To simply do what they were told.

In the same way that they worked on the rocket installation during the day, so, after their shift had ended, these young soldiers drank and ate and shat with equal impunity – the kind that was only possible with the help of the best military training in the world – training that had all but eradicated any nagging tendencies to second guess. Any pretensions toward moral ambiguity.

If none of the soldiers was really thinking very hard about what they were up to, they could be forgiven. The destructive capability of the weapon in question was so immense that it was really beyond anyone's comprehension. Very few people had so far managed to appreciate the scope of such an undertaking. Certainly not the scientists who had helped develop it. For them, a kind of willful numbness about the possibility of a nuclear Armageddon had set in some time ago, eroded relentlessly by the theoretical considerations of their investigations. And by now, of course, the science had pretty much gone out of it anyway. The physicists and chemists and sub-atomic specialists had all but outlived their usefulness. They were not on hand to watch these installations. They had done their job. The bombs had been built. Everything now came down to mechanics. It was simply a matter of execution, and that had been left to the military.

The young soldiers worked tirelessly. When their shift was over they went back to the barracks and ate a hearty meal, drank beer, played cards, and when it was time for lights out, masturbated vigorously into their sheets, much the same as the Wiebe boys would have done when they were in their prime. On a weekend furlough they sometimes went into town, got drunk at Jack's Bar, and tried to pick up the local women. Some of them succeeded, got those same women to take off their panties and spread their legs on the front seat of an open jeep while they pushed their swollen penises with great lust into their vaginas.

If one of these women was particularly promiscuous, she might have allowed a bashful but appealing Mennonite boy from across the line to do the same thing only a few hours before, perhaps across the seat of a pickup truck, so that the two batches of semen became mixed together. Then, if she became pregnant, she might never know whether the father was a young soldier preparing weapons of mass destruction, or a young man from across the line preparing to get up the next morning and slop the hogs before he dressed for church.

There was, in fact, a disproportionate amount of sexual activity taking place on both sides of the border. All across the valley – in the backs of cars, in bedrooms, under trees, hidden behind bushes, in church alcoves, under tractors, in granaries, porches, school basements – anywhere that provided the least bit of privacy – men and women, boys and girls, were copulating in haste and eagerness. Some primal urge had increased their sex drive tenfold. Men wanted to inseminate. Women wanted to be inseminated. The feelings were mutual. They experienced this increased need as a simple sensation of tremendous lust. If there was the real possibility of annihilation, so went the logic of their collective unconscious, there was going to be an awful lot of fucking before the dying. It explained a lot of things – like the women who came up from the States in their fancy cars to see if Abe Wiebe might want to make love to them. They were really just following their instinct.

Even the least handsome of men were not refused advances. Even the least attractive of women were pursued with vigour. Plain and uninteresting men and women, unremarkable in every way, could not believe their wild luck as one

129

after another they found themselves the object of someone's affection. All up and down the valley there was a sense of this urgency in these men and women. They sought each other out, undressed each other, coupled, and felt afterward – more than anything – that they wanted to go out and do it all over again. Even if it made no sense. Even if the increasing likelihood that they might all soon be incinerated made each subsequent act of copulation more ironic than the one before.

It was not unique to the valley, this sense of sexual urgency. It was happening – with greater or lesser intensity – all over the continent. The world. Soviet men and women were going at it with the same vigour. Sperm production in that region of the world was at an all-time high. More semen was flowing out of more Russian penises into more Russian vaginas than anyone could remember since the days of Stalin. The subliminal feeling that the juice of life needed to flow had an unmistakable cathartic effect. Each ejaculation took on a special importance. Became an affirmation of life itself. The possibility of regeneration. Even the President of the United States of America, and especially the vice-president, were not immune to these powerful urges, and found it necessary to inseminate a variety of women often and intensely.

All throughout the northern hemisphere people were having urgent and vigorous sex under a black and terrifying cloak of finality. It was a tremendous aphrodisiac – the equivalent of being on death row and eating a last, glorious meal, never to be digested. The only difference was that each serving was followed by clemency – by an unexpected reprieve – which was followed by another meal, and so on. And each one tasted as good as the one before. A student of anthropology, or sociology, or even psychology could have explained this as the primal drive for survival, the strongest of all human and animal forces. One that had to be listened to. That could not be ignored. Almost everyone felt it.

The young private at the barricade was no exception. He was having a fantasy just now, daydreaming in the sun. His reverie involved the beautiful young woman who had pulled up to the barricade in the yellow convertible earlier. He couldn't stop thinking about her pink angora sweater. Her white pedal-pushers. By now he had stopped enough vehicles with strange license plates to figure out that he'd unknowingly become the equivalent of a border guard. The people he'd been stopping all afternoon were all heading for the same place. The trees and buildings of a settlement were clearly visible on the other side of the line. The cars were full of people trying to get there without going through customs. What they were up to, he understood, was technically illegal. Not really allowed.

The occupants of the cars could have told him that it was more popular than ever for people from the valley to use the backcountry shortcut. That it was easier, even if the road was a little rough and difficult to negotiate, because things had changed at the customs office. The casual atmosphere was gone. The easy smuggling game had come to an abrupt halt. There was the bunker, of course, complete with two armed soldiers garrisoned inside, but even on the Canadian side, things were suddenly different. The customs officers were still unarmed, but a uniformed RCMP officer stood next to them as they asked their questions. Asked them in a different way. Looked at you differently.

The young soldier knew the people in the cars had all lied to him, just as he had lied to them. While they insisted, sheepishly, that they were just out for a Sunday drive, he insisted with an equal lack of credibility that there was a bridge out up ahead. It was obvious that everyone was lying to everyone, that neither side was really interested in the truth. Certainly not the young soldier. That wasn't his job. He had his orders. The fact that they were busy installing an intercontinental ballistic missile in the middle of a sunny Sunday afternoon, in full view of anyone who cared to watch, was beside the point.

But just now he didn't want to think about any of that. He wanted to fantasize some more about the woman in the yellow convertible. He'd made his way down into the ditch next to the road, pulled himself out of his skivvies, and was busy pumping away. For all practical purposes, he might just as well have stayed where he was, since he was just far enough from the site that no one would really see what he was up to. And there was certainly no one else around to see him. But then, he'd never been particularly bold about that kind of thing. Not like some of the other fellows in the barracks, who seemed to treat the whole exercise as some kind of spectator sport. They thought nothing of pulling their manhood out for everyone to see, then talking their way through the entire masturbation process – before, during, and after – in a kind of play-by-play fashion. They sometimes liked to finish up with a reference to the missile they were so busy installing. "Ready for launch...countdown...3-2-1...blast aaaaawwwwwwwwffffff!!!"

When it came to disposing of their emissions, every soldier had his own style. Some ejaculated up onto to their hard bare stomachs and rubbed it into their skin. Some spilled it over the side of the bunk and wiped it up with a sock or a pair of shorts. Others didn't bother about it at all, didn't care where it ended up, which meant that walking between the bunks in bare feet was not a good idea.

But those weren't the guys that made him most uncomfortable. That was reserved for the ones who wanted him to help them out. Who alternately offered to pay him or not beat him up in exchange for a hand job, or worse. He'd seen other men doing that, even sucking on each other, in the latrine stalls. So far, he'd managed to politely decline all such overtures. For him it was a private thing, and he wanted to keep it that way.

"Your uniform," the woman in the yellow convertible was saying to him in his fantasy. She was still wearing the same pink sweater and white pedal-pushers, looking up at him with those impossibly big, green eyes, running a hand through her long blonde hair, and the conversation they'd been having was about to take a decidedly pornographic turn.

"Excuse me?"

"Your uniform. I really like it."

"You do?"

"Yes. I like it a lot."

"Thank you."

"Time for inspection."

"Inspection?"

"That's right, soldier. Step this way."

"Ma'am?"

"You heard me. Get over here."

"Yes, ma'am."

"Closer."

"Excuse me, ma'am, but that's my fly you're unzipping."

"I know. There seems to be something in your pants here. Some kind of bulge."

"Ma'am, that's my cock you've got there."

"I know. Mmmm, it's getting bigger."

"Yes, ma'am."

"It's so big."

"Mmm... mmmm."

"Mmmmpfh..."

And so on.

The soldier was very eager to ejaculate. He was working himself up to the moment of climax. In this way he was not so different from the rocket only a short distance away. It, too, was being prepared for the optimal moment of thrust. Just like the young soldier, what it wanted most was to blast off. That was the reason for its existence. That was the essence of its

133

being. In this sense the young soldier at the barricade, the rocket, and the men bolting it down, all wanted pretty much the same thing. Thrust and explosion.

The young private was just about to do exactly that when he saw another vehicle approaching. He barely had time to stuff himself back into his pants and run back up to the road before the car pulled up. He stepped up to the driver's side as casually as he could, semen oozing out of the semi-erect penis inside his pants, and waited for the driver to roll down the window. When he got a better look at the occupants of the vehicle he forgot all about his erection. The driver looked okay, but there were two men with him who looked as if they'd stepped right out of a horror movie.

Abe Wiebe and the Martens brothers, on their way back from Jack's Bar, had decided to take the shortcut back across the line, just like everyone else. They knew all about the changes at the customs office, the silly questions, the waiting. Abe wanted to get back home. They'd stayed too long as it was. The American woman coming to pick up the schlopebank he'd made for her might still be there, waiting. He hoped she was. He badly needed a distraction. He wanted to forget all about Katie Klassen. But now here was this young soldier to put up with.

"What's up?" said Abe.

"Jesus Christ," said the soldier.

Oh boy, thought Jake. Here we go again.

"What can we do for you?" said Abe.

The soldier stared at each of the Martens brothers in turn. Jake was next to Abe in the front seat, and Cornie was sprawled across the back, sound asleep. There was a Sunday afternoon television western playing out of his mouth. "If I were you, Son," Richard Boone's deep baritone voice was saying, "I wouldn't go for that gun." He was talking to the gunslinger at the far end of the bar, a hot-tempered young man who mistakenly thought he could outdraw Palladin. The private mistook Cornie's broadcast for the radio and paid no attention. That, and he was busy trying to deal with the shock of going so abruptly from the exquisitely lovely woman in his fantasy to something as nauseatingly hideous as the sight of the Martens brothers.

He'd seen faces like theirs before, but only in pictures. Part of his training had involved being exposed to photographs of badly burned and disfigured survivors of Hiroshima and Nagasaki. The Korean War was still on at the time and the idea was to dehumanize the enemy. By the time they were through, the oriental faces up on the screen were supposed to evoke about as much empathy in a new recruit as pictures of demonic freaks. The program had succeeded beyond anyone's wildest expectations, and now when the young private looked at the two Martens brothers, he thought of them quickly and easily as less than human. It was really no trouble, since they looked inhuman already.

"Jesus," he said again.

"Look, we know about what's going on up there," said Abe. "We don't want to go over there and gawk. You know how annoying that can be, don't you? When someone just wants to gawk?"

"Excuse me?"

"We're on our way back over the line. Let us go and we won't give you any trouble."

The private reverted back to his original demeanour. Remembered what he was there for. "I can't do that, Mister," he said. "I got strict orders not to let anyone through."

"And what if we go ahead anyway?" said Jake. "What are you gonna do? Shoot us? With that big gun you got over there?"

The private realized he'd left his M-14 leaning against the barricade when he'd gone down into the ditch to masturbate.

He scrambled over to pick it up, stumbled back to the car with the rifle across his chest.

"I have my orders," he said.

"Sure. Sure," said Abe. "Now listen. I want you to back away from this car and let us pass." Abe had seen plenty of cocky GIs overseas in Korea. He was in no mood to put up with one here, on his own turf.

"You can't talk to me that way," said the soldier. He thought back to what the sergeant had said earlier that morning. "I'm the one with the gun, remember?"

"Right," said Abe and caught the surprised young private neatly on the side of the jaw with a deft jab. He'd learned to box in the army and knew how to throw a punch as well as a seasoned fighter. This particular blow was the kind that really didn't do much damage, other than to concuss the brain into brief unconsciousness. The private dropped his weapon and buckled into a heap.

"Snotty little cocksucker," said Abe.

"That was just like in the movies," said Cornie, who had roused from his sleep in the back seat.

"Are we turning around?" said Jake.

"The hell we are," said Abe. "Come on. Let's go home."

STEVEN ZACHARIAS was lying on his back under the shade of the cottonwood tree, propped up on his elbows. By that time Betty Unger had decided that if there was to be any meaningful progress in the area of sexual intimacy, she was going to have to, literally, take matters into her own hands. She'd unzipped the young poet's fly and, for the first time in her young life, taken hold of an erect penis. She understood perfectly that this was precisely the thing she wasn't, under any circumstances, supposed to be made to do. Nevertheless she found herself keenly interested. Allowed herself a long, dreamy look at the organ of so much fuss and bother. The idea of the penis had been so wrapped in riddles and half-truths that now, seeing it for the first time, she thought it a wondrous and magnificent creation. It seemed so harmless. Innocuous. A toy. A trifle. A doll. Yes. Very much like a doll to be played with. She felt not the slightest threat. She didn't feel dirty. Thought it, instead, a most inviting-looking organ. Its texture so pleasingly firm, yet soft. So hot to the touch. Humming and buzzing with life. She sensed its urgency. Its need to be stroked. Fondled. It seemed the most important thing in the world. To be able to do that.

She felt a surprising sense of exhilaration, then liberation, at the thought of what she was up to. So much so that she proceeded to do what even the other, older girls, had disdainfully claimed they categorically refused to do. She took the thing into her mouth. Rather than cheap or sinful, she felt immediately that she had come home to something. Understood instinctively that this was only the first of countless such organs that would pass between her lips. That she would see to it each and every one of them reached a climax there. Young Betty Unger didn't know it yet, but she was in the early stages of what would turn out to be a troublesome oral fixation. So troublesome, in fact, that years later, her condition would be diagnosed by a therapist as acute obsessive-compulsive disorder. By that time she would have developed a deep and urgent need for the taste of fresh semen on her tongue, the feel of it spurting hot and salty against the back of her throat. Would have come to feel, with the completion of each emission, as if she'd just had a tremendous thirst quenched.

The therapy itself would turn out to be something of a disaster. During one particularly graphic session, the doctor himself, against all better judgement, would become so aroused that he allowed Betty to give him a first-hand demonstration.

The idea of a woman like Betty was, after all, a highly pornographic one, even to a trained clinician – someone used to forsaking his own physiological urges for the sake of professionalism and proper decorum. Betty was the ultimate male fantasy, after all. What young man hadn't read about her in magazines like Playboy, where she'd been conjured into existence by staff writers who concocted her to titillate all their horny and gullible fantasies. But even those magazine writers, churning out endless sexual scenarios for edition after edition on those glossy pages – not even the best of them had ever come up with someone like Betty Unger. Who would have believed it? She was living proof that truth was stranger than fiction. The young doctor's indiscretion would eventually be discovered, but he would get off with little more than a token suspension, on the grounds that the act he had committed with his female patient did not actually constitute sex.

It was now Steven who was in over his head. Things were moving too fast. He couldn't think. Thankfully, Betty's head came up for a moment and when he looked down to see what was about to happen next, realized that by sheer coincidence, the shaft of his penis – bigger and harder than it had ever been – perfectly eclipsed the Minuteman Missile, upright now, only a few hundred yards away. When Betty took him into her mouth again, she appeared to be taking in the enormous rocket as well. It was enough of a distraction to keep him from giving Betty what she wanted. She was working very hard to bring him to a climax and, suddenly, all he could think about was the rocket, and all the possibilities of its destructive capability. If Betty was obsessed with ejaculation, he was obsessed with detonation. Too many aspects of the whole idea that he couldn't get away from. Too many avenues of imagination. Scenarios to work through. Deep and troubling, dark and disturbing.

The young poet found himself wondering just how close they were to ground zero. He'd recently discovered that the bomb did not go off on impact, but rather several thousand feet in the air. That way, he'd read, it could do much more damage. Kill many more people. It was that kind of logic that was making it difficult for him to maintain his erection, in spite of the fact that Betty was toiling over it with such fervour.

He found himself contemplating politics, as well. Wondered what the president of the United States would think about all this. John F. Kennedy, who seemed like such a nice man to him. Steven had seen him more than once on Martha's television set. Wondered how much of what was really important about this crisis had gotten through to the president. How much of what really mattered about the bomb. He guessed there probably wasn't a single poet among the entire group of people advising him.

The president could probably find out anything and everything he wanted to know about the subject. That certainly was not the case for the young poet. So many avenues of actual investigation were sealed off from him by distance and time and privilege. What little he'd been able to get his hands on had come almost entirely from the books his Aunt Martha supplied him with, but it was never enough.

It all came down to that moment of detonation. That, it seemed to him, was where the poetry would be. With the release of that much energy, what would be released in his imagination, he wondered? He had estimated that the ensuing fireball would be approximately twelve miles across, big enough to completely engulf Neustadt and all the other villages in the valley, so that in one way or another they would all be incinerated, evaporated, vaporized, cremated alive. But he'd also calculated that with enough forewarning, there might be time for him to make his way up to the crest of the Pembina Hills. From that vantage point, he thought, it might be possible to capture the poetry of the moment. It would be important to do that. It would be the most important thing.

It was for just such a purpose that he carried the cigarette case with him wherever he went. He felt for it in his pocket now. It was made of burnished steel, and inside it were several small pieces of white paper and a small pencil. If he did manage to make it to the top of the hill, there might be time to scribble a few quick lines and seal them inside the case before the furious fireball reached him. When they discovered his charred remains lying on the crest of the hill, as someone surely would – someone who came to the edge of the valley hours or days or months later to look down over the unspeakable destruction that lay below – they would find the cigarette case gleaming in the sun, and open it. And there, barely legible, would be a few precious lines of poetry, written in the last few frantic moments of his life. The imagery would be so compelling, the metaphors so stunning, the words so terrifyingly beautiful that all who read them would weep. He wanted that. That was important. That it should make them weep.

"It's really quite beautiful," said Betty. She was taking another break. It was her first time and she had no idea how long it took to get the job done. She would soon discover that other boys didn't take nearly as much effort to bring to the all-important conclusion.

"The tip," she said. "I like the tip especially." The young poet looked down and saw that she was still holding his erection strategically in place over the shaft of the rocket. "It seems a shame to hide something so shiny and beautiful." If she was deliberately playing a game of words to tease and excite him, he didn't think it was very clever. A cheap play on words. The crude simplicity of her metaphor disappointed him. Far too obvious, he thought. He was, on the whole, unimpressed by her lack of wit. The whole thing was having a less-than-positive effect on his state of arousal.

"It looks ready," she said.

"Ready?"

"To shoot. It looks ready to shoot." And she put her mouth over it again.

He looked up into the green canopy of cottonwood forming such an inviting bower over his head, at the sky behind it, clear and perfectly blue except for criss-crossing vapour trails from the warplanes. He looked out across the fields at the yellow and green crops that surrounded them, at the village only a few hundred yards to the east. He turned the other way and followed the fields up into the hills, purple and indistinct to the west, where the ominous black cloud was just about to swoop over the crest, slip silently down into the valley, the valley that had suddenly become precious beyond words.

"Now what do you suppose he's going to do with that?" One of the Zacharias sisters had just noticed the preacher, who lived directly across from them, slipping out the door of his summer kitchen with a rifle in his hands.

"Shoot something, what else?"

"But on a Sunday?"

"A Sunday is as good a day as any."

The other two were silent for a moment, each considering the veracity of this last statement. Neither of them could think of anything in the Scriptures that specifically forbade such activity on the Sabbath. They decided that it couldn't really be considered work in the fullest sense of the word, but more like a chore that needed doing. Like bowels that needed moving, for example. A necessary evil and nothing more. The preacher, they trusted, had good reason to be armed, and was not out with a gun for frivolous reasons. They watched him leave the yard and turn south, heading in the direction of Abe Wiebe's place.

They saw that he was clearly in an agitated state, and correctly guessed that it had something to do with what had hap-

pened in church earlier. The presence of people like Martha
Wiebe and the Martens brothers, and especially Abe Wiebe in
the congregation must have been upsetting for him. All of
them sitting in a small cloister, like some kind of outlaw gang,
listening to him deliver the most important sermon of his
career – its subject matter nothing less than the future of the
valley itself. At first the sisters had thought they might have
come to disrupt the proceedings, but they'd showed no out-
ward signs of brashness. They hadn't been loud or unruly. Still,
their presence had a disturbing effect on everyone.

They knew that the preacher, not to mention the elders,
had had some personal dealings with each and every one of
them. With Martha, there'd been the matter of her blatant disregard for the sensibilities of others, the latest example being
the television antenna on her roof. As far as the elders were
concerned, she might as well have strapped a golden calf to the
top of her house. As for the Martens brothers, their sin was
their insistence on leading a normal life, exposing their ugliness, unfortunate as it was, to women and children in the village, when it would have been so much better, they'd been
advised, to make themselves as scarce as possible – to try not
to let themselves be seen so much, by so many, so often. And
certainly not to go out cavorting with the likes of Abe Wiebe.

Even the young poet, who now roamed the valley with all
manner of sinful books in hand, filling his mind with garbage
and iniquity, had first come into their sphere of scorn a few
years ago when he insisted on singing black gospel songs in
Sunday school. When the preacher himself had punished the
boy for it with a good sound strapping, Abe Wiebe had come
barging right into the church and physically threatened him.
Told him calmly, but with great force, that if he ever laid so
much as a finger on the boy again he, Abe Wiebe, would per-
sonally come and thrash the preacher within an inch of his
life. The preacher, terrified, had tried to bluff his way out with

threats of his own, but it was common knowledge that he had been badly shaken by the incident.

For the preacher, the whole day had been strange from the beginning. It seemed that every item in his universe had shifted six inches to the right, or left, or up or down, he wasn't sure which. It didn't matter. What mattered was that nothing seemed to be in the place it was before. The way a thing sounded. The way a thing looked. The way a person acted. Even if that person was you. Even now as he saw the three sisters staring out at him, their cups perched neatly above their saucers, he thought of them differently. As more than merely intimidating or bothersome. As witchlike. Evil.

But they were right about one thing. The unexpected presence of so many outsiders in church that morning had thrown him off enough to ruin his sermon. He hadn't been able to deliver it with the kind of intensity and conviction it needed. Somehow, with Abe Wiebe and the others sitting there, it had come off as ineffectual. It was Abe Wiebe who was really the cause of all this troublesome erosion of authority. It could all be traced back to him. His open defiance. And there he was again this morning – daring the elders to do something. Say something.

And then, later, things had taken an even more troublesome turn. There'd been the usual gathering of people outside the church after the service, Abe Wiebe standing with a group of men, making small talk and laughing, far too lustily, as usual. And, quite suddenly, it had struck the preacher that perhaps they were laughing at him. Then he felt sure if it. Abe Wiebe was turning them all against him. That was the whole problem with him. He was so damn well-liked.

But it hadn't ended there. The worst thing of all was when he looked over at his wife, Anna, standing with a group of women nearby, the same as she would after any service, except that today there was an added animation in her conversation as

well. Instead of acting with the usual quota of reserve, she was
making gestures and remarks in a girlish way that was completely out of character for her. Calling attention to herself. And
then she did the most unconscionable thing. Abe Wiebe was
taking off his jacket – the sun shining hotter – rolling up the
sleeves of his white shirt, turning up his muscular forearms to
undo the buttons, folding the fabric back in three or four layers, his black suspenders showing now, talking the whole time,
laughing, arching his back a little when he did, slinging the
jacket over his shoulder and running his fingers through his
wavy hair. And there was Anna – the preacher's good and
wholesome wife – looking up at Abe with her mouth slightly
open, hips swaying a little from side to side, one hand on her
cheek, as if she were in a dream. It couldn't have been more
obvious if she'd laid down right then and there and spread her
legs wide. She was lusting after Abe Wiebe.

The preacher saw Abe look over at her and smile. Saw Anna
blush, straighten down the front of her dress, then go back to
talking with the other women. One of them said something
and Anna giggled – actually giggled – like a schoolgirl. And all
in front of him, in front of everybody. The preacher said nothing. Did nothing. But now he had come from their Sunday
afternoon conjugal rites, realizing that he had created a monster. Abe Wiebe had brought out the devil in his wife. In both
of them. How else could he explain how it was that he found
himself penetrating her with such evil intensity. Such unbridled lust. Such vigour. He hadn't been able to help himself.
Had never wanted her so much in all his life. The whole thing
had been reckless. His climax so hard and long and savage,
and with every thrust he'd imagined Abe Wiebe watching –
had punctuated each burst with a silent taunt in his direction.
"HOW do you like THAT, Mr. Abe WIEBE."

And to his amazement, just as he spit the last of his sperm
into his wife, he'd become aware of the fact that she was

144

writhing underneath him. And that was when he heard it – something he'd never heard before – a moan so long and deep and beautiful. A moan of pure pleasure. He knew little about such things, but it was clear to him that her womanhood had gone to a place it had never reached before.

Lying quietly on the bed beside her, the two of them still breathing heavily, the preacher had come face to face with the nasty possibility that all of this was Abe Wiebe's fault. That if the two of them had come to such a lovely conclusion, it had happened for all the wrong reasons. That Abe Wiebe had found his way into their most private moment, had infiltrated, contaminated, their most intimate sanctuary.

It was too much for his already fragile psyche. The neuroses he had been nurturing and cultivating all of his adult life spilled over into psychosis. The rational compartments of his mind shut down. All of his fears and resentments multiplied themselves upon each other until they congealed into a mass of schizophrenic paranoia. The only remedy for all of this chaos and cognitive dysfunction would be an episode of supremely irrational behaviour. An act of sudden and cataclysmic entropy.

And so while his wife slept – naked, happy – the preacher crept from the bed and tiptoed out of the room. He went straight for the closet at the back of the summer kitchen and reached for the rifle he kept up on the top shelf. He took down a box of shells next to it and loaded one into the barrel.

It was not unusual, even for a man of the cloth, to have a gun in the house. The inhabitants of the valley, religion and pacifism notwithstanding, were, in fact, a heavily armed bunch. There was always something that needed shooting: foxes in the chicken coop, raccoons in the garbage, skunks under the porch, rats under the granary, cats and kittens that had become redundant. Blind or old or rabid dogs, owls in the barn, rooks in the hayloft, snakes under the summer kitchen, hawks in the pasture, sick cows, crazed pigs, club-footed calves, broken-backed horses. The list went on and on – always something in need of extermination.

Virtually every household in the valley had an arsenal of rifles and shotguns for such eventualities. The preacher's house was no exception. In his case it was a high-powered .303 single shot long-barrel rifle which had belonged to his father. It was as good for getting rid of unwanted animals as any firearm in the valley.

By the time he got out to the street, the preacher had rationalized his action into a variation on the necessary extermination of vermin. He'd decided that Abe Wiebe was just that. Unwanted vermin. He would simply take it upon himself to rid the valley of it. He could dispatch his duties in this regard as well as any man. The rifle in his hand could obliterate the greatest and the least among them with equal effectiveness.

M ARTHA WAS BY HERSELF in her studio, sitting on a wooden chair, looking at a collection of photographs. Her father was back in his own room, having the second nap of the afternoon. She had put him through a lot today. She felt a little guilty about that now. She knew that one day soon he would go down for a nap and not wake up, and she didn't want it to be because of something she'd done. Insisted on. She didn't like to think he might die because she'd worn him out, even if there was a kind of ironic justice in that idea. She wondered if it was just her father who was really keeping her in the village. What if he did die? And there was no one left to take care of? Would she leave then?

She spent a lot of time in this room. Alone with her photographs. Thousands of them. So many pictures she'd taken over the years, She didn't think she'd ever be able to look at them all – boxes and boxes of them scattered all around the room. Up on shelves, on tables. Pinned onto bulletin boards, spread over every available piece of furniture, scattered across the floor, some hanging from clothespins on lines strung across the room. The closet was her darkroom. She had everything she needed. She could take picture after picture and develop them all herself there, decide whether they were successful or not. Whether or not anyone else should see them. She did sometimes share her photographs. Other times she kept the results all to herself. She was the final judge in all such matters.

And every one of them had to be black and white. Nothing else would do. The spectrum of truth, for Martha, had always rested in the endless possibilities that arose between only those two shades. It seemed to her that the human condition existed there, between those two extremes. That it was composed of infinite shades of grey. It was precisely that which, over the years, had become the subject of Martha's photographs. That, which she desired to capture. Its variety. Its scope. She herself had grown up looking at faded black and white photographs of mothers and fathers, aunts and uncles, grandfathers and grandmothers – mostly in stifling clothes, faces frozen into rigid obscurity. The people in those pictures had always seemed interchangeable to her. One exhausted Mennonite woman sitting in a wooden chair next to her expressionless husband looked pretty much like another. Face devoid of any participation in the moment. Only the shallowest sense of her presence in the photograph. As if the muscle and bone of her had been removed, from the inside. So that there was only the surface. The skin. Such a bleak, hollow image of the human condition. Such an astonishing lack of imagination on the part of the photographer. So little to take away from a photograph like that. Martha had vowed that she could do better. Much better. That her compositions would never be such a blasphemy against aesthetics. Against art. Against truth.

The first thing, she had learned, was to put as little distance as possible between yourself and your subject. To get in close enough to allow for the moment that would reveal the part of a person you wanted to capture. The part that would give life to the picture. Make it natural. Alive. A photograph needed to be taken that way, she was convinced, if it hoped to capture the idea of who that person really was. How they really were. People like Katie Klassen, and Abe Wiebe, and the young poet. She was looking just now at a series of photographs of the young poet sitting in her living room. She thought it might be some of her best work yet. He'd been looking through some books she'd brought him that evening, sitting in the burgundy armchair her father had always used before he stopped coming into the living room. Before the television.

There was one shot in particular she liked, where the poet was looking up at her, just beginning to say something. In his hand he held yet another volume on the nuts and bolts of nuclear warfare. She thought the photograph captured perfectly the depth of his curiosity. His need to know. But more important, there was something else in the grainy black and white image of his features. Something much more revealing. The subtle, more disturbing aspect of his research. The subtext of it was there in the shape of his mouth as he formed the words of his question. In the lines that gathered around his eyes and along his forehead. It was his fear.

And something of hers was there as well. An idea. A photograph was, after all, about two people. Not only the subject, but also the person behind the camera. A photograph could say as much about one as the other. And in this photograph, it seemed to Martha she had captured her ideas about the importance of the young poet to the valley. What better thing, she wanted the picture to say, for a young man of the village to have than the soul of a poet? What better thing for the valley to nurture? If a place like this could pull off something like that, she wanted it to say, there might yet be hope for the human race.

It was very important for him to stay, at least a little longer. For him to leave the valley now, divorce himself from it entirely, would result in writing that was merely full of anger, or spite, or worse – if he got himself an education – self-supe-riority. The kind of self-indulgent poetry that might make a few academics sit up and take notice, but that would fail to produce imagery and ideas bigger than that. If it took a whole village to raise a child, Martha thought, then surely it would take the entire valley to raise this poet. To make it possible for him to become a true citizen of the world.

And that was where she came in. She would help him stay long enough to get the job done. It was a heavy responsibility. To see him become an individual, with a mind of his own, with courage, conviction, and yet to have been nurtured by the place. Only in that way, she was convinced, could he hope to develop the insight that must come if he was going to write the things that needed writing. If he was going to speak, not only to the people, or from the people, but for the people.

Whenever she herself thought of leaving, she took out a few photographs like these and looked into them and decided that it was better to stay. That it was something she needed to do. Even if it wasn't easy for her to live in the valley. The under-pinnings of this need manifested themselves in the tacit understanding that she was a keeper of sorts. That she was needed, if not so much by her ageing father, then by those few who, like her, did not fit in.

In some ways it wasn't so different from being a missionary – work that was fast becoming popular among both urban and rural Mennonites. Many of them were taking turns running off to one underdeveloped country or another for a year or two of self-deprivation before returning to their bungalows and housebarns and church prayer meetings. The difference, Martha decided, was that she would not fly off to a poverty-stricken and disease-infested African country to save souls. There was enough work to be done right here in the valley. She would minister to others like herself. Those who needed to be shown the way – not to a Christian God – but to another, less institutional salvation. Those who needed to learn that in order to become that which they longed for, in or out of the valley, they would have to rely on their own inner way, and truth, and light. And that light was the very thing she wanted most to capture in the black and white images of her photographs.

The valley had always had a certain quota of misfits. The history of these people went all the way back to Russia, and a few countries before that. Almost every family had a story of someone in their past who had struck out as an individual – who had bucked the system for one reason or another – sometimes by choice, sometimes by chance. She wasn't sure just how the process worked, but somehow, through all the pressures to conform, individuals sprouted up who refused to do precisely that. People who refused, for one reason or another, to go along with the crowd.

It was precisely these people that Martha wanted celebrate. In a minute she was going to get her equipment ready and take it downstairs to the patio. The Martens brothers were coming later to have their pictures taken there. It wasn't the kind of thing she usually did – take pictures of people that were posed. But she was going to make an exception today. She was going to sit them down in their Sunday clothes on the wrought iron chairs out back and take their portraits. Just because they'd asked her to.

She felt she owed them that much for allowing her the other photographs. The ones she'd already taken of them in the workshop. When she'd first asked if it would be all right to do that, bring her camera into the same building that had nearly consumed them, they'd been reluctant.

"It's kind of dark in there for taking pictures," Cornie had said.

"Lots of junk to trip over," Jake had added.

"Not much room for visitors."

"We have to make a lot of noise."

Martha had sensed in their tone that what she was proposing constituted a kind of invasion for them. That this was the one place where they could truly be themselves. Where they were free from all the chattel of their visual debauchery. The more Martha heard, the more she wanted to capture them there, in the middle of such a safe haven, surrounded by it. And so she persisted. She had a sense that if she could just get in there with them, they would see that it was all right. That she meant no harm.

The fire had failed to destroy the Martens brothers completely. They had been saved by a miracle – some would have said a cruel miracle – and so had the shop. The fire had burned a hole through the roof and fizzled without so much as a bucket of water to douse the flames. No one could explain it. The damage was repaired and after the boys healed they returned to work there as if nothing had happened.

On the day they finally allowed Martha to step over the threshold, it was into another world entirely. From sunshine and heat and fresh air into darkness and dampness and the rank odour of gasoline and grease, concrete and rubber, smoke and ash. Everywhere there was the clutter of dismantled machinery and pieces of metal, all shapes and sizes and completely unidentifiable, scattered across the floor. Half-filled containers of oil and gas and piles of greasy rags. Wooden benches piled deep with tools and car parts, bins along the wall filled with nuts and bolts and brackets, the floor a maze of blowtorches and arc welders, crates and boxes, winches and anvils and planks. Just as they had insisted, there did not appear to be a square inch of room to move.

"It's a bit messy," Jake admitted, "but we like it this way."

"We know where everything is," said Cornie.

Martha wedged herself in between a stack of tires and a bank of old batteries and took a few shallow breaths. She promptly got out her equipment, then insisted they get to work as they normally would and forget about her as much as possible.

They were taking the engine out of a pickup truck that morning, getting ready to put it up on the heavy bench and rebuild it. It was no secret that they were the best mechanics in the valley. They seemed to be able to fix anything. Rebuild any piece of machinery. Martha studied them for awhile, her eye away from the camera, let them go about their work.

She found herself looking at their hands. She would certainly have to get some shots of them as well. You could learn a lot about a man just by looking there. But they were not the kind of thing you could photograph casually. You had to get good and close and intimate with them to do a really interesting pair of hands justice. Most men were happy to oblige, although there were exceptions. The preacher, when she'd asked him, had looked at her as if she wanted to photograph his genitals.

"Why do you want to take a picture of something like that?" He'd asked the question as if her request were some kind of perversion or fetish. As if the very notion were unhealthy.

"Why not?" Martha had answered. "They're only hands."

"Exactly. And so why are you so interested in them?"

Women, too, were often reluctant to have their hands photographed, but for different reasons. Sometimes it was just vanity or insecurity. But others displayed genuine surprise that there should be the slightest novelty in something they had always taken for granted. Why, they would often ask earnestly, would anyone be interested in what their hands looked like?

In the case of Cornie and Jake, Martha's interest lay in the fact that their hands were almost entirely covered in scar tissue, and so did not behave the way other hands did. The hands of most men in the village – her brothers, for example – had never been entirely free of grime, not because they didn't wash, but because the dirt and grease from their daily labours had worked its way into the cracks and folds of their skin so deeply no amount of scrubbing or brushing could remove it. To get rid of it would have required getting rid of the skin itself. And always there were the scraped knuckles, the bruises, cuts in various stages of healing.

That was not the case with the hands of the Martens brothers. For one thing, they had no fingernails, which had refused to grow back after the fire. And where the skin had come off in patches, it had been replaced by scar tissue, glossy smooth, too slippery for dirt and grease to cling to, the tissue so tough, cuts and bruises could not penetrate. Mostly, the skin on the hands of the Martens brothers resembled shiny patches of translucent reptilian armour.

But she was there to take pictures of their faces, and so she began. Most of them in quick bunches, while they were lifting out the engine, the two of them standing on opposite sides of the hood, each with one shiny hand on the engine, the other on the chain of the block and tackle they were using to lift it. Each wore the same dark overalls, buttoned halfway up the front, collar flipped up at the back of the neck.

And after she had developed, and carefully looked through them, she found it. The thing she had been trying to capture, in the very last picture she'd taken. Both of them were looking directly into the camera, not because she had asked them to, not because they were posing, but just because of the moment.

In this case, her nephew Abe had just stepped over the threshold to greet them.

When she showed them the photographs a few days later, they spent a lot of time looking at them. Stared, first one, then the other, into them, as if they were seeing themselves for the first time. Stared at something they hadn't seen before, but had always suspected was there. Martha understood that she had succeeded. That if, in other pictures, they had appeared to themselves as the leering demons that frightened children into hiding their faces in their mother's skirts, made adults stare in frozen disbelief or turn away in disgust – it had been the fault of the photographer. A trick of the camera. In these photographs, something else showed through. Something underneath that had always been there. The thing she'd wanted to show them in the first place. There was a lot Martha wanted to say about that picture, but no way to say it. It was always like that. In the most important moments. When it wasn't the words, but the silence that mattered. But it had something to do with their natural playfulness. Their remarkable courage.

"Can we keep this?" said Cornie. He held the photograph where they were looking up at Abe Wiebe coming into the shop.

"Sure. I'll make one for each of you."

"Make one?"

"Yes. I'll make you each a copy."

"But we don't want a copy."

"You don't?"

"We want this one."

"You don't understand. It'll be exactly like this one."

"But not this one?"

"No, but the same picture."

"We just want this picture."

"But I can make copies. I have the negatives."

"Negatives?"

"I can use the negatives to make more prints."

"But couldn't we just keep this one."

"Yes, of course, but...look. Why does this have to be so difficult?"

The two of them looked at her.

"I'm sorry," she said. "It's just that you don't understand."

"Oh. But we do," said Cornie, and looked over at his brother. "Don't we?"

"Yes," said Jake. "Yes, we do."

"All right. Keep that picture. And tomorrow I'll bring you another one just like it."

"Exactly?"

"Exactly. That way you'll each have one."

"That's a nice thing."

"A nice thing for you to do."

"It's nothing."

"Can you take more?"

"Now?"

"No. Sometime when we're cleaned up."

"When we're outside."

"When we're wearing our good clothes."

"I suppose I can. If you like. But it might not be the same."

"Sunday?"

"Sunday afternoon?"

"We'll come over after fastba."

"Fine."

Martha thought she had a pretty good idea what it was they'd seen in that photograph. The thing she'd been trying to capture all along. It was really a very simple truth. Something they had always carried around inside them, but revealed only in brief, unguarded intervals like the one in that photograph. A short, bright moment of dignity.

She looked again at the picture of the young poet with the book in his hands, staring so intently – at what? If a photograph could capture a moment of truth, the same was true, even more so, of a poem. And it was quite possible that the young poet would write such poems. Such a thing was not only possible, it seemed to Martha, but necessary. And so it was necessary to help him stay long enough to figure out that he could do that. He deserved that. The valley deserved that. Deserved to have itself held up to poetic scrutiny. In such poems – just as in her pictures – would be reflected both the soul of the creator and the place that created him. Unless. Unless it was all cut short by the blasphemy of that thing out there. That thing and a hundred others like it.

KATIE WAS WALKING DOWN THE STREET in her brilliant yellow dress. Somewhere, in one of the housebarns – she couldn't tell which one – a telephone was ringing next to an open window. She could hear it plainly. One long, two short. The phones here were still on the party line. That much hadn't changed. Everybody would know whose house was being called. People could choose to pick up the phone and listen in on the conversation if they felt like it. How many calls, Katie wondered, had the Zacharias sisters intercepted over the years? How many supposedly private exchanges were stored in the archives of their collective memory?

The phone was still ringing, but no one was answering. Katie imagined the telephone back in her apartment, thousands of miles away, doing just that. Ringing and ringing and no one there to answer. Some of the calls might be important. Agents. Producers. If they hadn't been able get her on the line, one or two might even have made the drive out to her place in their late-model convertibles, come up the walk in their Italian suits and Guccis, and knocked urgently on her door. No matter. There'd be no one to answer. By now somebody had probably gotten worried enough to call the police, who would have forced their way into the apartment, searched for clues as to her whereabouts. Perhaps rumours had already started to circulate – just as they had about Marilyn. If it could happen to her, would be the buzz, then it could happen to anybody.

Perhaps the police had come looking for Katie anyway. Even before someone reported her missing. She had, after all, been one of the last people to see Marilyn alive. Katie remembered everything about that morning, the two of them sitting next to each other, waiting for the call from the director. Katie knew exactly who she was sitting next to. Found herself surprisingly calm. Much more relaxed than Marilyn herself, who seemed to be in a state of high agitation. Not that Katie wasn't in awe of Marilyn, or intimidated by her. She was. But she'd learned something about her place in the business that helped her stay focused and at ease. Something she had refused to believe at first, but then come to accept. That she, Katie Klassen, was as smart and beautiful and talented as any woman in the business. It wasn't vanity. It was just simple fact. As for the men she had to deal with, they were another matter entirely. She didn't so much have to compete with them as get them out of her way. Katie had learned how to do both in a quiet and unassuming way.

Almost on a daily basis, handsome young men propositioned her in one way or another. Men with power. Money. Fame. Prestige. When she turned them down, it was often to their astonished disbelief. They were not used to such treatment from someone who was obviously new in town and trying to get established. At first the men she'd met were mostly small-time promoters and talent scouts and casting agents, but as she'd made her way up in the business they became slick-haired studio executives, casting directors, and cigar-smoking moguls who invariably threatened, after being spurned, that they would do everything in their power to make sure she never got anywhere in this town. A lot of the time it was like something right out of a movie. Life imitating art.

Not that Katie Klassen was entirely chaste during her stay in Hollywood. If she had, over the years, allowed some few select men into her bed, it was largely out of biological necessity. In spite of the fact that they were often rich and handsome and sensually exciting, any semblance of real lovemaking was too often informed by their hidden agendas of sexual conquest, of power and reputation.

But still, there was the undeniable need to feel the climax of a man inside her from time to time, a craving that simply could not be completely ignored, that grew stronger and stronger until it couldn't be pushed aside any longer. Katie had to be careful when this happened. Had to take care not to wait too long, to let the urge overpower her better judgement. After a while she knew when it was time. She only needed to send out a few signals and there were a dozen men ready to take up the challenge. They seemed to sense when such a rare moment was at hand. Those chosen were baffled and could not believe their good fortune, aware of just how unlikely their chances were in that regard. Katie always made sure it was someone who could do her absolutely no good in the movie business. Someone to whom she would owe nothing. Who could never come back to her and say that she was beholden to him.

If someone, perhaps a social scientist working toward a Ph.D, had undertaken a study of these individuals, collated and analyzed their more salient physical characteristics, for example, she would have noted some definite trends in that regard, among them the fact that all of these lucky individuals had rugged but gentle features, a full head of thick hair, and a pair of big strong hands. The hands were the most important thing for Katie. Without them there wasn't even any point in beginning. It was going to end in tears. At the very least, she needed to feel herself being held – really held – while she was being filled up, while her urgent need was being satisfied. If the social scientist had chosen to implement a field study as part of her investigations, she would have discovered another prerequisite – this one behavioural. It was absolutely necessary that during the course of the coupling, the individual in question not say a word. Utterances of even the shortest duration had the effect of completely ruining Katie's fantasy, the one the social scientist had no awareness of, the one she allowed herself to fall into every time. Where she could close her eyes and let what was happening become the sensation of another man inside her, the rush of that man's juices, the tremble of his loins against hers.

As for the few lucky men who found themselves on top of her in such times, they understood, instinctively, that they were not truly seeding her, feeding her, not putting into her what she really needed. That they weren't really penetrating her at all, but only the idea of her.

Katie and Marilyn were sitting in the studio backlot, on a set that had been made up to look like the front of a cheap diner in the middle of the desert. The set decorator had even sent a truck out to bring back a couple of huge Saguaro cactuses and had them dug into the packed dirt of the lot to add authenticity. The place was meant to look desolate. Forsaken. The script called for Katie to come running out of the diner, across the dusty parking lot, with a pair of pink high-heeled shoes in her hand. Marilyn would already be out there, walking toward a dirty waiting bus.

"You left these behind," Katie would shout. Marilyn would stop. Turn.

The camera angle would be from behind Katie's left shoulder, with her holding up the shoes, Marilyn facing her.

"Oh, thanks, Honey. That's sweet of you," Marilyn would say. "But you can keep them."

"What?"

"They're yours. Take 'em."

"But – you don't want them?"

"I won't be needing them."

"You won't?"

"Not where I'm going." And Marilyn would turn away from the camera. Walk slowly, deliberately, toward the waiting bus.

It was going to be the final scene in the movie – and if things went according to plan they could finish up the shoot that morning. It was another bit part for Katie, but not the kind she'd been hoping for. She'd thought there might be a chance at a close-up in this one. A head-and-shoulders shot. Katie had a pretty good idea that it might be all she needed. That if her face didn't end up on the cutting-room floor, the producers would sit up in their screening chairs and ask, "Who's that? Get her name." She was going to look particularly good today, too, because they were filming in natural light – the kind that showed off her magnificent bone structure, her remarkable complexion. But the scene was going to be all about Marilyn. And why not? She was the star. Katie's time would come.

Katie could tell that Marilyn was having trouble with her lines, repeating them to herself over and over again in a frustrated, impatient way. Nothing appeared to be sinking in. She seemed hopelessly preoccupied with something that morning, but Katie had no way of knowing whether that was normal, or whether there was something else going on. She thought of offering to help, since she had quickly and easily committed the entire scene to memory – knew all the lines for all the parts – but she didn't want to seem pushy.

Katie had been warned about Marilyn. That she had a temper. That she was unpredictable. She might forget her lines, they said, or not bother to memorize them at all. She might insist on very short takes – perhaps only a line or two at a time. Drive everyone around her nuts. But Katie wasn't much for rumours. She preferred to find things out for herself. She'd learned early not to put too much stock in what people in the business said about each other. Everyone in this town, she understood, had a hidden agenda.

"I've got a splitting headache," Marilyn said. Not to Katie. Not to anyone. Said it with an air of worry, as if it were a much more serious thing she was talking about. She picked up her purse and took out three bottles of pills, set them on the ugly green table next to her. She opened them each in turn and shook out a few pills until she had a small heap in her palm, threw them into her mouth in one motion, picked up a glass of water from the table and washed them all down at once.

"This shouldn't take long," said Katie. "They're talking about doing a quick shoot." She was trying to make conversation, something she didn't normally do. But she sensed that Marilyn needed it. Needed to talk.

"It's always a quick shoot," said Marilyn, without looking up. She lit a long filtered cigarette and sucked hard on it. "Everybody in this business is always in such a goddamn hurry," she said, and blue smoke poured through her nostrils. "Why should that rodent be any different."

Katie knew she meant the director. Looked over at him and realized that with his quick, jerky movements, his unkempt facial hair and round spectacles, it was an apt, if flippant, description. He really did resemble a mouse scurrying about.

"He's such a nervous little prick. He makes *me* nervous just watching him. I don't know why I agreed to this part."

"Oh, well, it's almost over."

"He still thinks he's got it over me, just because I let him fuck me once."

Katie had heard that kind of thing plenty of times before, but it still startled her each time one of them said it.

"That must have been years ago. When you were just starting out."

"He knows better than to try that shit with me now. What did he get out of you? Not more than a blow job, I hope."

When Katie didn't answer Marilyn looked up at her for the first time. Let the script fall into her lap. She stared into Katie's face. Into her eyes. Deeply, searchingly – her expression a mixture of gloom and surprise. "Who are you?" she said, as if she were asking the question from a long way off, from a long way inside herself.

"I'm the waitress." Katie picked up a pair of pink shoes from the prop table next to her. The ones she was going to hold up in the scene.

"No. Your name. What's your name?" said Marilyn. She was still staring. Leaning.

"My name is Katie. Katie Klassen."

"Where did you come from, Katie Klassen?" The way she asked made it impossible for Katie to answer. Then Marilyn seemed to get hold of herself. "I'm sorry," she said. "I didn't mean to stare like that. It's just that you look so...so...fresh."

"Excuse me." A man in a dark suit and sunglasses had come up beside them.

"Yea, yea what is it?" said Marilyn. "I said I'm working on it. Just give me another minute."

The man in the suit touched Marilyn's arm and indicated a limousine parked in behind them. Marilyn turned to see who it was. Shiny black limousines were a dime a dozen in Hollywood, but this one had something different about it. It seemed heavier to Katie. Thicker. Something about the windows. The doors. Completely impenetrable. The back window slipped down halfway and a man in sunglasses peered over the darkened glass. Katie thought he looked familiar. Thought she'd seen him someplace before.

"The gentleman would like a word with you."

"Gentleman," said Marilyn. She'd turned to look back down at her script. "That's no gentleman."

"Miss Monroe," said the man.

She turned to Katie. "There aren't any gentlemen in this town. You probably know that by now."

"Miss Monroe."

"Listen. Would you take a hike? Can't you see I'm working? Tell him I'm busy. And get out of my light." She pretended to go back to reading her script, but Katie could see she was not really taking anything in, that she was excited and troubled at the same time, and working very hard to seem uninterested.

"The gentleman says it's urgent," said the man in the suit and sunglasses. Said it in a low but forceful voice.

"Sure, sure. It's always urgent." She turned back to Katie. Looked at her again. Intensely. For too long. "This place hasn't got to you yet, has it?" She leaned in a little closer. "Listen. There's something you might as well know right off the top. They're going to try and take it away from you."

"Take what?" said Katie. She was feigning ignorance because she wanted to let Marilyn do this. It seemed important, somehow.

"People like him." Marilyn nodded her head in the direction of the limousine.

The man in the suit took Marilyn's arm, firmly. American men were always doing that. Taking women by the arm, jerking them around in one direction or another. Handling them like merchandise. Katie found it annoying. Condescending. The man was pulling at Marilyn now, trying to get her to stand up.

"Jesus," said Marilyn. "Would you get your hairy paws off me, you big gorilla."

"The gentleman insists on seeing you – now."

The man pulled harder at her arm. Stood her up.

"Goddammit, I'm gonna slug you, you big jackass."

"What's this all about?" said Katie.

"This?" said Marilyn. She leaned in close to her. "This is

what I was talking about. This is about what they want from you. It's about the way they treat you. It's about the deal you make. So you can survive in this place. But the funny part is, most of the time, you don't even know you're making it. You don't even know it's happening. Then, by the time you figure it out, it's too late."

The man took her arm again to pull her toward the waiting car. Marilyn wrenched her arm out of his grip and rubbed it. "It's about what you throw away and what you keep." She walked toward the car slowly, and with great dignity. When she got there the car window rolled down further. Katie could hear someone talking, but not loud enough for her to make out the words. Marilyn stood in front of the rolled-down window, arms folded. A man, his hair shiny and perfectly groomed, leaned out into the light. Katie recognized him immediately. She was a little disappointed. His large head seemed out of porportion to his surprisingly narrow shoulders. The face was more boyish than handsome. Almost delicate. There was nothing the least bit rugged about him but even from a distance, Katie sensed a kind of guarded self-assurance, a presence. Or was it a menace? He took off his sunglasses and Katie saw the power in his eyes. Confidence. That was the most dangerous thing in a man. She'd seen men with eyes like that before. Eyes that would try to make you do things, things you knew you probably shouldn't, but would.

Katie thought about Abe Wiebe's eyes, and how, whenever they looked into hers, they weakened her in such a surprising, disturbing way. Immediately. As if she had no will of her own. No man had ever stirred in her such a sense of complete vulnerability. Katie thought that Marilyn might be feeling the same thing, standing so close to this man. He put a hand out to reach for her. A surprisingly small and delicate hand. Katie thought of Abe's hands, large and muscular. How when they held you, you knew you were really being held. There was a sense of safety and assurance and submissiveness in that. In being held by a pair of hands like that.

Marilyn pulled away. Took a step back. "Don't touch me," Katie heard her say. "You think you can just prance in here and make everything all right. After last night? You've got another think coming. Who do you think you are, anyway? You think you can just walk all over people and get away with it? Just because...because.... Well, maybe with some people, but not me. Not me, you hear?"

The man in the car said something, but Katie couldn't make it out.

"Go to hell," said Marilyn. She was crying now.

The hand shot out again, surprisingly quick this time, and caught her by the wrist. Pulled her closer. She leaned into the window and Katie couldn't make out what they were saying. Doing. Then the man let her go and Marilyn straightened up, nodded, and walked back over to where Katie was sitting.

"Listen," she said quietly, "I have to go."

"Are you sure?" said Katie. "Are you all right?"

"I'm fine. Really."

"But what about the scene? They'll be ready to shoot in another minute."

"Tell them I'll be back." Marilyn's expression softened. Became more like a plea. "Tell them to wait for me. Will you? Tell them I had to go."

"Do you?" said Katie.

"What?"

"Have to go?"

"I do."

"All right," said Katie. "I'll tell them."

"And remember what I said. Don't let them."

"I promise."

Marilyn walked back toward the limousine. It seemed to Katie that it was a very long walk. That she was traversing a great arid desert of need. The man opened the far door for her and she got in. Just before the car disappeared, slowly, around the corner of the studio, Katie heard the whirr of the electric window and watched as it rolled shut. Something about the way it sounded. Something about the way it looked.

They'd shot the scene with a stand-in who was ready and waiting, as if they had anticipated that very thing. They reversed the shot and positioned the camera over the stand-in's left shoulder. Katie got the close-up she'd been after all that time. The one that practically guaranteed her success. That would turn her into that most implausible of female entities – the movie star. The big door would almost certainly open now. There was, after all, a huge gap waiting to be filled, now that Marilyn was gone, and Katie would be the one to fill it. She sensed it. Others around her did as well. Began to treat her with that disturbing yet intoxicating mixture of disdain and deference, the way they treated anyone on the threshold of attaining the very thing they themselves wanted more than anything in the world.

She was thinking, now, as she walked along the village street, about what Marilyn had said that morning. About the way she'd looked at her. Something about that look. Katie understood that Marilyn had been trying to tell her Hollywood was a prison of sorts. And now here she was, back in this place. A place of relative safety, but surely another kind of prison. She walked down the street. Behind her, the black cloud swept quickly and silently toward the village.

THE SMALL BLACK CLOUD that held so much electrical energy inside it was about to pass over Dickie's head. A ghastly concussion of light and noise would burst out of it, but just at that moment everything was very quiet. It was the time – the smallest bit of time – that always occurs just before a lightning strike. The instant when the cloud and the ground shake hands. Dickie heard it as a small, barely audible tick. In another split second, the entire charge of the lightning bolt would enter his skull dead centre. This particular lightning bolt had only one objective, the same as all other lighting bolts before and after it, which was that it wished to travel as quickly and efficiently as possible into the ground. That was what a lightning bolt did. That was the essence of its being. And because Dickie was wearing no shoes or socks, his stubby little toes curling into the moist green grass, he would make an excellent conductor for the massive electrical current that was about to enter his body. The tremendous lightning bolt would rip through his portly frame with deadly intensity.

Agnus Derksen, Dickie's mother, was at the kitchen window of her dilapidated farmhouse, such as it was, doing a load of dishes, and although she was aware of Dickie's presence out in the pasture, did not really take much notice of him. She knew Dickie must be nursing a goodly number of new bruises, since her drunken husband had given him another vicious beating only a few hours before. He was gone now, getting drunk across the line, as he did on so many Sunday afternoons.

Because she wasn't really paying much attention, she was momentarily blinded, not to mention deafened, by the concussion of the powerful thunderbolt, and failed to see the bolt of lightning actually strike Dickie. She saw only a bright flash, and when she could make him out again, he appeared to be executing a kind of jig out in the meadow. It was completely out of character. But there he was, one leg bent at the knee, foot placed correctly against the calf of the other, ballet style. One arm flung out wide, the hand utterly expressive, the other poised artistically above his head, while he performed a perfect pirouette. If that wasn't strange enough, Dickie opened his mouth wide – wider than she'd ever seen it, impossibly wide –

and out came the most glorious, the most exquisite note of song Agnus Derksen – or anyone else for that matter – had ever heard. No one had ever heard more than a few thin squeaks and grunts out of Dickie, and now here he was, doing what no one had ever thought possible: making, not just a noise, but a stunningly beautiful one at that. Singing magnificently out across the valley. It was completely beyond her comprehension. She thought she must be dreaming. And then she noticed something else: a lazy curl of white smoke rising from the top of Dickie's head.

In fact, a scientist familiar with the effects of a direct lightning strike on the human body would have explained all of this to her easily enough. They were doing a lot of that, lately. The scientists. On radio and television shows. In books and magazines. Explaining all kinds of things. It was becoming quite fashionable for them to go around insisting that things people had always found remarkable or novel were really nothing of the kind. That, examined within the context of proper scientific method and theory, they were perfectly ordinary. To be expected. Necessarily so.

Magazines like *Popular Mechanics* and *Scientific American* had become prevalent. People had a voracious appetite for their cut-away diagrams and illustrations of good old American ingenuity. They just couldn't seem to get enough of having the nuts and bolts of things explained to them. Something about it made everyone feel better. Even the scientists. The bomb had done that to people. Scared them into believing that it was really just fear of the unknown that was making everyone so nervous. And even if the explaining was done in language devoid of human emotion, couched in a hopeless and blasé teleology that took the wonderment out of everything, at least it was better than being scared all the time.

In this case, the scientist would have explained to Dickie's mother that it was merely an overload of electrical current that was responsible for his highly unusual behaviour. That the disruptive power of a million-or-so volts of electricity coursing through his body had caused the circuitry to malfunction in, admittedly, spectacular fashion. The scientist might have added that Dickie was technically dead by the time he performed these same manoeuvres, and that they were, for all intents and purposes, the involuntary movements and emissions of a corpse.

There was also the matter of Dickie's exceptional physical proportions to be taken into account. He was built something like an under-sized sumo wrestler, with a cavernous and powerful chest cavity. Being struck by lightning was precisely what his vocalizing equipment needed in order to reach its fullest potential. A trained musician could not have produced a note so perfectly pitched, with such stunning resonance and clarity, such sheer power. It hung there in the air, expectantly – a note that dwarfed, that mocked, the finest ever sung by any basso profundo on the stage of La Scala. The pitch happened to be B flat, and a trained musical ear might have expected it to fall, possibly, into a graceful A natural – as it would have if Dickie had been singing, say, *Barber*. But Dickie wasn't singing *Barber*. And so the B flat hung there. One note. Impossibly long. Impossibly loud. Growing ever richer, ever stronger – the sweetest note of music ever heard in the valley. In the country. In the entire world.

The scientist making such a valiant effort to remain unimpressed would have gone on to explain to Mrs. Derksen that normally, when a person received that kind of massive shock, all the air in his lungs would be expelled very rapidly, in one quick and unremarkable gust of expectoration. But since Dickie's vocal chords happened to be constricted – to just the right tension, he might have added – thanks to the nature of his congenital defect, things took a rather more spectacular turn. The process was further augmented, he would have informed her, by the fact that Dickie happened, at that precise moment, to be straining to look up into the sky, and, in his excitement, gulping down a huge lungful of air. Add to this the fact that he had a forty-eight-inch chest and a diaphragm that would have been the envy of any opera singer, and you had the ingredients for the mother of all notes.

The B flat Dickie had produced, thanks to this unique combination of factors, found itself travelling unimpeded through the rarified air of the valley, and up into the hills. It carried across the border, and quickly reached the men busy installing the anti-ballistic nuclear missile not far away. They were just crawling out into the open again, after huddling under various pieces of machinery, anticipating the short but powerful thunderstorm. As it turned out, the angry little cloud had produced only a brief sun shower. Already the sun was back out, shining on their upturned faces as they listened to a sound they had never heard before – would never hear again.

The note hovered around them, even as a brilliant shaft of sunlight shot out from behind the cloud, sparkled gloriously on the wet tip of the rocket, on the warhead they had been bolting down there. It cascaded out across the entire valley, greener and fresher now than ever, thanks to the purifying and nutritional benefits of the thunder shower – water, ozone, nitrates, ions, electrolytes – all of them smothered in the rich elixir of Dickie's joyful noise.

# PART *four*

I N NEUSTADT, AS IN EVERY OTHER VILLAGE IN THE
valley, there was a school near the centre of town, and
next to it a small unremarkable bungalow, with no barn
attached, that served as the residence for the teacher.
Such a building was necessary, since the task of educating the
young inevitably fell to a stranger from someplace else. There
were almost no homegrown scholars in the valley. They were
usually brought in from the city.

Those who came to teach rarely stayed for more than a year
or two. That was about as long as they could stand the gossip
of people like the Zacharias sisters, and the second-guessing of
the village elders, who meddled their way into everything that
went on inside the school until they found something to disapprove of.

Local residents referred to the building as the teacherage,
and looking at it now as she walked by, Katie was stung by its
suffocating lack of appeal. Having to live there, she thought,
would surely suck the life out of anyone. Its construction was
novel only for the fact that it lacked the usual attachment of a
barn. It looked about as inviting as a granary, so hapless was
the architecture, so unremarkable the walls and windows. If it
was intended to reflect the personality of its inhabitant, then
such an individual would need to be as mediocre and unen-
terprising as possible. Even the tiniest spark of imagination

would need to be extinguished in order to survive there. Thinking back, most of the teachers Katie could remember had fit the requirements nicely, including Peter Giesbrecht, the man who'd taken her out of the village all those years ago.

Katie watched a group of girls playing on the swings and teeter-totters in the school yard. They were the same girls who had been playing among the hollyhocks at the border earlier – who would have been the first to see her if she'd been allowed to take the shortcut into the village. She stopped to watch them for a moment. So innocent. So carefree. So vulnerable. So ready for the world, and yet not ready at all. So quick to be good and kind and loving, so easily injured and disappointed and let down. Was there anything in the world with more potential for joy and sorrow?

Katie saw the sky darkening above them, felt the chill of the wind that fluttered their skirts. Ruffled their hair. She knew what was coming. Remembered how quickly something unexpected could sweep down out of the hills. When the girls looked up and saw the cloud bearing down upon them they instinctively ran toward the schoolhouse and up the steps. One of them tried the door but it wouldn't open. They huddled under the small overhang in a cluster. Katie thought she'd better get in somewhere herself, but she didn't want to leave the girls like that. They seemed so helpless. Would they just stand there and let their dresses get soaked, their shoes ruined? She ran into the yard, up the steps, and tried the door herself.

"It's locked," said the older girl.

"Wait here," said Katie. "I'll be right back." The wind was coming up hard now, the rush of it kicking dust into the air.

Inside her teacherage, Tilli Nickel was having a maddoch schlope of her own. She was very tired. Another week of teaching so many children in so many grades all in one room had worn her out. She was having a dream just now, about a funeral. She knew – and yet did not know – whose funeral it was. She was there herself, dressed in black – and yet she was not. There was a coffin. That much was certain. Elders at the front of the church. A congregation of villagers – yet not one face she recognized. Among them, scattered here and there, women who clearly did not belong to the valley – a surprising number of them, young, attractive, mysterious – dressed in black outfits that ranged from modest to outrageously provocative. Some wore elaborate black hats low over their eyes so that only glimpses of their striking faces appeared from time to time. Others arrived in low-cut dresses that revealed a shocking amount of perfect, pale cleavage. Each was keenly aware of the other's presence, so that the church was absolutely electric with a kind of feline energy. Each woman's presence a shameless admission that she had known the man in the coffin – in the Biblical sense of the word. There to mourn his passing publicly, all of them, this man they had once been intimate with. They had come to see him one last time. Put their hands on his lifeless body. Stand over him. Touch his folded hands with their jewelled fingers, weep their tears onto his breast. And Tilli Nickel was one of them. And yet, she wasn't.

Tilli looked at each of them and wondered if their jealousy was new, if they had somehow failed to imagine that there would be others like them. Tilli had never been under any such illusion. And yet, she carried inside her a fierce possessiveness. Each time her eyes met those of still another younger, prettier, smarter woman glancing out from under her hat, it was with the unspoken message that she, Tilli, wasn't like any of them, that there was something they did not know about her, that made her different. That if all of them had shared a little of themselves with Abe Wiebe, she had done much more than that. Had sacrificed much more. There was an unmistakable element of defiance in each of her stares because, in her own way, Tilli Nickel had won.

She had stayed in the village long after another teacher would have left. Stayed because even though Abe Wiebe no longer paid more than passing attention to her, paraded around with other women right in front of her, she'd made it up in her mind that she wasn't going anywhere. That when the novelty finally wore off, when he was tired of all the running around, she would still be there, waiting for him to notice her again. She was going to outlast them all. She hated herself for being so in love with him. Hated life in the village. But the whole thing had become a mission for her. A reason to get up in the morning.

While the storm approached outside her window, Tilli slept on. It wasn't the first dream she'd had about Abe Wiebe. She was in love with him as only a shunned woman can be with a man who doesn't want her any more – with that tenacious mixture of fanatical devotion and stubborn hope – strengthened, rather than weakened, the longer it went unrequited. There had been times lately when she thought she might be winning. When it seemed to her that, give or take a few mini-skirted housewives from across the border, he was getting tired of all the skirt chasing. That any day now he would walk up to the door of the teacherage and knock, the way he once had.

The knocking woke her up. Was it possible? She got out of bed and put on a dressing gown. Was it him at the door? Another knock before she opened the door and standing there, instead of Abe Wiebe, was one of the women from her dream. The most beautiful and threatening of them all. Except that she wasn't dressed in black.

"I'm sorry to bother you," said the woman, "but the children," and she turned to indicate the girls all huddled against the door of the school. A gust of a cold wind blew in through the door and flared Tilli's gown. She realized then that she wasn't dreaming any longer. That this woman, with her unearthly beauty, was real. But who was she? Another one of Abe's so-called customers from the States?

"They need to get inside – now," said the woman. "It's going to pour any second."

"Of course," said Tilli. She picked a set of keys off the table, hurried out the door ahead of Katie, and rushed up the steps of the school. She unlocked the door in one easy motion, opened it, and yelled for the children to hurry in.

"Go on," she shouted. Katie came up the steps behind her and together they herded the children inside. Some of the girls wanted to stop in the doorway to take off their Sunday shoes, place them neatly in a line along the wall next to the door, the way Miss Nickel would normally have expected them to, but there wasn't time. The sky had darkened ominously. There were small, quick flashes of bright light.

"Never mind that," said Katie. "It doesn't matter about the shoes. Just keep them on. " She lifted one of the smaller girls bodily over the others blocking the entrance. Then they were all inside and she had just closed the door when the first sheets of rain pelted against it. But it was a very compact, angry little cloud causing all the trouble, and it would only be a moment before the sun was out again, the sky blue, the wind calm, as if nothing had happened. The children, all huddled in the foyer of the school, were chattering amongst themselves, looking up at Katie, unable to reconcile her prodigious beauty with their own girlish awkwardness.

"Who are you?" said the girl in the pink dress. She was, in fact, Katie's niece, and would grow up to be almost as beautiful. She and the young poet would discover each other years from now, long after they had both left the village. They would come back for Aunt Martha's funeral, and at the cemetery, enduring the preacher's interminable blather, they would stare across the coffin at each other. Later, they would end up side by side on one of the wooden benches in the church basement, surrounded by the noise and clatter of knives and cups and spoons, by black-coated men buttering buns and kerchiefed women pouring coffee. And they would discover, in the midst of such parochial sociability, a surprising degree of comfort. A new and unexpected wisdom would be born that afternoon in each of them. While they sat, ate, talked, and shed many of the notions they'd been clinging to so stubbornly about marriage and children. They would become the parents of two boys and a girl. The girl's name would be Katie.

"Now Sadie," said Tilli. "That's impolite." But she was equally curious.

"Don't be silly," said Katie, and reached out a hand to Tilli. "Katie Klassen."

The name did not invoke any particular reaction from Tilli. Her position in the village dictated that she keep to herself as much as possible, and moreover that she remain steadfastly out of the loop where local gossip was concerned. As with other teachers in the valley, she was far more likely to be the object of rumour and innuendo than a participant in it, especially since word had got around that she might have allowed Abe Wiebe into her bed. And so Tilli did not connect Katie's name with any stories of a beautiful young woman who'd left the village years ago to become a movie star. A woman who, supposedly, still had Abe Wiebe turned inside out. Who was the secret motivation for all of his misadventures. Tilli was, instead, working under the mistaken assumption that Katie was another one of those young American housewives who had lately been coming up to the village under the pretence of buying one of his schlopebanks.

"Tilli," she said, and took Katie's hand. "Tilli Nickel. I'm the teacher here."

All the girls were staring up at Katie, at her apple green eyes, at the radiance and glow of her. They craned their necks and sensed that they were in the presence of something special.

Even in the dim of the darkened interior, Katie, in her yellow dress, shone above them like a small, benevolent sun.

MARTHA WIEBE stood at the open window of her upstairs room. Smelled the approaching storm. She pulled the curtains aside and looked out, saw the preacher walking down the street with the rifle in his hands. Thought little of it. Something needed killing, she guessed, and surely a preacher was as good a man as any for that, especially if there was suffering involved. When she thought of suffering she wondered how many of his own parishioners must sometimes toy with the notion of shooting him, or perhaps even themselves, just to put an end to one of his interminable sermons. She'd considered as much herself, only that morning.

From the window she could see the rocket in the distance, fully erect now, waiting to be lowered into the ground. A penis, she thought. What could be more obvious. An enormous penis. Mother earth, the hole in the ground. What else could the launching of such a rocket be but the ejaculation of a nation?

She had no interest in taking pictures of it. It seemed a silly act. Ignorant. What meaningful information could such an image possibly convey? Such photographs would be no different than the lifeless portraits of her dead ancestors. What would be the point of wanting to stare into the emptiness of that. The void. Better to wait and get one of her father, say, watching the billowing mushroom cloud. The eerie glow of incomprehension across his face. The inconceivable becoming conceivable. A brief and final understanding. That would be a much better portrayal of the truth. Moments of truth were always about people, thought Martha. Not about the technology they produced. To think otherwise was simply naive.

She spotted Dickie Derksen standing in the middle of the pasture, looking up at the sky. She'd seen him do that many times. Sometimes the young poet was there, too, next to him, pointing at something in the air. Martha thought that one day soon she would have to take her camera down there and get some photographs of them doing that. And some of Dickie by himself. He had an interesting face. Of course, there would be those who thought her insensitive for it, just as they would about the pictures she'd taken of the Martens brothers, but she didn't care. If they considered it cruel, the subjects of those photographs understood that it was just the opposite.

Martha picked up the telephoto lens and looked through it. She could make out Dickie standing in the open pasture, barefoot. She liked that idea of that. As if he'd grown there right out of the soil. In a way that was true of all of the valley's inhabitants, but Dickie was different because he still seemed so profoundly connected to it. To this place. Perhaps looking up into the sky like that was his way of reconciling the larger world with the valley, something Martha had never been able to do. But you could love a place and yet despise it, couldn't you? Hold it up to ridicule and praise at the same time? Wish to be gone from it, and still long for it? It was the paradox of these two extremes that informed Martha's daily existence. This constant struggle to bring larger, more complex sensibilities to a place where sensibilities had never been allowed to develop. This dogged insistence that ideas which flourished in the one should not be allowed to wither and die in the other.

Martha ran her fingers over the many photographs scattered across the table. Picked one up at random. Sat in a chair next to the window and examined it. It was the last picture she'd taken of her four brothers together, before they died so suddenly, one after the other. The four of them were seated around the supper table, each holding up a chicken leg, mouth open, teeth glistening, about to take an enormous bite. Martha remembered that she'd taken it the day she returned from one of her trips, and that the boys were so happy because this was the first meal she'd cooked for them in the better part of a month. There weren't many shots like that. Such moments of sociable humour were all too rare in the household. As robust as they were physically, the boys had always cultivated a deep and impenetrable solitude. Even when their mother was still alive, they had never been a close family. There was always an aloofness in each of them – in the way they carried themselves through a day, an evening, a night. A quietness of manner. Of mind. They always seemed more content out of each other's company than in it. Martha herself was no exception. She, too, was afflicted with an unexplainable but powerful need to be left alone. It was as if each of them had been born with a built-in need to exist within the confines of his or her own interior space.

The boys spent their waking hours in work and solitude, content to build Martha a new bread oven every year, grind up the wheat, sift it, and store it in bags in the barn attached to the house. The barn also contained the cows they milked and the pigs they slaughtered for sausage, and it was altogether such an efficient operation that they almost never had to leave the village. Companionship was necessary only within the context of the day's activity. Work that needed to get done or food that needed to get eaten. The rest of the time they spent alone. While one played a radio softly next to the bed, another repaired a chair out behind the house. If one squatted in the middle of the yard to play with the dog, another polished the car in the barn, or built a birdhouse in the shop. There was in each of them a tacit willingness to be the companion of his own lone self, whether they were across the yard from each other, across the hall, or only across the table.

There existed a compelling contentment to their shared solitude, even in the expenditure of their sexual energy. On her way to her bed at night, walking down the corridor between the boys' rooms, Martha could sometimes hear the muffled sounds of their fierce and urgent masturbation. She imagined them with fists clenched around their sturdy erections, jaws set, pumping at themselves. She sometimes stayed to listen, in spite of herself, to the involuntary moans that escaped them as each, in turn – and occasionally in quirky, unplanned unison – brought himself to the necessary conclusion.

When they were done and all was quiet again Martha, still in the hall, would sometimes listen to their even, rhythmic breathing through the doors, as one after another, they fell into deep and unremarkable sleep. She would allow herself to inhale the pungent aroma of freshly spilled semen as it penetrated the undisturbed air of the dim hallway. After that she would slip, quietly, into her bedroom, aware that even such private rituals translated into a chore, because she would have to change the sheets again.

She understood now that perhaps the reason things hadn't changed – the reason none of the boys had ever taken a wife – might have had something to do with the fact that they hadn't needed to. Martha had made things too easy for them. Had cooked and cleaned and looked after their needs as well as any wife might have. Better.

But she had never allowed herself to be completely defeated. There came a time every year – a time her father and the boys dreaded – when she packed up her suitcases and one of them drove her to the train station in Winkler. They knew they wouldn't see her again for three weeks, perhaps as long as a month. When it was time to come home, she always phoned a day or two ahead to let them know she was on her way back and if the place was a pigsty when she got there, she was turning right around and heading back out again. They never tested her on this threat, and it was the one time the boys – and even her father – would spend an entire day trying to make the house look presentable for her.

When she stepped in through the kitchen door and began her inspection, she did so with her suitcases, one in each hand, poised above the kitchen floor. If one of the boys offered to take a bag for her she would pull it away and lift it that much higher off the ground. She would not set them down until she was satisfied that she'd come home to a civilized place. When she finally did allow herself to lower the heavy bags to the floor, all the boys would run to help her with them, barely able to control their glee. Things would get back to normal now. There would be decent food to eat. Clean underwear. Towels. Bread.

None of them ever asked her where she'd been and Martha never volunteered an answer. There was always plenty of gossip around the village about where she went on these trips, especially from people like the Zacharias sisters, but it didn't bother her. She was immune to that sort of thing – had been for a long time now. She'd become strong-willed in a way that cost her dearly sometimes, but also paid dividends. Everything, Martha learned early on, had a price. It was only a matter of how much you were willing to pay.

She walked over to the shelves now and pulled out an album. It was one she hadn't looked at in a long time, but today she felt the need to reacquaint herself with its contents. It was a collection of photographs she'd taken of Abe Wiebe and Katie Klassen when they were still together. The very first picture was one of the two of them walking down the shady village street toward the camera, leaning into each other the way they often did, in that understated, yet unmistakable way that said so much. They had been a couple like no other. If you subscribed at all to the notion that God made people for each other, then here was undeniable proof. If you wanted to get an idea of what Adam and Eve might have looked like, then you need only look at these two. It was as if they had been made by the hand of God himself. Moulded in the image of his perfection. Flawless specimens of the human form.

Next to Katie, other pretty women of the village were just that – merely pretty. They simply could not compete. Became skinny little girls. Not one could radiate her charm, her elegant sensuality, could make the act of simply turning her head a gesture of pure aesthetic genius. Katie's attractiveness was not the kind models displayed in the magazines that young women smuggled back from across the line – copies of *True Story*, and *Cosmopolitan* – all interchangeable. Hers was a beauty completely her own, belonged to no one but her. No magazine photograph could ever hope to capture it. So much of it lay in the animation she gave to the smallest gesture, the least movement of her mouth, her magnificent hands. Her beauty was not static, but fluid. It had as much to do with the way she moved and spoke and breathed as with her bone structure or skin texture.

The same was true of Abe Wiebe. His was not the image of the quintessential handsome man that appeared on those magazine pages. His animal movement captured a notion of masculinity not accessible to any mere model. His good looks were much more than that. They contained deeper elements of ruggedness and strength, of gentleness and sensitivity. Other handsome young men looked like awkward adolescent boys next to him. Not one of them could carry himself with such assurance. Such understated power. Not one could show a smile with such a mouth full of white teeth, a laugh so manly, yet infectious, appealing in every masculine way.

When the two of them were together it was all multiplied. Each intensified the other. In each other's presence their movement became so effortless, their mannerisms so elegant, that those nearby could only watch from a distance, in wonder and amazement. Martha looked again at the picture of the two of them walking toward her, down the village street. She'd taken it only a few days before everything went so terribly wrong. It seemed to Martha that in the photograph they were an absolutely impregnable fortress. That they walked in armour, shielded from the pettiness of others. From their jealousy, their unsophisticated provocation, their vulgar enmity. They were immutable. Unreachable. Invincible to everything. Everything, it turned out, except each other.

When the two of them parted, even the most cynical of the valley's inhabitants understood that something rare and precious had been lost. Even the most unrefined men, the most repressed women of the valley sensed as much. Even the faintest, most distant romantic notions had been brightened by the comet that was Abe and Katie. The two of them were clearly meant to be. And now they weren't. Hadn't been for a long time. According to local wisdom, the ways of the flesh were, after all, the ways of sorrow. And pain. And so in the end it all fit perfectly into their notions of worldliness. Of vanity. Any possibility for a happy future forfeit, they would have said, by default.

The truth was that neither Abe nor Katie had ever been the slightest bit vain. They had, after all, been brought up in a culture where the most predictable reaction to their perfection was often disdain. Where their amazing good looks were more likely to be seen as a liability than an asset. Katie in particular, was often treated more like a leper than a goddess. And yet, Martha had the sense that in some begrudging way the two of them had always been secretly celebrated by the inhabitants of the valley, even as they were being openly shunned.

Martha thought the same might be true for herself. Did people look at her with a confusing mixture of begrudging admiration and harsh disapproval? She was certainly a misfit when it came to her demeanour. Much too bold and independent. She made everyone uncomfortable with her bravado. Not that she acted like a man. She was not masculine, but then, neither was she feminine in the way a woman like Katie was. She did not consider herself unattractive, but rather as a big, strong, handsome woman, without the worn look so many of the village women carried around with them. Perhaps it was because she'd never had children of her own. How many babies did it take before even the lithest slip of a woman lost her girlish figure? Before her sinew and bone became tied to an endless string of unrewarding and mind-numbing tasks? Before all possibility of personal aesthetics became subordinate to toil and care and childbirth?

And then, quite suddenly, the idea struck her. It was time for her to become the object of her own inspection. Time to get a good look at herself. She picked up the camera from the table, adjusted the shutter speed, the lens aperture, set the timer button. Today, she would turn the lens on herself. Of course, it would have to be black and white. Anything else would interfere with the truth. The search would be contaminated by colour. Would hide the very thing she was looking for. The very thing she was trying to illuminate. So often in her photographs, she would discover the thing she'd been trying to capture – the thing waiting to be found – in the most unlikely place: in the negative space of the photograph – in the absence of light. Away from the subject. She would look there, and suddenly, it would become clear. And if she stared at a picture of herself, standing naked in this darkened room, perhaps that was where she would look. In those places. Yes, there was no way around it. She would have to be naked.

She would get undressed, shoot the photos, then develop them in the little darkroom she had created out of the closet. She'd hang them up to dry there, and only later, perhaps much later, when she was once again dressed and relaxed and composed, would she allow herself to look at them – one by one – inspect them closely. Stare intently into each one, just as others so often did when she handed them a picture of themselves. Stare, as if they had just figured themselves out a little better. The camera could do that, sometimes. Provide that opportunity.

And she must try it on herself. Look for the very thing she'd searched for in the endless hours of staring into photographs of other people. She wanted to get a good look at herself. She needed to do that today. There was something she wanted to discover. Something her own naked body might be able to tell her. She wouldn't know what it was until she saw it. This thing she'd never quite been able to figure out. But it was suddenly very important that she find a way to present herself to herself. The mirror wasn't going to do it. She'd tried that the other day, stood naked in front of it for a long time. But nothing had happened. Nothing at all. It had only made her self-conscious. She understood why now. She had not been far enough removed from her own naked presence. She needed more distance, more perspective. The camera would give it to her.

She set the camera on the tripod so that it faced the open window. Sat down in the chair. Took off her clothes. Slowly. Deliberately. Got back up and headed over to the window again. Sat back down again. Got up. Walked over to the camera. Pressed the timer button. Walked back to the window. Pulled back the curtain. The smell of rain in the air. The sky growing dark. A gust of wind. The camera click. Something about that. About the idea of that. Taking pictures of her naked body made her feel deliciously illicit. Naughty. Brave. Incredibly alive. She positioned a finger strategically. Began to move. To undulate. Gyrate. The camera clicked. Her hips were liquid. Her knees watery. Her arms not her own. She was ready. A bolt of bright lightning – an all-but-simultaneous rattle of thunder that blinded and thrilled her. The camera clicked.

In the photograph Martha's naked body would be illuminated by the most unearthly white light coming in through the window. It would pour over the curves of her pale flesh and expose it in ways she had never thought possible. Behind her, in the shadow of the lightning, a part of the photograph that seemed completely impenetrable. She seemed to be moving forward, away from there, into the light, at great speed. Not to be standing on the floor at all. To be in mid-air. About to levitate out through the window.

THE PREACHER, walking briskly down the village street, was on a mission. He felt more like a man than he ever had in his life. He carried the gun tightly in both hands, one finger on the stock, one on the trigger, oblivious to the thunderhead that had snuck quickly and quietly over the edge of the escarpment and swept silently down into the valley. He was going to find and kill Abe Wiebe. Hunt him down and dispose of him.

By this time his state of mind had progressed, by degrees, from vanity, to jealousy, through revenge, all the way to the profound conviction that the act he was about to commit constituted nothing less than God's work. If no one else had the courage to do what was necessary, then he, as a watchdog of community morals, was going to have to do it himself. Christian charity was out of the question. In matters such as this there could be no turning the other cheek. He would have to kill Abe Wiebe, not because he had become the object of his wife's unadulterated lust, not for evoking in her such a blatant display of carnality, but because he represented a threat to everything the valley held sacred. Corruption on such a level could not go unchallenged. It was really a question of moral leadership.

The preacher was so engrossed in all this convoluted rationalization that the bright flash and all-but-simultaneous crash of thunder – close enough to shake the earth underneath him – were completely unexpected. The effects of so much sudden light and noise were twofold. First, the violent concussion of the lightning bolt short-circuited the preacher's autonomic nervous system and caused an involuntary contraction of his trigger finger. Second, the seismic and auditory components of the shock wave completely masked the report, and simultaneous kick, of the rifle.

The end result was that the preacher resumed walking, unaware that he had just inadvertently fired the high-powered rifle he was carrying. The bullet left the barrel of the gun at three times the speed of sound, travelling in a southerly direction at a slightly upward angle. A quick extrapolation based on that combination of velocity and trajectory indicated it was going to catch Abe Wiebe, who happened to be leaning against the hood of his car on the other side of the border, some distance to the south, square between the eyes. It would, literally, come out of the blue, and strike him dead before the back of his head touched the hardened dirt of the road he was standing on. His theory – the one he'd clung to in Korea, about a single shot not being enough to kill him – would turn out to be wrong.

And it would all happen right there in front of Jake, who would claw and crawl his way up the hood of the car, trying desperately to get away from the gruesome horror of what he had just witnessed. The crush of tissue and bone as the back of Abe's head exploded.

"YOU'RE NOT FROM AROUND HERE," said one of the girls.

Katie looked over at Tilli, then back at the girls. Didn't know the answer.

"You're so pretty."

"You're the prettiest lady I've ever seen."

"Do you like my dress?" said the girl in the pink dress.

"Yes," said Katie. "It's such a lovely shade of pink."

"My mother says dresses like that are a sin," said the older girl.

"Does she?" said Katie, in a way that was lightly dismissive.

"That's right." The older girl stared up at Katie defiantly. "She says girls who wear dresses like that are going to hell."

"You're going to hehh..ell, you're going to hehh..ell," sang the girl with the braided hair.

"Am not," said the girl in the pink dress.

"Are, too."

"Am not."

"Are, too."

Miss Nickel put a hand on each of their shoulders. "That's enough. Stop it, both of you." The older girl wriggled her shoulder out from under Miss Nickel's hand and stared up at Katie. There was hardness in her eyes. A coldness. The same look Katie had seen just a few minutes ago in the eyes of the Zacharias sisters as they stared at her from the window. It gave her a shiver. A little knot in the pit of her stomach. It was just this kind of thing she had run from.

The harshness of the older girl's reproach shook Katie enough that she felt the need to look out the window for a moment, to try and collect herself. When she did she saw the preacher walking down the street, seemingly oblivious to the rain, carrying a rifle in his hands. She was not particularly alarmed, although she thought it odd that he didn't wait until after the storm. She remembered that there had always been men with rifles in the village, men who were out to shoot some creature that needed killing for one reason or another. A pig or cow about to be slaughtered. A calf that was crippled. A cat that was surplus. A dog that had gotten old. And then there were the pests: rats and badgers, weasels and owls, foxes and coyotes, all the wild animals that interfered in one way or another with the smooth and efficient operation of the farm. Things obviously hadn't changed much in that department.

Her father had been no exception. She could remember one incident in particular. A stray dog that had come wandering into the yard, hobbling and half-starved. It lay down under one of the cottonwood trees and stayed there, unable to go any further. Katie brought out some milk and pork rinds for it, stroked its matted fur, asked it a few questions, the way humans do to animals who cannot understand them. She tried out a few names without success, then went back into the summer kitchen to get some water and there was her father, about to step out into the yard, a loaded rifle in his hands.

"What's that for?" she asked, already knowing the answer.

"Stay here," said her father.

"What are you going to do?"

"Get inside the house."

"Papa?"

Her father looked down at her, jaw set, eyes narrow. "I told you to get inside."

"But Papa."

"You heard me."

Katie had long ago learned never to call her father's decisions into question, understood that there were harsh consequences for such impertinence, had seen them on her mother's face. But this time she couldn't stop herself. "But why, Papa? Why do you have to shoot it? Why can't we just let it go?"

Her father set one foot on the threshold.

"I'll get it to go away. I will. Just let it rest for a minute."

"It won't go now," said her father, and indicated the empty dish in Katie's hand. "You've fed it."

"But it isn't doing any harm."

"It is not a question of harm. That animal is of no use to anyone."

"What about me, Papa? Am I of any use to anyone?"

"You are testing my patience, daughter."

"Do you want to shoot me, too?"

He went to step out into the sunlight.

"No. I won't let you," said Katie, and made a grab for the gun, pulled at it, tried to wrestle it out of his hands. Her father did not move. Held the gun firm. Let her struggle. Pitifully. And then he looked down at her with such cold eyes that she had to let go.

He stepped across the threshold and walked out into the yard. "I hate you," she shouted after him, and ran out the back door of the summer kitchen. She hurried out of the yard, but there wasn't enough time. She still heard the shot when it came.

In Los Angeles people used guns and rifles, too, but not for shooting animals. Mostly they shot each other. It happened all the time. Katie had seen it herself once. Standing in line, waiting to be called as an extra, she watched a thin, frail-looking man being led out of the police station across the street. There was a burly, plainclothes detective on either side of him with a hand clamped on each arm. The man looked as though he might have been beaten up. Even from across the street Katie could see that he had a black eye. A stocky pedestrian in a cheap suit and a fedora walked up to him briskly, pointed a revolver and fired. Katie thought the shot sounded like a cheap cap gun, the kind one of her brothers would have shoplifted out of the five-and-dime store in Walhalla. The frail man clutched his chest pitifully and fell backward into the arms of the detectives escorting him. No struggle. No shout of pain or anguish. Complete submission to the bullet. The thing that struck Katie was how casual the whole episode seemed. Like some kind of business transaction. She realized later that the manner in which the man in the fedora had taken the life of his victim wasn't much different than the way her father would have disposed of that dog back on the farm.

Looking out the window of the teacherage now, at the preacher carrying the rifle, she had no reason to suspect that he might be out to do another human being harm. He was a man of the cloth, after all. And besides, wouldn't the animal in question already have holed up somewhere, anticipating the weather? The thought never crossed Katie's mind that the preacher might be out to shoot another human being. And not just any human being. The one human being, above all others, she would have wanted to see alive at least one more time.

Lightning flashed white through the window. A blast of energy shook the walls and rattled the panes.

"Is it the bomb?" said the girl in the pink dress.

"Of course not, silly," said the older girl. "The bomb doesn't sound anything like that."

"How do you know what the bomb sounds like?"

"But there was a white flash," said the girl with the braided hair. "Teacher said there'd be a white flash. Didn't you, Miss Nickel?"

"We know what to do," the girl with the kerchief said to Katie.

"Teacher showed us."

She and the girl with the braided hair scampered down under their desks, knelt on the oily wooden floor, and covered their heads with their arms. They resembled two humble worshippers performing some ritual of deference on the floor of a temple.

"Sarah. Amy. Please," said Miss Nickel. "You don't need to do that now. It's nothing like that. It's just a thunderstorm."

The girls got up and rubbed their knees, straightened down their dresses. "We do it when we see a white flash. Isn't that right, Miss Nickel?"

"That's right. But there isn't going to be any white flash."

"But we just saw one."

"Teacher?" said one of the other girls. "What happens if we don't hide under our desks. What happens then?"

Tilli Nickel looked over at Katie helplessly. "They make us do that. All the schools in the valley. The people from the department. They insist that we teach the children these ridiculous drills. It's humiliating."

The girls had moved off to another part of the room. They were drawing on the chalkboard, playing Xs and Os. "In here," said Tilli, and stepped off to one side. Katie followed her into a small room full of old textbooks. "I'm going to have a cigarette," said Tilli. "Do you want one?" And without waiting for an answer she closed the door, took a pack of cigarettes out from behind one of the higher shelves, and lit one. She blew the smoke over Katie's left shoulder.

"He's not here, in case you're wondering, " said Tilli.

"Excuse me?"

"Or maybe you already knew that."

"I'm sorry. I don't know what you're talking about."

"Don't tell me. You came up to buy one of his benches. Right?"

"Benches?"

"Don't play dumb with me." There was a sudden menace in her voice.

"Really, I don't know what this is all about, but I think you've got the wrong person."

"Sure." Tilli folded her arms. Leaned against a bookshelf. "It must be a terrible disappointment for you." She took another long pull on her cigarette. "You're not the first, you know."

"I'm not?" Katie felt trapped by this woman's stubborn, if misguided provocation.

"And don't think you'll be the last." Tilli blew the smoke out in a harsh cloud of white. "He's very popular. If you get my drift. Or should I say his benches are."

Katie tried not to breathe until the smoke had cleared a little. "I think I'd better go and see about the children."

"This is just a game for you, isn't it?"

Katie was struggling now to keep her composure, something

she thought she had learned to do so well in Hollywood. And now here she was, calling upon all her powers just to deal with this misguided woman.

"Look. I don't know who you think I am, but you're making a mistake."

"I think it's the other way around."

"Excuse me," said Katie, and tried to get by, but Tilli blocked her exit.

"Women like you are a dime a dozen to man like Abe."

And then, suddenly, Katie knew who this woman was talking about. She brushed past Tilli, who crushed her cigarette out on the floor and followed her out of the room.

"A dime a dozen," Tilli said again.

So he was here. He hadn't been killed in Korea. Hadn't drunk himself to death in some foreign country. Hadn't married a beautiful young Korean woman who had his baby before she died quite suddenly of fever and Abe found himself a widower raising a young boy who grew up to be as handsome as Abe himself by the time Katie met him one day after he'd come to Hollywood to be a movie star, and they had a conversation in the course of which she discovered who his father was which set off a series of events that led them back to each other. Katie had a hundred scenarios like that one. A thousand. She thought she had conjured up every possible eventuality for the way in which the two of them might ever come into each other's company again – every one except this, the most obvious. That he would simply return to the village. But then, Katie hadn't thought she was ever coming back either, and here she was.

The little girl in the pink dress ran over from the blackboard. "Do you want to play?" she said to Katie. She held out a piece of chalk in her hand. "You can have pink."

"Sure," said Katie, her heart pounding. She felt something seeping in through the walls of the school, the windows –

penetrating every pore in her skin. It was like nothing she'd ever heard before. She thought at first she might be the only one hearing it. That it might be the sound of her own scalding blood screaming through her veins. She'd never felt so alive. But then the children heard it, too. The sound of it silenced them all into a wonder. A single note – that hovered above them, smothered them in a blanket of sweet sound. The lights went out. Miss Nickel tried the switch. Nothing happened.

"What is it?"

"Sounds like... someone singing."

"An angel."

"Don't be silly," said the older girl.

"Up in heaven," said the girl in the pink dress.

"It's nothing like that."

The girl in the pink dress looked up at Katie. "Do you think it could be an angel?" she said.

Katie looked down at her. Didn't know what to say. Had never been asked such a question. Couldn't think.

"Well?" said the older girl. "Do you?"

"Maybe she's an angel," said the girl in the braids, pointing at Katie. She was thinking how the note's perfection matched perfectly that of the beautiful woman who had appeared out of nowhere and taken them to shelter, and who now stood in their midst.

"Trust me," said Miss Nickel curtly. "She's no angel."

They all ignored her. The girl in the pink dress took Katie's hand. Held it tightly. Looked up into her face, and Katie down at hers.

"The rain," said the girl with the pigtail. "It's stopped." She opened the door and they stepped out into the fresh air.

WHEN ABE WIEBE saw the angry little cloud sending out a swath of rain that cut cleanly across the floor of the valley, he stopped the car. He knew if that much water fell across the road they were travelling on, it would become instantly impassable. The surface would turn into a slick soup on which no vehicle could hold its tracks. Even the best driver would be unable to avoid slipping quietly and relentlessly off the road and into the ditch.

He got out and leaned against the warm hood of the car to watch the progress of the little black cloud, moving at an amazing speed, dropping a dense, narrow wall of water as it went. It was going to douse the village for sure, but it was touch and go as to whether any rain would actually fall on the road where it went through the ravine and crossed the border into Canada. That was always the worst part.

The bullet accidentally fired out of the preacher's gun continued to speed silently toward the centre of his skull. It was headed directly for the small, smooth patch of skin between his large and gentle eyes. It knew precisely what it was going to do when it got there. It was going to slam into the front of his head, dislodge a good portion of his skull and brain, and exit out the back. The shot would, in its damage and effect, all but dismantle his cranium.

The missile site was off to the left. Already the sun was back out there. The rain had just missed it, cutting a line along the border, just to the north, as if the black cloud, somehow cognizant of the boundary it was skirting along, was reluctant to cross over. As if, in spite of its malicious will to do quick and terrible harm, to spit lightning and drive hard rain down on the inhabitants below, it was really a cowardly little thunderhead.

Jake got out of the car and hoisted himself onto the fender next to Abe. From there they could see the men at the missile site crawling out from under various pieces of machinery, places where they had taken refuge, certain that they were about to get soaked. But not a drop had fallen on them. The wall of water had narrowly missed them, cutting so close they could hear the pellets stinging the earth only a few feet away. The rocket, suspended from a monstrous crane by ropes and chains, hung above them, clean and dry, glistening in the new sunshine.

Abe was looking at it now, thinking about its ridiculous proximity to the village. He was getting ready to go over there in a minute and say something. Do something. Yell at somebody. Call someone a stupid bastard. Maybe punch somebody. Knock some sense into somebody. He knew he had to do at least that much. He might even start up that enormous crane, swing the rocket around like a sling until it broke free and flung itself to the ground in pieces. He was going to let them know there were a lot of people close by who did not appreciate what was happening. Who were angry, and frightened, and confused, and if nothing else, someone was going to get a bloody nose and fat lip for allowing it to happen. They were not, by God, going to get away with it scot-free. If he stayed here much longer, seething, he could definitely work himself up to something like that.

"What's this?" said Jake. He'd noticed a car in the distance, coming down the road toward them at high speed. Abe was about to turn and see for himself when a vicious bolt of lightning forked out of the angry little cloud and writhed toward the ground. The bright flash blinded him for a second and made him flinch. There had been something there. Where the lightning hit. Something, or someone. Abe thought he'd made out a human figure just as the bolt hit, but it was hard to be sure, especially now that he couldn't see all that well. It might just be a tree stump or a barrel.

The crash of thunder that reached him almost immediately was powerful enough to make him flinch again, just as the car came up behind him. It did not stop, but instead, picked up speed and continued down the road. By the time Abe turned, first one way, then another, to see who it was, the car – a Cadillac convertible with the top down – was accelerating rapidly and erratically away from them down the road.

"Hey. It's that guy," said Jake. "From Jack's Place. The loudmouth American." There were two men in the front seat, and even from behind Abe recognized the driver as the real estate agent from the bar. He was wearing the same ill-fitting fedora, cocked a little to one side, the same greasy suit. The man in the passenger seat looked familiar, too, but Abe couldn't place him. The two of them were leaning against each other, heads touching, like they might be singing a duet. The car was weaving from side to side, as if the driver were not really steering, but letting the tracks worn into the hard dirt keep the vehicle on the road.

"Drunk," said Jake.

"Passed out, I bet," said Cornie, up from his nap and standing next to them now. The car accelerated rapidly, heading directly for the missile site.

"Listen," said Jake.

"What in the hell is that?"

"A trumpet?"

"Somebody calling?"

Dickie's note had come surging in behind the thunder.

"Where's it coming from?"

"Over there," said Cornie, and pointed to where the lightning had struck.

"Some kind of singing?" said Jake. They both looked at Abe, but he wasn't listening to them again. He'd been like that all afternoon. Holed up inside himself. But Abe had just noticed something that had nothing to do with lightning bolts or missile sites or unusual sounds. Something much more engrossing. A shaft of brilliant sunlight had pierced through the first small opening in the dark cloud, shining like a magnificent spotlight on the southern tip of the village, on something sitting there in Katie Klassen's yard. Surrounded by dripping cottonwood trees and green grass, shining like a small sun of its own, was a bright yellow convertible. The bullet had not yet reached him, but Abe felt as though he'd just been shot. As though his heart had just exploded up into his throat, and it was all he could do to swallow it back down.

"Sounds like – like rejoicing," said Jake.

Cornie Martens, still waking up, opened his mouth to yawn, but then he went rigid, eyes wide, jaws locked in position.

THE REAL ESTATE AGENT left the bar not long after Abe and the Martens brothers, and took Harry with him. The two of them headed for the missile installation in the new Cadillac he'd just bought for himself. He wanted to show Harry what was making him so much money. He wanted to shoot some film, too, with the new 8mm movie camera he'd bought at the J. C. Penney store the day before. He thought maybe Harry could get some footage of him leaning on the car, with the missile site in the background. Something to show his grandchildren.

The camera was a marvel of technology for its time. Almost nobody had one, which was what he liked most about it – the fact that he could afford one and hardly anybody else could. But as with every other technological innovation he'd ever owned, it would turn out to be a short-lived novelty. It was always like that with people like the real estate agent. Theirs was a life of continual irony. A treadmill of buying things they turned out to have no use for. Of being the ones who wanted most what they needed least. People who went out and bought an 8mm movie camera with all the bells and whistles, only to discover that there was disturbingly little they cared to get on film. That their lives really weren't very interesting.

Harry had agreed to go along because he was very drunk, and felt the potential to be meaner than he had ever been in his life. He thought today might be the day he went to the next level. Pulled off something he'd never tried before. Not consciously, at any rate. What Harry wanted to experience, plain and simple, was the act of murder. He knew he'd been working his way up to it for a long time now, and the real estate agent would make as good a victim as any. He was stupid, and slow, and he would be completely surprised when Harry turned on him. That would be so glorious. That look of incomprehension on his face when Harry pulled out the knife and came for him. Harry always carried a pocket knife.

But he didn't want to just punch holes in the real estate agent with it. There would have to be more to it than that, or what was the point. Perhaps Harry could stab him in just the right places to incapacitate him first. Stay away from arteries and veins. Target muscles and tendons. Render him harmless, but not dead. And then Harry could tell him – gently, lovingly – all about the mutilation, the humiliation, the pain, that was to come. That was when the real fun would begin.

When they pulled up to the barricade, the young private was just picking himself up off the ground, where he had been lying since Abe Wiebe had cold-cocked him for being so snotty. He'd suffered a mild concussion, and was still disoriented, not quite sure exactly who he was or what he was there for.

"You okay there, Son?" said the real estate agent out of the car.

"Huh?"

"Yeah. I'm fine." He braced himself against the car. "What can I do for you?" The disoriented private had forgotten almost everything about why he was there, except that he was supposed to ask questions.

"Not a thing, Son, not a thing. You sure you're okay?"

"I think so. Just a little groggy that's all."

"What happened?"

"I don't know. I guess I slipped."

"Slipped? Slipped on what?"

"I don't know. I don't remember."

"You've been out in the sun too long, son. That's your problem. You should get indoors for awhile."

"Yes, sir. I will, Sir." The young private was confusing the real estate agent with the sergeant.

"We can give you a lift, if you like."

"No." The private had a sudden and urgent sense that he was supposed to stay where he was, even though he had no idea why. "Thanks. I think I'd better stay here."

"Well, we'll be going then, if it's all the same to you."

"Sure," said the young private. "Go right ahead. Don't mind me." His state of confusion would not allow him to remember that he was supposed to keep people from getting through. "You take care now," he said, and waved them on weakly.

They were just getting up to speed when Harry spotted Abe Wiebe and Jake Martens.

"Hey," he said. "It's those assholes from the bar."

The real estate agent handed him the camera. "You should get them on film," he said. "Probably never had anyone take their picture before. Probably get a kick out of it. I'll get out and talk to them. You shoot some film," he said. By that time Harry was busy trying to think of a way to film himself mutilating the body of the real estate agent. That way he could watch it over and over again. He pressed a button and the camera began to roll. It was pointing straight up at Harry's face, recording every expression written there.

"I'll just pull up ahead of them here," said the real estate agent. He slowed down, manoeuvred the convertible around Abe's car. Just at that moment the flash of lightning – the same bolt that was killing Dickie Derksen, that caused the preacher to fire his gun – turned the sky white. The same flash that temporarily blinded Abe Wiebe, made him flinch. Then there was the thunder that came immediately after, which caused him to involuntarily turn his head and shift it six inches to the right. The result was that the bullet which had been on its way to his skull zoomed harmlessly by and smashed, instead, into Harry, still filming himself in the passenger seat of the real estate agent's brand new Cadillac convertible, which was coasting by at that precise moment. The bullet smashed into Harry's chest, travelled cleanly and silently through his beating heart (while the camera recorded every nuance of surprised horror on his face), then out the other side of his chest, where it made a remarkably neat and tidy exit wound. It then entered his left wrist, struck a bit of bone which miraculously failed to alter the shape of the bullet but had, instead, the effect of radically altering its trajectory. It turned sharply upward, made still another neat exit wound out of Harry's wrist and – still in pristine condition – entered the real estate agent's skull, where it converted a large portion of his brain into pulp before exiting out the other side, leaving his hat neatly in place.

Both men were killed instantly and fell dead – one of irreversible brain damage, the other of massive heart trauma – against each other, like two valentine lovers, heads touching. One additional effect on the real estate agent's body was a sudden and violent straightening of his right leg, which caused him to jam the accelerator to the floor, so that instead of coming to a stop, as he had intended, the car sped crazily down the dirt road.

By the time Abe Wiebe had turned, half-blinded – first one way, then another – to see who it was, he saw only the backs of their heads, and the Cadillac convertible accelerating rapidly away from him. The occupants appeared to be asleep, not because they had lost consciousness, but because they had lost their lives.

As for the bullet, it continued on at precisely the same speed and trajectory it had been travelling before it caused so much carnage, at a slight upward angle. No one knows what happened to it after that.

"WHAT THE HELL IS THAT?" said the sergeant, who had stepped out of the bivouac to see what was going on. A lot of men were just crawling out from under pieces of machinery. The sergeant had been left in charge, only because it was a Sunday, and the two regular officers in charge, both from Philadelphia, had managed to snag a cargo plane from Grand Forks Air Force Base to fly them back to their families for the weekend.

"Air-raid siren?" said one of the soldiers. The sound continued to carry out across the fields. Ahead of it rolled the last remnants of thunder.

"I've never heard anything like it before," said another.

"What do you think it is, Sir?" said one of the enlisted men to the sergeant.

"I don't know, exactly," said the sergeant, "but five'll get you ten the Commies have something to do with it."

"Commies, Sir?"

A lot of the young soldiers might have indulged in a few epiphanies of their own, but they were highly trained men, and most higher forms of human emotional response had been drilled out of them. This afforded them a kind of collective immunity, especially people like the sergeant. But for at least one of the men on hand the training had not been entirely successful. He still carried within him some few remnants of human emotion that could only be described as sensitive. This particular young soldier had been drafted into the army, just as most other eligible young men of limited means had, for a two-year tour of duty. He felt as out of place as it was possible to be, not because he was in North Dakota – the last place in America he would have visited voluntarily – but because the whole concept of spending all day and night in the company of boorish young men was utterly distasteful to him. He couldn't stomach their simplistic bravado. Their willful ignorance. The humdrum daily grind of enduring their lack of imagination.

He, for one, was aware of the fact that they were near the international border. He had, in fact, wandered in that direction on more than one occasion to get a better look and discovered a village there, just across the ridge, nestled under the tall cottonwoods. He thought of it as – and it was the only word that would do – exotic. The look of it. Such peace. Such tranquility. Here, he thought, was the opportunity for such a simple, yet rewarding life. Life in one of those housebarns under the cottonwood trees seemed so idyllic.

He'd even met a girl. Under one of the tall, solitary cottonwoods that grew along the border where he took his off-duty walks. He'd discovered her sitting there alone one afternoon and stopped to say hello. She told him she was from the village. The one he could make out in the distance. Then she told him she liked his uniform. He was pretty sure he was in love with her. She seemed so incredibly innocent to him. He didn't think there was a girl in all of the United States of America as innocent as she. He was going again tonight, if he could get away. They were going to meet and he was going to get her to tell him all about the village. The valley. The people. And he was going to spring the news on her that it was his intention to desert. He was going to cross the border one of these nights and never come back. And would she help him? Give him safe haven? He was willing to work. Work hard to earn his keep. The girl's name was Betty Unger, and now, when he listened to this sound – the sound of Dickie Derksen's incredible note – it conveyed an obvious message to him.

"Sounds like... like – joy," said the sensitive young soldier.

The sergeant looked over at him. "What in hell did you just say?"

"Sir?"

"You heard me, soldier." The sergeant glowered at him.

"Nothing, Sir. I didn't mean anything."

"Use that word around me again and you'll find yourself on twenty-four-hour latrine duty."

"Yes, Sir."

Some of the other men snickered. The young soldier tried to stare one or two of them down, but with no luck. He wanted to be brave for Betty, but it was no use. He lowered his head in embarrassment while the others went on talking about the strange sound.

"Where's it coming from?"

"Hard to say."

"It's like it's coming right out of the blue." And indeed the sky was blue again. Already the dark little cloud had moved off speedily to the east.

"But there's nothing up there."

"That's not really accurate," said the sensitive young soldier. "There's at least one B-52. I saw it just a minute ago. And probably a couple of Voodoos as well."

"Are you being smart with us, soldier?" said the sergeant.

"No, Sir."

"Because if you are, I'm going to kick your ass for you. Right here. Right now."

"It's just that they said there was nothing up there."

"I want you to shut up."

"Yes, Sir. I'm sorry, Sir. I was only trying to be helpful."

"Get away from me."

"Yes, Sir." The soldier took a few steps back.

"Tell me something, corporal," said the sergeant to the man next to him. "What would it take to fire that thing?"

"Sir?"

"Launch it."

"Sir? You mean right now?"

"I mean right now." The man he was speaking to was a skilled technician, but, like everyone else on the site, he had only a very small job to do. A job meaningless out of the larger context. One small cog in the wheel of redundancy. "I'm talking to you, soldier. I want to know if we can get that thing into the air – if we have to."

"Permission to speak freely, Sir," said the corporal.

"For Christ's sake get on with it, corporal."

"Well, Sir, the thing is – the thing about the rocket is, well, it's just hanging there. I don't know a whole lot about it, but I really think if we're going to fire it, it needs to be down in the silo."

"You do."

"I do."

"I don't give a damn if it's hanging upside down between your goddamn legs, boy," said the sergeant. "I want to know if we can fire that goddamn thing."

"I really don't think so, sir."

"You don't sound very sure of yourself." The sergeant turned to the adjutant beside him. "Get me the manual."

"Sir?"

"The manual. What are you – an imbecile? The manual for that goddamn rocket. Get it. I want to have a look at it."

"I don't think I can do that, Sir."

"You don't."

"No, Sir."

"And why not?"

"Because, well, because there is no manual, Sir."

"No manual."

"No, Sir."

"That's ridiculous. How do they expect us to put that damn thing together and send it up without a goddamn manual?" The sergeant knew very little about the nuts and bolts of the installation procedure, but he couldn't be blamed for that. He'd never been put in charge before. Had no business being in charge now. He knew that as well as anyone. But here he was. "You," he said to another uniformed soldier standing nearby. "What do you do here?"

"Me, Sir?"

"Do I look like I'm talking to anybody else?"

"I'm the crane operator, Sir."

"Crane operator."

"Yes, Sir."

"Tell me something. What would it take to put that thing back on the truck and haul it on out of here?"

"Sir?"

"You heard me."

"But why would we want to do that, Sir?"

"*Why would we want to do THAT, Sir?*" the sergeant was mocking their answers now. He was frustrated. "Listen to me. I don't know what that goddamn sound is but I've got a pretty good idea it might be some kind of radio frequency designed to scramble our radar defences. And if it is, that means the Russian ICBMS are on their way over the pole right now. You understand me? They're going to blow the living shit right out of everything around here, son. This place is going to look like the surface of the moon in about twenty minutes. Now, dammit boy, we have to think damage control. I want you to put that thing back on the truck and haul it out of here."

"But where would we take it, Sir?"

"Up there." The sergeant pointed north. "Over the god-damn border, that's where. They'll never think to look there."

"Who, Sir?"

"The Russians, you idiot."

"I'll drive," the sensitive young soldier volunteered. He was thinking about a chance to see Betty Unger.

"I told you to get the fuck away from me," said the sergeant. "Jesus," he took off his helmet to rub his forehead, "I got such a fuckin' headache." He leaned against the fuselage of the rocket with his other arm. At the precise instant his finger-tips came into contact with the missile, the stored-up electrical charge it contained immediately realized that it had found a way to get to ground, as all charges of electricity wish to do, and promptly used the sergeant's body as a conduit. He sparked like a cartoon skeleton and fell silently into the maw of the open silo pit.

Before any of the men had time to react, a Cadillac convertible travelling at high speed veered off the dirt road, careened up onto a mound of dirt piled up next to the missile silo, became airborne, and struck the rocket full force twenty feet off the ground. The missile, with the car stuck to it, swung in a large graceful arc like the pendulum of a giant grandfather clock. The occupants of the vehicle appeared to be two men in some sort of embrace. They fell backward out of the car just as the rocket swung back and disappeared into the hole after the sergeant. No one saw the 8mm camera, still rolling, fly out of the car and land in the hands of the sensitive young soldier. He caught it like a football, promptly turned it off and stuffed it in his packsack. He would use it to film the quaint little village and send it, camera and all, to his sister Alice. Show her the place where he'd chosen to start his new life. Alice lived with her husband and children in Dallas. He'd been staying with them when he got his notice that he'd been drafted into the army. He would get Betty to film him saying he was okay and not to worry. Maybe get some footage of Betty as well, walking toward him down the shady street.

Alice would be relieved to discover that her brother was all right, but she would worry that he was still a fugitive from justice. As for the camera, she and her husband would find – after taking a few spools of film (dad goofing around with the kids in the pool, mom bringing in the birthday cake, the family dog running across the lawn) – that it really wasn't good for much and sell it at a yard sale to a man named Zapruder.

On the next swing the last of the straps holding the rocket in place let go. The missile lurched, dropped several feet, lurched again, then swept the crumpled car ahead of it into the gaping hole before plunging into the silo along with it. There was a tremendous cacophony of dust and noise. The commotion of metal tearing. Concrete collapsing. And then nothing at all. Only the sound of Dickie's note.

THE LIGHTNING BOLT that struck and instantly killed Dickie Derksen turned out to be only the most spectacular of three. Another, much smaller bolt had flashed out from behind the cloud and struck the top of the Minuteman II Missile about to be lowered into the underground silo. The rocket, hanging as it was from an enormous harness, strapped in on all sides, and suspended from the rubber-tired crane, had simply absorbed the energy and stored it up for future use. Held the tremendous charge of static electricity in escrow until such time as it found a means to deposit it into ground.

The warhead attached to the rocket, fully armed, had at no time been in danger of exploding. The lighting bolt had no effect whatsoever on it. It was really a very difficult and tedious process to make an atomic bomb detonate. The net effect of the lightning strike, then, was merely to charge the entire rocket, bomb and all, with enough electricity so that the next person who came into direct contact with it would be instantly electrocuted in the same way Dickie Derksen had just been. That person was the sergeant. His headache was gone now, because he was at the bottom of a tremendous pile of rubble, buried under the crumpled ruins of the brand new Cadillac, the massive wreck of the broken Minuteman II nuclear missile, sandwiched between the battered and bloodied bodies of Harry and the real estate agent, all of them smothered in solid fuel rocket propellant.

Another charge of lightning had escaped from the front of the cloud at precisely the same instant and struck the top of the gigantic television tower – still busy broadcasting its network television programming – and momentarily turned the tip a bright orange. It had done no actual damage, except to briefly and radically alter and intensify the electromagnetic waves the tower was emitting. The effect of these mutated emissions was quite startling. When they reached Cornie Martens, for instance, in the middle of his yawn, he began to shiver and vibrate. His mouth opened wider than it ever had before. The radio waves emanating from his cavities were more powerful than he could ever have imagined.

So there was the tremendous note coming from the already dead, but still erect and vocalizing Dickie Derksen. Add to that the momentarily altered and magnified signals coming from the television tower. Finally, throw in the intensified waves coming from the mouth of the yawning Cornie Martens, fresh from the back seat of Abe Wiebe's car. The beams of energy from these three sources, by sheer coincidence, converged at a focal point precisely where ground zero would have been in the event of an atomic detonation. There, high above the valley floor, they met each other and congealed into a metamorphic ultra-high frequency pulse the likes of which was unprecedented. Even the scientists so busy explaining how everything that seemed remarkable in the natural world was really just ordinary were going to have trouble explaining this one to people.

The synchronicitous convergence of necessary and sufficient conditions required to produce it had never occurred before. Would never occur again. It was a once-in-the-universe event. The only thing even remotely close to it had occurred on January 17, 1877, in Salsburg, Austria, at the home of a composer named Ludwig Von Beethoven. It consisted of a momentary wormhole that travelled up through the floor of his studio, became magnified by the tightly drawn strings of the piano he was sitting at, and burrowed its way into the cochlea of his inner ear. He was stone deaf by that time, and wasn't supposed to be able to hear anything at all, but here was the unmistakable sound of something turning, whining. He had never heard anything so unearthly before. The official scientific explanation would have been that he was merely suffering from tinnitus, which he was. There was, indeed, the constant noise of ringing in his ears – a high-pitched whining hum and buzz that never left him, all possibility of hearing replaced by just that. But this was altogether different. There was only one explanation for what he was hearing. He was listening, he realized, to nothing less than the sound of the universe spinning on its axis. The music of the cosmos. Of God himself. The notes came furiously after that. *"Uberm sternen zelt,"* the sopranos would sing, *"muss ein lieber vater vohnen."*

The effect of Dickie's note, amplified out of all proportion by the freak waves from the energized television tower, augmented by the frequencies coming out of the yawning Cornie Marten's mouth, formed a triad which combined to create a superwave of pulsating electromagnetic energy. The sheer power of this tremendous beam of rarefied energy was sufficient to temporarily paralyze any functions performed by electrical devices or equipment in the vicinity.

Everything shut down. Everything went dead. All the motors on all of the machines in the valley – gas, diesel, electric – died simultaneously. Everything was knocked out, including the television sets. All motors and radios, all telephones and fridges, all stoves and cream separators and church organs. All the engines of post-war technology had to stop what they were doing. The note rendered the same effect sometimes reported by individuals who claimed to have experienced close encounters with alien visitors. A particularly astute UFO investigator had already determined that a disproportionate number of sightings occurred near television towers and transmission lines, but they had yet to discover that, in an even more surprising development, a large percentage of those reporting such close encounters happened to be on their way home from the dentist.

Even the fighter planes high up in the sky went into a prolonged, unpowered, glide. While the waves travelled through the upper atmosphere, the high and heavy whine of the B-52 flying fortresses ceased. The false thunder of the F101-B-Voodoos fell silent. Above and below, across the entire valley, everything froze under the rarefied waves of fused energy.

All across the valley people were rising from their maddoch schlope, and getting ready to sit down to fastba. A few stragglers had stayed behind in their bedrooms, still watching their newly acquired television sets, but the note soon put an end to that. Everyone had to stop what they were doing. Everything stopped. There was only the awesome reverberation of Dickie's B flat.

Men and women and children emerged from housebarns and stood on porches, in the doorways of summer kitchens, in the middle of yards, on back steps, and looked up into the sky. Listened. Wondered. Beasts, too. Cows and chickens and dogs and cats. Birds and bees and dung beetles. Even in the trees, the great cottonwoods that towered over everything, the leaves

213

ceased their rustling. All was quiet. Not so much as a shiver or a quiver in any living thing. And yet, none were fearful. Children did not cower. Dogs did not whimper. Peace settled over the valley. Unimaginable, unfathomable peace.

Anyone with the slightest inclination toward epiphany accomplished as much on the spot. Dickie's mother was no exception. Even as she watched her son's stumpy body topple over stiffly, silently – still singing, arms positioned perfectly, one at his waist, one above his head – she had a profound, insight. It was a terrible irony, she realized, that only at the moment of his death had her son found a way to reveal to the world the enormity of his gift.

The fact was that everybody was really thinking the same thing. It only seemed different to them. Merely manifested itself in different ways. Something like the idea Katie had been reading about in *Mind, Knowledge, and The Nature of Nature,* her latest book of philosophy. The author claimed that it was possible for a group of people to be looking at something yellow, for each of them to identify it as being the colour yellow, and yet, for each of them to be seeing a different colour. Only none of them knew it. Could ever know it.

In fact, it was nothing like that at all. Even epistemology and metaphysics had been temporarily suspended. Everything Katie, or anyone else for that matter, had read on those two subjects was suddenly of no consequence. The idea of knowing something became meaningless. The same for belief. For faith. To say of an idea that it was a fact, a belief, an opinion, ceased to have meaning. Ideas about particular or individual pieces of knowledge vapourized. To speak of that which was possible as opposed to that which was not made no sense. Truth, for the moment, rested not in knowledge or belief, not in the abstract or the concrete, not in black and white or colour, not in pleasure or pain, because Dickie's note had put a moratorium on all such phenomena.

People were really all just thinking one thing. The same thing Mr. Beethoven had tried so hard to explain to the world in his ninth symphony. The one he wrote after his dysfunctional hearing apparatus had been invaded by cosmic beams. *Seit umschlungen, millionen,* he wrote. *Diesen kuss der ganzen welt.*

All across the valley, notions typically associated with thought – conjecture, hypothesis, theory, logic – had been suspended. For one brief moment it was another kind of consciousness that was ruling people's minds. It came from a place in their collective subconscious they almost never bothered to look. A place that belonged not to the presence of something, but to its absence. To the world of silence. Of stillness. There, in what people thought of more and more as negative space, lay the one true wish they hadn't known they had. The one all their actions were really trying to make come true. All acts of art, commerce, cruelty, forgiveness, religion. All of them wishes, really. The unspoken desire to become one flesh. One body. One soul.

As for things like the rocket, and the jet fighters and television tower, they might as well have ceased to exist so long as Dickie's note hovered over the valley. The physical world of man-made technology became redundant. It was – at that precise moment – of no consequence. All of its beauty and ugliness became static, like one of the old photographs Martha disdained so much. The entire domain of technology, and all the teleology that went with it, was nothing more than an idea – and not a particularly compelling one at that.

All over the valley, and even down into the States, people were having epiphanies. People who had never had one in their lives – never would have but for this rare moment. Most of them were people who wouldn't have known an epiphany if it came up and bit them on the ass, and so a lot of them mistook it for something else. Something pleasant, like the feeling

215

just before or after a good meal, or sex, or an enjoyable book, or a particularly pleasant bowel movement.

Clearly something was happening, but no one was sure exactly what it was. And inside each of them, something felt different. They, each of them, felt more whole than they ever had in their entire lives. Felt that they had come to a place that was special. And all of this because the waves that had passed through their bodies were of a different kind than they had ever experienced.

The hard-core scientists would have attempted to explain that there was really nothing supernatural going on. That the super-conductive electromagnetic waves created by the combination of Dickie Derksen's note and Cornie Marten's mouth and the television tower had managed to access, directly, the wiring every human being had for experiencing spiritual revelation. Everyone had it, they would insist. They just didn't know it. Even psychopaths like Harry. The only difference, they would claim, was that his wiring was faulty.

Fortunately, none of this mattered to the people having the experience. They were too busy feeling things, unexplainable things. Feelings of worth. Of dignity. Of sanctity. Everything and everyone became, for one brief moment, sacred. Each soul became a sanctuary for every other soul. There was, in everyone, an unexplainable feeling of love for the entire universe. They were, each of them, part of something much bigger. Dickie had created something that would not soon be duplicated. The taste of it was indescribable. A small sliver off the secret cake of life.

Luckily the whole thing lasted only a few seconds. Lucky because the world would never have been able to stand itself for more than a few short seconds under such demanding conditions. Such a heightened state of enlightenment. When it was over things would pretty much go back to the way they always had been. Almost. But not exactly. The silence that followed the note of the wail would be just a little deeper than anything that had preceded it. A little more profound. Even though it didn't feel like it, things would be ever-so-slightly altered. People would go back to being cruel to each other, insensitive, unkind, dismissive, coarse, crude – but perhaps, hardly detectable, infinitesimally less cruel, infinitesimally less often, infinitesimally less willingly. They would find it just the tiniest bit more difficult to execute acts of barbarism. The necessary and sufficient conditions required to manufacture a monster like Harry, for example, would have been reduced by the minutest factor.

And the thing that all of them were thinking? While they were listening to Dickie's note? Whether they were having a profound and life-altering awakening, or just a little kink in their psyche; whether they were in the middle of an orgasm, or at the moment of their death? What all of them – even people like the Zacharias sisters – were thinking, while the spectacular note filled them so completely, was: "Yum."

ALL ACROSS THE VALLEY, people were having epiphanies. When Dickie's note reached them their reactions varied, depending on how they were wired and what they were doing at the time. For most it was a quiet moment of reflection and revelation. For some, it was more intense. Everybody felt something. The feeling was so delicious that it intensified those already engaged in such pastimes. For many, it was just that the air had never been so fresh, or food so tasty, or the song of a bird so lovely. Others were wired for deeper experiences. Things they'd never felt before. Thought before. Of course, it was all tangled up in whatever they were doing at the moment. Whatever was occupying their consciousness.

For Steven Zacharias, it was a feeling of intense climax, since Betty had finally succeeded in bringing things to a conclusion. He thought at first he might be making the noise him-self, since he was experiencing a kind of titillation he'd never known. The lightning and thunder, and then Dickie's note in behind it, were like a thrilling symphonic finale to the moment. As for Betty, the acrid aroma of fresh semen, mingled with ozone in the air caused by the lightning, and the musky dampness of the roots at the base of the rogue cottonwood tree all smelled to her like life, and deepened her fixation.

The tremendous concussion had made her pull her head up quickly. The young poet, propped up on his elbows, saw the smaller charge strike the top of the rocket. From his angle it appeared to strike the tip of his erect penis, still erupting, as well. He winced and sat up. Listened to the sound of Dickie's note wafting across the valley.

"Do you hear that?" he said.

"Hmmm," said Betty dreamily. Thunder was still rattling around inside her skull. "I'm surprised I can hear anything," she said.

"Listen."

They stood up. The Pembina Hills in behind them had turned a spectacular purple as sunlight washed down across the face of the slopes in the wake of the cloud.

"What is it?" said Betty.

"Some kind of note," said Steven. "Some kind of singing."

"But where's it coming from?"

"It seems to be everywhere."

"Look," said Betty, and pointed. "What's that?"

They could make out Dickie's stumpy outline in the dis-tance. He appeared to be performing some kind of crazy acro-batic stunt. Even more unusual, there appeared to be a thin and misty plume of smoke rising from the top of his head.

"Come on," said Steven, and took Betty up by the hand.

"Where are we going?"

They ran out from under the shelter of the cottonwood

tree, and across the open countryside toward Dickie, while the note of incredible beauty and grace reverberated across the valley and echoed up into the hills, carried on the rarefied and electrified airwaves just in behind the thunder. And even as they ran toward Dickie, the feelings inside the young poet were the first inklings of an idea that would spread across the valley, the continent. And he, Steven, was going to be the first minstrel of its song. He would, literally, take the idea and run with it. Spread the word to places like San Francisco and Vancouver. The word would be love. And the motto would be: Make love, not war.

THE PREACHER, on his way to kill Abe Wiebe, was still walking down the street, soaking wet, when the rain stopped as suddenly as it had started. The sun came out. When he looked up, a brilliant shaft of light blazed down out of the sky, directly onto the modest steeple of the white church. It lit up the glistening, galvanized roofing and it seemed to the preacher the whole building was awash in the light of the Lord. It was a remarkable moment of grace for him. It could have been more than that – a moment of deep spiritual awakening that turned him into a new kind of man. Unfortunately he lacked the capacity for that kind of conversion, and had to settle for something less spectacular. The best he could manage, given his lack of vision, was to change his mind about the word lover. Perhaps there might be something to be said for it after all.

He would break his promise. The one he'd made never to let himself go that way again. He would leave off resisting. Allow himself to give in to the possibilities of carnal pleasure. What was faith, after all, if not a kind of giving up? Submission. Letting go. Who was he to deny himself such a possibility?

The end result was that he threw his gun down, not because he was repulsed now by the sight of it, by the idea that only a moment ago he had wanted to use it to do harm to a fellow human being. No. He threw it down because he was repulsed by the idea that he might have used it and inadvertently robbed himself of this opportunity for enlightenment.

He would go back to his wife, back to the bed where she lay sleeping, wake her, and ask her to pray with him. Pray for understanding and guidance in the new arena of love they were about to embark on. Then they would make love again. Give themselves over to the moment. Without malice. Without anger.

The preacher had no idea what he was in for. His wife, waiting for him to come back to bed, unaware that he had slipped out of the house with his gun, was going to get what she'd always wanted. A chance to strut her stuff in bed. He was going to let her try things she'd always wanted to do. Have her way with him for once, and in the process, she was going to give him – and herself – more pleasure than either one had ever dreamed possible. Fingers would dance across terrain previously untraversed. Tongues would explore orifices never before ventured into. New sexual frontiers would be crossed on a weekly basis. It would be the first of many Sunday afternoons of spectacular lovemaking, the best kept secret in the village. That in the bedroom of the most pious couple in town, sexual adventure ran rampant. Even the shared fantasies of the Zacharias sisters would fall short of the lusty and vigorous copulation that took place there. The only giveaway would be the occasional cry of delight, of joy or pain that escaped from the open bedroom window. If the sisters thought the noises coming from the preacher's house unusually primal, they would attribute them to speaking in tongues, something they themselves practised from time to time, or possibly self-flagellation, another favourite of theirs.

The one stipulation the preacher had was that they must restrict their lovemaking to Sunday afternoons. It would henceforth be remarked by more than one parishioner that the preacher's wife appeared to be getting younger and fresher every week, that they could not recall her sitting through the service with such a smile on her face. That she must surely have come into a state of grace, as if the very light of the Lord were shining out of her. God, they would surmise, was surely visiting his spirit upon her. What the preacher's wife had visiting upon her were, in fact, tiny precoital orgasms, as she anticipated the wild ride she was going to take on her husband's adequate, if not spectacular, erection in only another hour or so.

For Martha, it happened at the moment she heard the note, felt the lightning flash across her full-bodied nakedness, heard the camera click. The note filled up the room, filled her up, the way nothing else ever had, penetrated every pore of her being. For a moment she thought of her body as not merely her own, but the body of every woman, everywhere. As belonging to one thing. One entity. The note sang into the deepest recesses of her energized body. Into places she had never thought existed. And with it, finally, in a rush of juices and shivering flesh, the thing she'd been trying so hard to give herself for so long.

The cry of her ecstasy, when it came, blended in beautiful harmony with the note coming through the open window. A spectacular fusion of pitch and timbre. Waves of sound overlapping, intertwining. She was caught up in something. Something big. It went on and on, wave after wave, each crest punctuated by a tremendous pouring forth. Sound multiplying the sensation. Sensation multiplying the sound. A symbiosis of crackling energy.

MARTHA'S FATHER ISAAC, in his own room down at the end of the hall, heard all of this glorious noise-making and sat up in bed.

"What is it," he said in Plaut Dietsch. "That what there singing does. That hears me oh but very fine." Said it like a little boy. Just to himself. To hear the sound of his own voice as a way of reassuring himself. "That are the angels, no."

So far as Isaac was concerned, these unearthly musical trumpetings were in all likelihood the last thing he would hear. He had decided that he must be dying, breathing his last few breaths. The Lord had come to call him home in spectacular fashion. His experience of death would manifest itself in biblical proportions. He was making one more failed attempt to get it right.

"They come now." He meant the angels of the Lord. "Now must I with go, that hears me."

He allowed himself to fall back onto the pillow. "Fire of evening," he said in Plaut Dietsch. "Home to sleep." He closed his eyes and a long, shallow breath trailed out from between his lips.

KATIE, standing with the children in the doorway of the school, had much same reaction that Abe had when he saw her yellow convertible glistening in the sun. All of her wiring was preoccupied with one overriding thought. He was here. He, too, had come back. This was a pilgrimage. All the intellectualization she had constructed, she understood, had been a ruse. All that business with the study of metaphysics. Of epistemology. Trying to distinguish the real from the imagined. All that had been the cosmic equivalent of smoke and mirrors. She hadn't come back to see whether the place was still real. The place she'd come from. Would always be from. She had come back to find out whether she, Katie, was still real. That she hadn't slipped away – like Marilyn. Had not disappeared. And yet, that must be the very thing she did now. And he must do it, too. If only they could make themselves small enough, long enough, to find a way. A way to make each fit the other.

It wouldn't come down to words this time. Words about what he wanted or she wanted. It was words that had caused all the trouble last time. Had gotten in the way. It was going to have to go beyond that. They were going to have to make themselves smaller than that. There wasn't anything she needed to tell him he didn't already know about her. Nothing that had happened to either of them in the intervening time would make any difference. None of that was important now. None of that mattered. She found herself in a state of controlled excitement. Quiet giddiness.

THE YOUNG PRESIDENTIAL AIDE stepped into the Oval Office and walked briskly up to the desk. Jack Kennedy sat up in his chair and the makeup woman stopped what she was doing. She stepped back a little and exchanged glances with the aide. The secret service men glanced over at Elby.

"Mr. President," said the young aide, "there's a call for you."

"Not now. Can't you see I'm busy?"

"I think you'd better take it, sir."

"Excuse me?" said Elby from his chair. "Did you hear what the man said?"

The aide stared straight ahead, a complete lack of emotion on her face. "It's SAC on the line, Mr. President. Grand Forks, North Dakota."

"North Dakota? said Elby. "Where the hell is that and what have we got up there?"

"Minuteman Missiles, sir," said the aide. "Quite a lot of them." There was just the tiniest hint of sarcasm in her tone.

"I heard something about that," said Elby.

"I think you'd better talk to them, Sir."

"All right, put it on the speaker phone. Hello.... Hello?... I can't hear you."

"What in Sam Hill?" said Elby. There was a highly unusual sound coming out of the speaker phone, like nothing any of them had ever heard before. Dickie Derksen's incredible, augmented, B flat – even filtered through all that electronic gadgetry – was unmistakable.

"What is it?" said the president.

"That's what I'm calling about, Mr. President," said the voice on the other end of the line. "It seems to be coming from the missile site. We have a direct line patched through, sir. I thought you should hear it."

"Missile site?"

"Yes, Sir. One thirty-seven, to be precise. There's been an incident."

"Incident?"

"Yes, sir. One thirty-seven appears to have sustained some kind of attack."

Elby's chair came off the wall with a thump. "Jesus Christ," he said. "They've gone and done it. The goddamn commie bastards have gone and done it. I knew it. I hate to say I told you so." He looked at the president.

"Now hold on, Elby," said the president, "let's not jump the gun here."

The suits put on their jackets and buttoned them.

"Goddamit," said Elby, and stomped his cowboy boot down on the floor while he poured himself another drink.

"Any casualties?" said the president.

"I'm afraid so, Mr. President."

"But what the Christ is that Gawdawful noise?" said Elby

into the speaker phone.

"We don't know. But we've lost all our power over here. Everything's down. We think the noise has something to do with it."

"But what is it?" said Elby.

"A B flat," said the aide.

"What the hell are you talking about?" said Elby.

"The pitch, sir. The note. It's a B flat." The aide also happened to be a highly trained musician. She had, in fact, given up a promising career as a concert pianist to come to Washington and enlist as a member of the president's personal entourage. All she wanted now was to be near him. She was ready to throw herself in front of a bullet to protect him, if it came down to that. Her family didn't understand any of it. She didn't really understand it either, except that she'd seen him on television one evening, felt a deep personal connection, and made up her mind then and there about what she wanted to do. It was happening to so many young people in the country that they'd come up with the idea for the Peace Corps just to get them off the streets of Washington.

"Nobody gives a rat's ass about that," said Elby. "What we want to know is – what the Christ is it? What the hell is making it?"

The sound wasn't having much of an effect on Elby, or on any of the other men in the room. They didn't have the wiring for it. But the young aide and the president were different. They were particularly attuned to its frequency, just like some of the people back in the village.

The young aide heard, along with the note, a ringing in her ears, something she'd never heard before. It was not unpleasant. It sounded to her like the music of the stars. As though she were listening to the constant high-pitched whine of the universe spinning on its axis. She found herself humming Beethoven. The Ninth Symphony, to be precise. The *Ode*

*To Joy.* Mouthing the words to herself. *Bruder,* she mouthed. It looked to an outsider as if she were puckering her lips at the president. The men in the room elbowed each other and snickered.

"*Bruder,*" she sang out loud.

"Brooder?" said Elby. "What in the hell are you talking about, little girl?"

"*Fruede schoener goetterfunken tauchter aus eeliesium,*" she sang. Felt the words and music reaching across a great span of time and into her soul.

"Would you get her hell out of here?" said Elby to one of the men.

"No. Wait," said the president. "I want to hear this."

The makeup woman smiled at the aide. At the tenderness in her voice, her words. It certainly wasn't something she'd seen much of in Hollywood.

The noise ceased abruptly. Nothing but silence.

"What's happened? Are you still there? Hello?" said Elby into the phone.

"It's stopped, Mr. President," said the voice on the speaker. "Just a moment. Wait. Things appear to have returned to normal. I have a report that all systems are back up and running. Everything seems to be under control, sir."

"Thank God."

"No imminent danger."

"Fine. That's fine."

"Sorry to disturb you, Mr. President."

"No trouble at all, soldier. Glad to be of help."

"Thank you. Mr. President."

"Don't mention it." He pressed a button on the phone.

"Will that be all, Mr. President?" said the aide. She wanted to get back to work, sorting and puttering and fretting for him in the outer office.

"Get me Moscow," he said to her.

"And I don't want to talk to anyone but Khrushchev him-self. Make that clear."

"Yes, sir."

"Well?"

"But what about the television broadcast?"

"That will have to wait. Just get me Moscow on the phone."

"Now hold on there," said Elby. "I thought we agreed you were all done talking to that commie bastard?"

"I've changed my mind."

"About what, exactly?"

"The whole thing. All of it."

"Christ, Jack, you can't do that."

"I can. I have. Something just came clear to me."

Jack Kennedy had decided that he was going to call up Nikita Khrushchev one last time. Talk to him – human being to human being. Tell him that they should both take their fingers off the button. That it wasn't worth it. It never had been. It never would be. He was going to reach across that newly erected wall with an olive branch.

"I think you're making an excellent decision," said the young aide.

"If anybody gives a rat's ass what you think," said Elby, "you'll be the first to know. Will somebody please get her the hell on out of here before I do something I'm gonna be sorry for."

"I'll get you Moscow immediately, Mr. President," said the aide. She smiled triumphantly at Elby, and made her way to the door.

"You goddamn cunt," said Elby, and went for her. She stopped in mid-stride. Stood her ground. A couple of secret service men grabbed Elby by the arms, held him in check. "When I get you alone," he leaned closer to her, "I'm gonna tear you a new asshole."

"Excuse me, Mr. Vice-President," she said, her voice steady,

"I have a call to make." When she'd gone Elby pulled his arms free of the agents and walked over to the bar to pour himself another drink.

The president smiled to himself while he waited for the call to come through. He felt as happy as he had in a long time. It was the space between people that was causing all the trouble, he realized. And if he, Jack Kennedy, could do anything to get rid of it, it was his sworn duty as a public servant to do just that. When this was all settled he wasn't going to stop there. He was going to get out and start meeting people. Take Jackie along for a change. He was going to start getting more involved. Travel the country. The world. Say hello to folks. Shake their hands. Look them in the eye. Talk to them. Really talk. He thought he might even go down to Texas. Meet some of Elby's people. Find out what made them tick.

A BE WIEBE, transfixed by the sparkling yellow convertible in Katie Klassen's yard, finally understood why he had come back. It was clear to him now that all the business with schlopebanks and missile silos and bored American housewives had been just so much window dressing. All along it had been something else. True, he'd never been completely free of the valley. Never would be. He'd admitted that much to himself long ago. But now, for the first time, he found himself face to face with the much more compelling admission – that it was really something else he'd come back for. The possiblity of it.

When he saw that the angry little cloud had missed the road where it crossed the border, and that it would be possible to use the shortcut, he signalled the Martens brothers to get back into the car and they sped off.

"What happened?" said Cornie. By that time he was back

to normal, no worse for wear, except that he was very tired. He didn't really remember much.

"You don't remember?"

"No."

"You did that thing again."

"What thing?"

The intensity of the note, and his role in its creation and execution, had caused a temporary malfunction in his short-term memory.

"You know, with your mouth."

"I did?" Cornie rubbed a hand across his shiny jaw, which was sore.

"Only this time there was some other stuff along with it."

"What other stuff."

"It's like you were part of something...I don't know...something bigger."

It wouldn't be until much later that it began to come back to him. Quick flashes that would make him want to weep uncontrollably. These episodes would be mercifully few, but remain with him for the rest of his life.

"Bigger?"

"There was this...this sound."

Cornie looked at him uncomprehendingly. "You mean something from the tower."

"No. It was something else. It was – bigger."

"Bigger."

"It's hard to explain. Kind of like a voice. Like singing. And you were part of the song. Like you were frozen into it."

Abe wasn't paying attention. All circuitry of his brain, all its computational power, was preoccupied by only one thing at the moment. All he could think about was the fact that Katie was so near. About the possibilities it presented. Things he'd always dreaded and secretly hoped. He was busy just now running through the multitude of scenarios. What his first words would be. If he could get them out. If she gave him the chance. If he pulled up to the house and she was standing there next to her yellow convertible. If it really was Katie. And he saw her that way. Just standing there waiting for him to say something. That would be the hardest thing. It would be all he could do to breathe at that moment, never mind say something. Just pull air into his lungs and push it out again.

What if he moved toward her a little? What would be her reaction? Would she freeze him on the spot with one look? Or would the laws of physics take over? Propel him toward her. He'd never entirely escaped the pull of her gravity, that was certain. Had always been in orbit around her, however distant, like a comet. And now she would be so near. The pull so strong.

What if she let him come close enough to see the flecks of hazel that were bound to sparkle out of her impossibly green eyes? Oh, the ache of that. Or worse, what if she spoke? Would he be able to hear the words? Or would they be undecipherable, lost on their way to his ears by the movement of her lips, the look of her mouth, the flicker of her tongue between such excellent white teeth. What if she said something terribly important? And he missed it? Couldn't make himself hear it? Comprehend it. Respond to it.

Abe drove right by the chaos of the missile site without so much as a second glance. He wasn't the least bit interested at the moment. The prospect of atomic warfare was of no concern to him. All ideas of finality, of last chances, hinged only on the possibilities presented by a shiny yellow convertible parked at the edge of the village.

"Hey, look at that," said Jake. He was looking out the window at the carnage of the missile site.

"Holy shit," said Cornie. "What the hell happened?"

"Looks like there was an accident."

"You can say that again."

The young soldiers at the missile site didn't care about any car driving by. They were all in one form of shock or another. There was a lot of confusion. Some of them were milling around the maw of the open silo like crazed ants around a wounded queen. Some knelt at the edge of the pit, staring down into it. Some stood frozen to the spot, stunned looks on their faces. The tip of the rocket portruded from the ground at an odd angle while the frayed ends of the crane straps flapped in the breeze above it. A car horn honked unendingly from someplace deep under the ground.

They'd lost their commanding officer, and the technology they'd worked so hard to assemble lay in ruins. If Abe's car had been another vehicle intent upon further sabotage it could have accomplished as much without the slightest resistance. No one expected a second attack.

"That's a hell of a mess."

"Hey, look." Jake pointed at something on the road ahead. "What is it?"

"It's that guy's hat. The guy from the bar." The real estate agent's hat had blown off just before impact and now it was lying in the middle of the road. Abe didn't stop. Didn't even slow down. Flattened the hat with both sets of tires. He took the car through the ravine and up the other side, onto the nearly deserted village street. No one there knew yet that Dickie had been struck by lightning. No one knew about the two men killed instantly by the preacher's stray bullet. A rogue bullet that was even now on its way to do more damage at some unknown time. Some unknown location.

There was still a little water dripping off the cottonwood trees, but the sun was out and everything smelled fresh. Abe took a deep breath. There was something about the smell of the village. Something familiar, yet new. Katie's yellow convertible sat on the green green grass in front of her parents' abandoned house. It sparkled in the brilliant sunshine. The rain had not touched it.

Abe stopped his car and got out. Cornie and Jake got out, too.

"We'll walk from here," said Cornie.

"We have to go get cleaned up now," said Jake.

"We're getting our pictures taken. Over at Aunt Martha's."

"Fine," said Abe. "I'll see you later."

The two of them walked away down the street and left Abe to stand there, which he seemed quite content to do. He watched the two of them until he saw them turn off the road and disappear behind the cottonwood trees. He was about to step into the yard when he saw a woman in a yellow dress coming toward him from the far end of the village. She was a good distance away, but he knew instantly that it was her. Saw the way she burned. There was a girl in a pink dress with her, running up ahead of her, hopping and skipping. Hers? He didn't care. He turned and walked toward her, his heart hammering against his chest.

Katie walked along the shady village street from the opposite direction. Tilli Nickel had sent all the children home. The girl in the pink dress was just about to run into her own house to tell her mother about the beautiful angel who had rescued them from the storm. Miss Nickel had gone back to bed to try and finish her dream. She wanted to get back to the funeral. Wanted to see whether Katie Klassen had been one of the women in her dream.

Katie's mind was racing. It had started the second she'd figured out who Tilli Nickel was talking about. A lot of it, she'd already decided, would have be settled without words. The usual expectations for a scripted first exchange would have to be cast aside. All talk of lost chances. Of prizes. Of what was lost and won. None of that would do. And most important, there would be no talk of forgiveness. It was long past the time for that. After all, what, really, was there to forgive? Except everything. And nothing.

What if all he did was hold his arms to her? What then? Those great sculpted hands reaching for her. Would the power of such a gesture defeat her completely? Rekindle all the same feelings? Make her forget everything she had taught herself about control?

When she saw Abe coming toward her, she stopped. Knew instantly who it was. Couldn't breathe.

"What's the matter?" said the girl in the pink dress.

"Nothing," said Katie, shocked at the completely foreign sound of her own voice. "I'm fine."

"Come on," said the girl in the pink dress, when they'd resumed walking again. "Just a little further. My house is that one." She pointed, but Katie wasn't following the line of her finger. She was calling upon all her powers of concentration just to put one foot in front of the other. The road was a shiny ribbon. It seemed suddenly slippery. It was all she could do to keep from falling off. How could she possibly hope to stay on it long enough to come face to face with the man coming toward her? Especially since the street was so deserted. There was no one else around. Why?

A car came up the street behind them. Honked its horn. They stepped off to the side to let it pass, but a red shiny convertible pulled up next to them and stopped. The woman behind the wheel – made-up, attractive – started to say something, stopped, mouth open, looked at Katie for a full five seconds, froze, then she seemed to shake herself free before she looked down at the girl in the pink dress. "Hi, honey," she said, "I'm looking for a man named Abe Wiebe. Do you know if he lives around here?"

She took out a cigarette and lit it, inhaled deeply and blew the smoke in Katie's direction. "He makes benches," she said. She held the cigarette out wide while she looked down the front of her blouse, brushed at something there. "You know him?" She threw a strand of hair back from her face, checked her lipstick in the mirror.

"Sure," said the girl in the pink dress. She'd just seen Abe Wiebe walking gingerly toward them. "That's him right there."

"Well, what do you know?" said the woman. "Thanks, honey," she said, threw the cigarette down at Katie's feet, and just before she drove off, she looked at Katie defiantly, as one woman does to another when there's something she wants her to know. Something she wants to give away.

By the time she'd pulled even with Abe – who didn't give her so much as a sideways glance but kept right on walking, staring straight ahead – Katie had turned to jog, then run, back along the street, into the first house that looked familiar through the haze of her vision, and there was Aunt Martha, of all people, as if she'd been waiting for her all this time. And Katie did what she'd done all those years ago – as if no time had passed in between – and threw herself on Martha's ample shoulders.

The Zacharias sisters watched it all from the window of their darkened kitchen, teacups and saucers in hand.

"That took a nasty turn."

"I'll say."

"Got what she deserved."

"What did she expect?"

"What goes around comes around."

"Gone to blubber about it to Martha."

"A lot of good that'll do her."

"I suppose she'll go back where she came from now."

"Do you think?" There was an air of regret in this conjecture.

"Back to that Holy Wood.

"You mean Hollywood."

"What?"

"It's Hollywood."

"What did I say?"

"You said Holy Wood."

"Oh."

When Abe saw that Katie had turned he took off on a run after her. He wanted to catch her. Explain to her. But he would sound ridiculous. What sense would it make to say that it was only because he needed to be in the company of a beautiful woman from time to time? How it was like fresh air to him. What would it sound like, if not a cowardly lie, to try and tell her that it had only been one disappointment after another? That he had never been able to breathe in the air of any other woman without it becoming stale. Choking him.

He ran for only a short distance before one of the village boys, gesturing and shouting, grabbed him by the sleeve and told him to come quickly. Something about an accident. Out in the pasture. Something terrible had happened to Dickie Derksen.

# PART *five*

ON THE DAY OF THE FUNERAL, THE ELDERS sat up at the front of the church, stiff in their long black coats, like so many badly shaven undertakers. The church was packed. Funerals, always popular in the valley, ranked even higher than weddings in the hierarchy of social occasions. They inevitably generated more enthusiasm, evoked more intense feelings than even the most elaborate wedding could muster. The collective consciousness of the valley was chock full of oppression, suffering, death and destruction – almost all of it on the part of their ancestors – and the inhabitants were always willing to invest more of themselves in sorrow than celebration. The fact that this was the funeral of someone who himself had been a victim of suffering and oppression all his life only added to the already charged atmosphere. People like the Zacharias sisters were beside themselves with anticipation. It was all they could do to maintain some sense of decorum and not tear off their clothes, babble in tongues, and fling their naked bodies against each other, as they occasionally did within the more private confines of their home.

The preacher had never seen so many people in the church. He took it as a sign of his importance in the religious life of the community. The church elders considered it proof of the effectiveness of their vindictive and spiteful leadership. The fact was that a lot of the people in attendance were there not because of, but in spite of, them. Still, people like the preacher were always eager to take personal credit for something when the opportunity arose, and today was no exception. He was a typical cleric in that regard. He smiled ingratiatingly at his wife, who was sitting in the front row a few feet away from him.

By the time Dickie arrived in a shiny black limousine hearse, the church was so packed with men and women, boys and girls, that others had placed themselves strategically on the steps outside, on the grass next to the open windows, anywhere they could participate, even remotely, in the proceedings. According to the rumour that was circulating, Dickie was being buried in such fine style thanks to a secret benefactor. No less than the Zacharias sisters had it on good authority that the occasion was going to be particularly lavish thanks to a substantial donation made to the funeral home, with the proviso that the donor remain anonymous.

No less than the funeral director himself, a handsome and husky man with a fiercely righteous head of black hair, rolled the coffin in regally, opened the top half of the lid with utter grace and aplomb, and oversaw the placing of a number of elaborate bouquets around it. The casket itself was glorious. A gleaming swirl of cherrywood grain and polished brass, it was the most beautiful thing Agnus Derksen had ever seen. It glistened under the sunlight coming in through the open windows and reminded her of some marvellous gigantic maple walnut dessert Dickie would have dreamed of devouring. She wished he could see it. He had certainly never been surrounded by such luxury. Neither had she, for that matter. She imagined the coffin in her sparse sitting room, there for her to enjoy at her leisure. Any time she felt like it she could run her hands along the smooth polish of it, while she described to Dickie the regal luxury of his final resting place. But there would only be these precious few hours to enjoy it, and then she would never see it again. Would have to content herself with only the memory of such loveliness and elegance.

Dickie's stepfather was not in attendance. His absence at the funeral was attributed to drunkenness. No one missed him. Certainly not Agnus Derksen. If anything, she was relieved that her husband had, for all intents and purposes, vanished from the face of the earth. She had no idea he was at the bottom of a missile silo. It was going to take a while to dig him out of there, and his remains, when they were recovered, would become part of a massive, covert investigation into the events that led up to the destruction of Site 137. His body would be shipped, along with the those of the sergeant and the real estate agent, to Roswell, New Mexico, along with the other, larger pieces of evidence, such as the rocket, the warhead, and the convertible. The research would be conducted by the usual assortment of intelligence agencies, which meant that it had almost no chance of success.

In the interests of national security, and in order to keep publicity to a minimum, the site would be decommissioned. Once the debris and the bodies had been removed, the silo would simply be filled in with concrete and bulldozed over. The thinking was that since there were already enough nuclear missiles to bomb every man, woman, and child on earth back into the Stone Age several times over, one warhead more or less wasn't going to make much difference. The site would become just another abandoned military installation, one of the many hundreds and hundreds to dot the North American landscape by the end of the century. The land would be returned to the original owner on the condition that he return it to seed. The following summer, children playing among the hollyhocks at the edge of the village would once again be able to look over the border and see only waving wheat. A visitor unfamiliar with local history would never guess that a missile installation had once existed so close to the border. The only remaining evidence of its presence would be an exceptionally robust circle of wheat stalks where the silo had been, as if a giant cow-pie had once been deposited there. The effect would, in fact, be much the same, except that the added richness of the soil would be the result of phosphates left behind by the residue of the spilled solid rocket fuel propellant.

The viewing of the body was taking a long time. If people wanted to get a good look at Dickie, their curiosity was understandable. He had, after all, died in even more spectacular fashion than his father. But to their surprise, or disappointment perhaps, they discovered that not only had Dickie's face been remarkably well preserved, considering the ferocity and violence of his death, but dressed as he was in a sparkling new tuxedo, hands neatly folded across his massive chest, he looked positively handsome. Agnus Derksen thought he had never looked so good, and that it seemed a shame to bury him. There was a freshness about him that was striking. He appeared, more than merely happy or content, to be positively enraptured with some unseen entity in a way that animated his features, even in death.

The steady stream of people filing deferentially past the coffin reacted, again and again, with a mixture of surprise and disappointment, then moved on to offer their condolences to Agnus Derksen before returning to their pews. A lot of them were people who had never given her so much as a passing nod. But Agnus thanked them all in the same way, told them how much it would have meant to Dickie. If some of them seemed a little awkward, a little sheepish about their presence, they had good reason, since up until that moment most of them had never wanted anything to do with Dickie.

Some were complete strangers. People she'd never seen before in her life. She accepted all of their overtures with polite equanimity, unencumbered by second thoughts as to why they might have felt the need to come and pay their respects. She was not nagged by the possibility that morbid curiosity might have had something to do with it. Hers was the touching simplicity of a mother's grief. She had lost a son. A son she loved. As she loved all of her children. That and nothing more. Nothing less.

When the Zacharias sisters took their turn, they surrounded the coffin and launched into a forensic examination. For them, it was not so much a viewing as a post-mortem. They inspected the body like a trio of pathologists, turning over a hand, touching a cheekbone, poking a rib, lifting an eyelid. In a moment of reckless bravado one of them slipped her hand deftly under the lid and ran her bony fingers over Dickie's nether regions on the chance that he might be naked below the waist, as cadavers sometimes were. Each of the sisters had, in her time, fondled more than a few male genitalia in just such a manner. They maintained the stubborn belief, based on a story one of them had heard, that on rare occasions the phallus of a male cadaver maintained itself in an eternal state of posthumous erection. None of their investigations had, to date, substantiated that allegation, but that wasn't going to stop them from continuing their quest. In Dickie's case there was the added incentive of the rumour that had long been in circulation regarding the size of his endowment – a last chance to satisfy their curiosity. When the lucky sister found the object of her search she let out an audible gasp and pulled her hand away quickly. There would be plenty to talk about later.

The next to approach the casket was Martha's father, Isaac. He'd been wrong about the angels, who hadn't come for him after all, and now he wanted nothing more than to look down into the coffin of one more person he had outlived. Martha wasn't there with him, as would normally be the case. She had deliberately placed herself farther back in the line. She knew perfectly well, as did everyone in the church, what was about to happen next, but she wouldn't be there to catch him this time. This time, she was going to leave it to somebody else. It would serve him right if he injured himself. After all, she'd tried to leave him at home, but he had insisted on coming. Claimed he was under a certain obligation to make an appearance. He was expected, he said.

In the end she had relented a little and made sure there were two sturdy and fit-looking men in behind him, even if they were complete strangers. No one seemed to know who they were. Distant relatives from the city, perhaps. Long lost nephews. There was definitely something foreign in their mannerisms, but they had a sombre look about them that perfectly suited the occasion. Martha was sure her father would be in good hands.

They were, in fact, special agents, sent up from Roswell by the US Central Intelligence Agency. They were there to investigate the strange and powerful energy waves that had emanated from somewhere in the region. The unexplained energy surge – composition unknown, source unknown – that had wreaked havoc at the missile site. Caused all of their instrumentation to malfunction, their backup systems to fail, their planes to lose power, then inexplicably regain it. The pilots of those planes were even now suffering through yet another debriefing, trying desperately to explain how it was possible that their engines had cut out and then restarted themselves. None of them had ever had anything like that happen to them before, except for a flight sergeant with very bad teeth, and he wasn't making any sense. So far, all the evidence pointed to a major electromagnetic disruption of some kind. Whatever it was, it had clearly compromised the military capabilities of the United States Armed Forces.

The special agents had been sent to investigate the source of the energy. They had sophisticated monitoring devices strapped to their bodies. Instruments that could detect any waves being emitted, any chemical gases, electrons, isotopes being given off. They were walking laboratories. The infrastructure of their standard issue plainclothes undercover suits was loaded down with equipment. Sensing devices were clicking and buzzing away under there, recording the slightest variations in levels of every conceivable emission. So far all they managed to pick up were some low-level alpha waves coming from the vicinity of the coffin, as well as some others from an area of the congregation occupied by what appeared to be a pair of Hiroshima survivors.

The two men were also the only two people in the church who didn't know what was about to happen next. When Isaac reached the casket, having approached furtively, in small steps, already unsteady on his feet, wavering from side to side, he clasped the edge of the coffin, eyes wide, and took in an enormous gulp of air. Then he did what he'd been doing at funerals for as long as anybody could remember. He straightened up rigidly, clutched one hand to his chest pitifully, threw the other out in front of him as if he were trying to stop traffic, and fell back on his heels in a dead faint.

The special agents reacted like the highly trained professionals they were and caught him instinctively, the way they would have if Isaac had been a wounded president, for example. They had no idea he pulled the same stunt at every funeral. That the whole thing had become a bit of a tradition, to the point where, if the interment of your loved one did not include a fainting by Isaac Wiebe, you felt you had been snubbed. It was a kind of validation of a loved one's passing. The equivalent of a military flyby. The Zacharias sisters, who made a habit of gauging the piety of the dear departed by the veracity of Isaac's swoon, were impressed. Dickie must surely have entered the gates of heaven.

The agents took his fainting as a sign that the waves of

energy emanating from Dickie's body might be more powerful than their readings indicated. They conveyed Isaac gingerly to a nearby pew, then checked and rechecked the readings on their concealed electronic equipment, to see whether they could detect any verifiable surges of increased energy.

When it finally came around to the young poet's turn, he was pleasantly surprised at Dickie's appearance. There wasn't the least bit of contortion or pain in his face. No sign of suffering. His features seemed to have been altered, energized by the lightning bolt, as if his systems had not yet shut down completely. Lifeless though he was, his expression seemed frozen into a kind of suspended elation. As if he had died on the threshold of a great discovery. Of some ultimate epiphany. And because there were, in fact, still considerable amounts of energy coming from inside Dickie's body – the kind the young poet was particularly susceptible to, he felt an unexplainable increase in his own vitality. An acceleration in all his systems. He was suddenly ravenous. For food. For sex. For drink. For poetry. He wanted to live himself silly.

When it was his turn to offer his sympathies to Agnus Derksen he took her hand and held it. Said nothing. Failed to utter a single word of comfort or condolence, hopelessly intimidated by the compelling notion that, given the nature of the circumstances, anything he said would sound hopelessly disingenuous. Contrived. Hollow, since he felt so very much alive. *I'm so sorry,* he might offer. Too obvious. *My condolences.* Phony. *You have my deepest sympathy.* Pretentious. But Agnus, by that time, had gone into a kind of autonomic response mode. Her cognitive functions were on overload. She had never dealt with so many people – well-intentioned though they were. And so she took no notice of him one way or the other. The young poet had wanted to say so many things to her. About Dickie. Instead, he moved on, and went back to his pew without a word.

The preacher's sermon hardly made mention of Dickie. Instead the parishioners were treated to an abbreviated version of the usual platitudes and Bible passages. Dickie's note had failed to change the preacher in any fundamental way. His petty self-importance remained firmly intact, but he did keep things mercifully short because his wife was eager to get back home and have sex.

Abe Wiebe and Katie Klassen sat on opposite sides of the church, as far away from each other as possible. Katie in a dark dress, modest in every way, with a high collar and only a hint of black lace trim along the buttons down the front, sat very straight in the hard wooden pew, looked anywhere but at Abe. The garment Martha had brought for her failed miserably, as had every other item of apparel she'd ever worn, to hide her utter loveliness. Abe, crushingly handsome in a smart-fitting black suit and tie, was sandwiched in between the Martens brothers, and spent most of his time looking down at his hands.

Aunt Martha, sitting next to Katie, smiled to herself at the thought of it all. Here they were, the two of them in all their glory, shaming every modest cut of wood, every inornate window frame, every self-deprecating ceiling joist into submission, trying to make themselves inconspicuous, when in reality, they blazed, one on either side of the church, like two bright fires.

Nobody had seen them since Sunday afternoon. While people were busy talking about what had happened at the missile site and making preparations for Dickie's funeral, Katie and Abe had stayed, not only out of each other's company, but out of sight entirely. They had, as if by mutual agreement, taken up a hermitlike existence – put themselves in quarantine, each in their respective places. Katie at the abandoned home of her parents, Abe in his workshop.

In all that time neither had left the yard. And yet the string of energy that ran from one house to the other was all but visible in the dark, the sound of it humming like a telephone wire, crackling and sparking as you walked down the street between the two places.

By the day of the funeral the Zacharias sisters had worn themselves into a state of frenzied, exhausted anticipation. Their reconnaissance had been somewhat hampered by the fact that many of the people who would normally have augured much of the gossip through the village had left for Paraguay in a great hurry.

"This business with the hiding. It can't go on much longer now."

"Childishness, that's what it is. Plain and simple."

"It only adds to their shame."

"They're going to have to come out now."

"Let's hope they can keep their hands off each other."

That night, unable to sleep, images of carnal lust firing through her brain, one of the sisters had caught a glimpse of Abe as he walked the length of the deserted street, stood perfectly still under a naked moon in front of Katie's house for more than an hour, then walked back home. Another had seen Martha walking along the street with a black dress draped over her arm heading in the direction of Katie's house. The third had intercepted a call from Abe to the Martens brothers one afternoon.

"I need you to give me a hand."

"With what?"

"You'll see when you get here."

Word had it that Abe Wiebe was building something special in his workshop, something bigger and more elaborate than a schlopebank.

"Funeral's day after tomorrow."

"I know. That's why I need you to help me."

"Lots of people going."

"Everyone. I even bought a new spade. Down at the J. C. Penney Store."

"That nephew of yours says he's gonna read a poem."

"Says he doesn't care what the preacher says."

"Says you'll set things right if the preacher tries to stop him."

"Never mind about that now. Just get over here. And bring that big sander of yours."

"Sure thing, Abe."

"And that coping saw you bought last year in the States. Bring that, too."

When the church emptied, Abe and Katie stayed a good distance from each other, but not so far as they had been inside. Everyone made their way out to the cemetery, which was just in behind the church. A small collection of modest headstones rested under a stand of cottonwood trees. Everyone gathered quietly around the gravesite. An afternoon breeze gently swayed the branches above. A black and orange oriole sang brilliantly there. A pair of yellow finches flitted in and out of sight. The day seemed made to order for Dickie. The kind of day he would have loved nothing better than to stand out in the open and gaze up into the heavens. Green grass. Fresh air. Blue sky. And in the distance the Pembina Hills sparkling a silky lavender in the sun.

Standing next to Dickie's coffin, most people had only the faintest notion as to why they'd really come. That it had little to do with morbid curiosity or paying their respects to the dead. They sensed, dimly, that thanks to Dickie's note, they'd been allowed to participate in a rare and special moment, a glimpse into something beyond their daily vision. They had tuned in, for just a moment, to the possibility of something else. Something bigger. A brief interval, in which – thanks in part to the wonders of network television and modern dentistry – they had been given a taste of something rare. The flavour of it was still on their tongues, and Dickie Derksen, assisted by ten million volts of electricity, had been the catalyst.

At the gravesite, the preacher was about to start up again, ready to give another generic eulogy for a boy he knew nothing about, for whom he had never taken any time. When he'd come for his obligatory visit to the household of the deceased, there was so much Agnus Derksen had wanted to tell him about Dickie. So many of the things that made him special. Things she hoped he might mention at the funeral. But the preacher hadn't wanted to hear any of it. Cut her off almost before she began. Made some witless inquiries about her husband's whereabouts instead. Agnus Derksen had wished something then. That her wicked husband should return one more time and inflict himself on this preacher for being so insensitive. Harry would have done it, too, if only because the usual object of his abuse had been taken from him, and somebody was going to have to pay. That's the way it was with people like that. Somebody always had to pay.

Steven Zacharias walked up, stood next to the preacher, and said, "I wrote something. For Dickie."

"That's fine. I'll read it later."

"It's not for you to read. It's for Dickie."

"Yes, fine, then. Give it to me."

"You don't understand. I'd like to read it out loud. Here. Now."

"Nonsense," said the preacher. "Give it to me."

"Not until I've read it out."

"You'll do nothing of the kind," said the preacher, and made a grab for it.

The young poet pulled away. "I really don't see why I shouldn't be allowed."

"Look. I'm done talking. The answer is no. Now would you kindly step aside and allow me to proceed."

The young poet stood his ground.

"Would someone please remove this obnoxious person?" The preacher looked into the crowd for support.

"Certainly," said Abe Wiebe, and stepped forward. He walked up to the preacher, took him firmly by the arm and led him off to the side.

"Wait. Not me, you fool. Let go of me. What do you think you're doing?"

"Just doing what you asked, Reverend." Abe held his grip on the preacher's arm.

The preacher looked around wildly. "Are you people just going to let him get away with this?"

Nobody moved. Thanks to Dickie's note, they were just a little less willing to behave like sheep. A little more reluctant to allow themselves to be browbeaten into submission by self-serving entreaties.

"If the boy would like to read," it was Agnus Derksen who spoke now, "then I want to hear."

"You heard the lady, " said one of the special agents. He and his partner walked up and stood, one on either side of the young poet, dark glasses hiding their eyes, each with a hand inside the breast pocket of his suit.

"Nobody moves," said one.

"And nobody gets hurt," said the other.

The special agents were not really literary types. They had no interest in subverting the abuse of power by a small-town cleric. If they were aiding and abetting a coup of sorts, it was simply a matter of good sound investigative procedure. They had been trained to leave no stone unturned. No scrap of information was too small, too insignificant for their investigation. No avenue that might lead to a breakthrough would be overlooked. Not even poetry.

"For Dickie," said Steven, and proceeded to read.

ANTIDOTE

Now in the shivering
stomach of our unconfirmed
regret you, Dickie,
fester
like the inside of a mouldy
peach pit.

One of the special agents took out notepad and wrote
something down.

Musty,
strangely aromatic,
perhaps poisonous,

The other turned on a hidden tape recorder.

the seed
a possible antidote
to all our cancers,

The two of them glanced at each other. Nodded knowingly.

who ever thought
it would turn out
to be you?

A nudge and a wink.

Now
we are left to ponder only
the dogged genius
of your departure.

If Dickie's funeral turned out to be the literary debut of the young poet, it was not a particularly rewarding or poignant one. Certainly, it failed to move anyone to tears. And that might have been the end of it except that Martha Wiebe took it upon herself to begin applauding. Methodically, forcefully, loudly, persistently. She wanted to clap for Steven, but mostly she wanted to clap for Dickie. For the revelation that genius could manifest itself in the least as well as in the greatest. If only, she thought, everyone could make himself as small as Dickie, what possibilities there would be for the world.

The first to join in was Abe Wiebe, who had found himself pondering the notion of unconfirmed regret, and what it meant to him. And then Katie, who had felt that very shivering in her stomach, just as the young poet had described it. Felt it now. After that Cornie and Jake Martens joined in, and then the preacher's wife, and Betty Unger (fixated on the idea of a musty aroma), and even the sensitive young soldier (out of uniform and soon to be AWOL) who was in love with her.

But when the two secret service agents began to clap, it put everyone else over the top. The applause became thunderous, punctuated with the occasional hoot and shout and whistle. They were caught up in the moment because all that boisterous, lusty, impolite applause was giving them just a little of the taste they remembered hearing in Dickie's note.

The preacher sensed that something very dangerous had just taken place. A revolution of sorts. His natural vindictiveness kicked in, and he decided that literature was to blame. That it was even more evil than Abe Wiebe, and he must do everything in his power to eradicate it from the valley. He took his wife, who followed reluctantly, by the hand, and stomped off.

Dickie's mother knelt over the coffin ready to be lowered into the ground, patted it gently. Ran a hand over the smooth surface. Something about the way she did that made the applause stop. She looked up at Steven.

"That was a nice thing you did," she said.

He held the paper out for her to take.

"Most people never wanted much to do with my Dickie." She took the paper from him. "I saw you."

"Saw me? Where?"

"Out there." She gestured in the direction of the pasture.

"Oh."

"I watched you from the window."

"That was his favourite place."

"He used to tell me all about it when he came in. Tell me everything you said."

"He told you?"

"Oh, yes."

"Spoke to you?"

"Yes. Why?"

"But I didn't think he could."

"Could what?"

"Talk. I didn't think he could talk. Nobody did. Dickie never spoke to anybody."

"He never felt comfortable – doing that."

"But he talked to you?"

"Is that so hard to understand?" She saw the look of confusion on Steven's face. "A boy can always find a way to talk to his mother." She rose and backed up a few steps. "All right," she said. "Finish it."

The men on either side of the coffin took up the straps, Abe and the young poet and the Martens brothers among them, and began to lower Dickie slowly and carefully into the ground. Then, one after another, they took up the spades they had carried with them and plunged them into the black, fertile earth piled next to the grave. The shovelfuls of dirt made hollow, satisfying sounds as they landed on the lid of the coffin deep in the ground. It was not unlike the sound of distant thunder, loud at first, and then quieter and quieter as the grave filled up.

There was something so comforting for Agnus Derksen about the way the earth thumped onto Dickie's casket. The good solid sound of that. A little hollow at first, and then deeper and deeper, more and more reassuring, more and more right that earth should fall, first on the wooden casket, then earth on earth.

The grave was only about half-filled when Abe Wiebe did something completely unexpected. He stopped, straightened up, looked over at Katie Klassen, standing a little apart from the others with Martha, waited for her to look back up at him, and held the spade out to her. The others stopped. No one moved. Everyone waited. For a moment the breeze up in the trees ebbed, which made the birds hold off their singing. It was a long time before she finally stepped forward and took the spade gingerly out of his hand. She stood there with it until Martha grabbed the spade out of Cornie Martens' hand, who gave it up willingly, and came up beside her.

"Come on," said Martha, and bent down, pushed the spade into the soil, dug it in deeper with the heel of her shoe, and waited for Katie to do the same. Katie plunged her spade alongside, and the two of them lifted out the dirt and let it fall into the grave. The young poet gave his spade to Betty Unger, who took it and joined the other women in their work. There was only the sound of the breeze, which had resumed, rustling high in the cottonwood trees, the even rhythm of the women's laboured breathing, of their simple effort and toil, the machinery of their muscle and bone, until the grave was not only full, but a generous mound of damp, rich earth had been piled over the top, as was the custom.

Then Martha gave her spade to Abe, and stepped back, as did the others, all except for Katie, who had lost herself in the work, and didn't notice at first that it was just the two of them now, thumping the backs of their spades down onto the damp earth, running them along the sides, smoothing and shaping the fresh mound of earth. When she looked up and saw who it was on the other side, she hesitated for a moment, spade firmly in both hands, and it seemed to everyone present that much was exchanged in that long look. And then they fell to work once again, patting down a bump here, filling in a depression there. They worked with a careful concentration, as though this task was the most important work they had ever done. In each movement there was a quiet dignity. A reverence. It seemed to Martha that in each gesture something deeper resonated, something full of hope, and promise. They kept at it until they had sculpted a firm, rectangular monolith over Dickie's grave. Finally, the two of them straightened up and stood across from each other.

"Good," said Agnus Derksen, and turned to leave. The others followed. They would make their way to the church now, for a meal in the basement. They walked in small clusters and pairs under the cottonwoods. The young poet, for one, was eager to get back. He was ravenous. Hungrier than he had ever been in his life. Felt that he had never worked up such an appetite.

Then it was just Abe and Katie, resting against their spades.

"We should go back, too," she said.

"I don't think we can do that."

"We can't?"

"They say you can never go back."

"I didn't mean it that way."

"Well, I don't think this valley will ever be quite the same, if that's what you mean."

"Sometimes a place needs changing."

"And what about the people? Do they need changing, as well?"

"I don't know. Do people ever really change?"

"Don't they?"

"That's the big hope, isn't it? The one they feed us over and over again in the movies and books and television."

"Don't forget the Bible. Better throw that in while you're at it."

"You believe in it, then."

"The Bible?"

"That people can really change. That they can be transformed."

"And you think it's a Hollywood fairy tale."

"You have to admit, it's a pretty romantic idea."

"This place could use a little more romance, if you ask me."

Abe took the spade from her and folded it into his. Then he swung them both over his shoulder with one hand and they began the walk back to the church, side by side. A slight but unmistakable leaning, one into the other, that only the most studious observer would have detected, found its way into the fluid rhythm of their walk.

Behind them, a high-pitched whine, the sound of something turning, spinning, hummed from deep beneath the ground.

## ACKNOWLEDGEMENTS

Thanks go out to my wife, Brenda Sciberras, to Chris Dirks, Edna Alford, Bruce Eason, Kimmy Beach, Robert Kroetsch, Geoffrey Ursell, Nik Burton, Joanne Gerber, to Helen Elias, DJ, Bill, Wendy, Transcona Springfield, the Manitoba Writers' Guild, and to many others not mentioned here for their suggestions, guidance, and support in the creation of this book.

Special thanks to the Manitoba Arts Council for their assistance.

## ABOUT THE AUTHOR

D AVID ELIAS is the author of two other
books of fiction – *Places of Grace,* published by Coteau in 1997 and *Crossing the Line,*
published in 1992. His work has also appeared
in many journals and periodicals in Canada
and the US. His short story "How I Crossed
Over" from *Places of Grace* was a finalist for the
1995 Journey Prize. David Elias holds a degree
in philosophy from the University of Manitoba
and divides his time between teaching and
writing. He is also active in the Winnipeg
Philharmonic Choir.